LIVING AT NIGHT

MARIANA ROMO-CARMONA

LIVING AT NIGHT

Mariana Romo-Carmona

MARIANA ROMO-CARMONA

Spinsters Ink

Duluth

First edition October, 1997
10-9-8-7-6-5-4-3-2-1

Spinsters Ink
32 E. First St., #330
Duluth, MN 55802-2002, USA

Production: Helen Dooley   Lori Loughney
              Joan Drury   Ryan Petersen
              Emily Gould   Kim Riordan
              Marian Hunstiger   Liz Tufte
              Claire Kirch   Nancy Walker

Library of Congress Cataloging-in-Publication Data
Romo-Carmona, Mariana, 1952–
    Living at Night / Mariana Romo-Carmona — 1st ed.
        p.   cm.
    ISBN 1-883523-22-2 (alk. paper)
    1. Puerto Ricans—United States—Fiction.   I. Title
PS3568.O56547L5   1997
813'.54—dc21
                                                      97–26929
                                                         CIP

Printed in the U.S.A. with soybean ink on recycled paper

Acknowledgments

In the process of writing this book I have acquired a joyful debt of gratitude to many people, and I would like to acknowledge them. June, for her confidence in me. Adriana M. Romo and Juanita Ramos Díaz, whose early reading of drafts came with thoughtful and thorough feedback, and Sarah Schulman for her encouragement. Ibis Gómez-Vega por el susto, she knows why. Ann Stokes at Welcome Hill, for the snow storm. Joan Drury, my editor on this project, whose care and respect I couldn't have imagined. Everyone at Spinsters. And most of all, the residents at the Mansfield Training School who taught me something about love.

Dedication

To the women who raised me,
some of whom are younger than I am.

1

It was the night before Halloween and I was twenty-one, or would be if I survived the next turn and made it to work on time. I'd just had a fight with my girlfriend, and I was driving at breakneck speed over poorly lit back roads to avoid being late. My car rattled and screeched along, frightening no one but rabbits, raccoons, and myself, when I hit a pothole and the convertible top of the Valiant snapped loose on both front corners. I ducked. The top slipped halfway back and bounced over the backseat like a slinky as I drove.

Driving these roads at any hour, taking curves with the edge of my tires until they squealed, these were the things that made me feel I belonged to this place. The woods, the rivers, and the roads—which, I knew by their fragrance in any season—made me part of the landscape, though I had no illusions of being the typical New Englander. But which of the people I knew could really say they were? I was the only Puerto Rican around for miles in any direction, and at least my old car and I were something special.

The fight with Millie was over my birthday party the following night, which I didn't want to celebrate with everyone else, meaning the nine other lesbians in the area. Not just all the others, though, one woman in particular. Scooter, Millie's ex-lover. I was jealous. Just not about to admit it.

"You're jealous," Millie crossed her arms.

"Nah, I just want my own birthday party, not a Halloween party—that's for kids!" I waved my arms around to make my point.

"It's not for kids, it's a sacred night to all the women who reclaim their feminine power and worship the Goddess. You should be happy to share it."

"Well, why do I have to share it with Scooter?"

"See? You are jealous!"

So, we were having a party. For me, there was no direct relationship between witches and being gay, but for Millie, and for the few friends we could name between the towns of Ashford and Willimantic, we were practically a coven.

I took an illegal shortcut through the woods, my hands frozen to the wheel, my eyes watering with the cold and the dust I was raising. I sent a deer scampering toward the lake behind the Training School, watched the back of its legs in the foggy beam of my headlights. When I shut off the motor, it was 11:35 exactly, five minutes late. I went running down the limestone path to get into the building, down the tiled hallway, through the laundry room, and slid on my sneakers to see the charge aide give me the look I dreaded.

"Don't run, you'll fall, *Gracia*," she said.

"*García*," I returned. "Sorry I'm late."

The ward was quiet. Our residents, whom we had to call "clients," were asleep, and all of us third-shift aides stood waiting for our assignments or the coffee to be ready, whichever came first.

I picked up the clipboard to do a bed check with the second-shift aide when Fran, the charge, called me.

"You're going to work at the hospital, Gracia." The news startled me more than my last name, always mispronounced, no matter what pains I took to correct people. "Christina took a turn for the worse. They need an aide at all times," she finished in the pseudo-army voice she used when she wanted to be serious.

Some envious looks followed me as I left the ward. According to the rumor mill, when Fran played favorites, she gave out the hospital assignment, which meant sitting all night instead of scrubbing and mopping floors. To me, it was ridiculous. I'd much rather work and keep moving at night than grab a chance to sleep curled up on a hard-backed chair, watching over one of our people. But for a lot of the aides, the game was trying to get their money's worth from the job: stay awake all day and then steal sleep at night.

When our clients were sick, they would be sent from the Training School for the Retarded to one of the area hospitals, but one of us had to go with them because real doctors and nurses don't know how to handle retarded people. Or so Fran had told me.

I went out again to the parking lot and secured the top down on my car. I latched it securely on both sides and banged the clasps with the heel of my hand, probably fracturing my wrist. Christina, the one I was going to watch, was rather young and looked practically normal. She was usually very quiet, and sometimes she sang. A pale, blind girl with straw-colored hair, she had a smile that seemed to have just landed on her features and stayed. I think it was the way she sang to herself, the way she walked around like a fairy creature in her own world, that made me so fond of her though other people thought her strange. She had been in my ward for only a few months when she was transferred to another building for higher-functioning people. I remembered her, always quiet and pleasant in the mornings, never waking during the nights. We hadn't heard anything more about her until the previous week, when I was sent to the Willimantic hospital for five nights to watch her sleep. Christina was such a "good kid" that no one had noticed when a congested cold had turned into pneumonia. She lay still at night, her thin hands on the sheet, barely turning her head once in a while. The last night I was there, before my days off, her condition had improved, and she was taken off the respirator. When I left on the fifth morning, I had thought she'd go back home in a few days. Home. For her and for the others, the ward was home.

As the fog lifted, I could see a few stars. I headed east to 195 for the slightly longer route, then south toward Willimantic. I wanted to see the expanse of sky around Mansfield Hollow along the way and the moon shining on the bittersweet bushes at the curve at the bottom of the hill.

"Bring anything to read?" A nurse showed me into Christina's room. I sat down, staring at my client. Seeing her again was a shock. She was connected to the respirator, her heartbeat was monitored. She had catheters entering and leaving her. She had grown paler, her face and hands puffy, edema disfiguring even her fingers.

"I'm glad they sent you," continued the nurse, tucking the sheets, glancing at the oscilloscope. I checked the blue plastic tag pinned to her uniform that read *G. Ramerez, R.N.*, and thought that nobody could spell anything in Spanish in this part of Connecticut. "The other girl fell asleep," she said to me, with her hands on her hips.

"Is she going to die?" I whispered, motioning toward Christina.

"Nah, she'll be all right. You like *Vogue?*"

I sat motionlessly for a long while, listening to Christina breathe evenly, in sync with the air sac, punctuated by the beeps on the monitor, watching the little dance of the light measuring her heartbeat. At 3 A.M., I smoothed her sheet. Her hands were cold.

"I'll go get you another blanket," I told the sleeping Christina.

"Unh," I thought I heard her say and turned to look at her, my heart beating fast.

"Unh," she said again, moving her hands. I rang the buzzer clipped to the bedsheet, and two nurses came in.

"Pobre chica," said G. Ramerez, R.N., and I responded, "What, what! ¿Qué le pasa?" my mouth feeling funny, rusty from not uttering a word in Spanish for so long.

"Oh, she just needs to cough up the phlegm. She'll be all right," said the other nurse, tending to the catheters. I wondered, did they get together on this, how do they know she's going to *be all right?* Meanwhile, G. Ramerez was back, bringing me a bologna sandwich and another *Vogue.* She patted Christina's head.

Christina seemed to feel better. I pulled up the blanket and stood next to her holding her hand. My mind felt empty. Then I sat down and devoured the sandwich. I walked around the bed, looked at Christina, and talked to her once in a while.

"Christina," I whispered. "Remember when you used to sing?" Just faintly, her eyelids fluttered.

At five-thirty, the sky started to lighten. I stretched out in the chair as much as I could and leafed through the two magazines, not seeing or reading them, but feeling as though I'd done that before, in another hospital, on another long night. With a start, I put the magazines down. I could see it happening so clearly: it was when Mami had been so sick, me watching her, my sister running after the doctors. The last thing I ever wanted to think about.

I felt so stiff. I wished I was back at the ward, mopping. Right before seven, another aide came to take my place. We said hello to each other but didn't bother with names. She was a big woman, friendly, and looked more awake than I thought I could ever be again. She took Christina's pale hand in hers and seemed to warm her instantly.

"How we doing, honey?" she greeted Christina in a Maine drawl. "We gonna get you off this hose today?" Christina managed a smile even under her closed lids and her still face. I left her in good hands.

The phone blasted me out of my core. I knocked everything over in my path to silence the evil ringing. Cursing, I changed my mind and put the receiver to my ear.

"Where are you?" Millie's clear voice. "You said you'd only sleep until two!"

"What time is it?" I ventured, dragging the phone back to bed.

"Six," she answered impatiently. I looked around my two-room apartment. I'd never find my clothes in this mess.

"Erica!" Millie intoned. "Wake up, this is your party. Remember?"

I promised Millie I would be at her house in seventeen minutes, the shortest travel time I had clocked on the back roads from Willimantic to Eagleville Lake, in Coventry. My first night back to work usually hit me like a ton of bricks and left me sort of hung over.

Clearing a space for the telephone on the floor, and then a space for my feet, I stretched down to touch my toes. An inventory of the clothes, shoes, books, and last month's phone bill was enough orientation for my brain. Under a cupboard in the small kitchen, I spotted the old cat's dish, sticky and covered with lint, and a cat toy with the stuffing knocked out of it. I felt *unresolved guilt*, as Millie would put it. I threw the toy in the trash. ("Toti is sick, Erica," Millie had helped with the decision. "And she's bleeding there, who knows what she's got." "Do you think she's in pain?" I had asked the attendant at the ASPCA.)

She probably was in pain. But, she'd come to me when I moved into the place, looking for a home and someone to take care of her. How could I take her to die? I washed the dish, remembering that there was another one in the yard behind the building. Six-fifteen. I tossed the clean dish in the trash, made a mental note to put a plant in the other one, and figured out what to wear.

The small house by the lake was already humming by the time I arrived. There were orange candles glowing in every window, carved pumpkins on the doorstep, and the music was turned up loud. As I pulled in the driveway, I saw one witch and two of our old friends from the dorms going inside, wearing some kind of funny blonde wigs. Getting extra sleep had cost me the time Millie and I had planned to spend alone together. I looked for my friend Tina's car, but I didn't see it. She'd promised she and her sister would come. I went in.

In the fireplace, a fire roared as if it were the middle of winter.

"Happy birthday!" Millie hovered over the faded carpet in a long, black dress and gave me a quick kiss. Too quick. The blondes (Shelley and Beth dressed as two of the Andrew sisters) and a couple of other witches, whose voices I didn't recognize, joined in, singing and shouting greetings.

"You're beautiful," I whispered to Millie.

"You're late," said my witch, drifting away to busy herself with an orange birthday cake. The coven followed her.

It had taken me longer than I thought to achieve the George Sand look. Besides, it was the only costume I could easily transform when it was time for me to go to work. I kept a sweatshirt and a pair of sneakers in the car, which I could trade for my old silk shirt with the puffy sleeves and the riding boots. I consoled myself over Millie's coolness by watching the furious sunset over the lake.

"Erica!" A hand tousled my hair, and I cringed away. "Happy birthday! I thought you were working tonight!"

"I am," I said drily to the tall woman who'd been Millie's lover before me. "So, do they celebrate Halloween in Puerto Rico?" She was my archenemy.

"No, they celebrate my birthday, what do you think?"

"The crowd's over by the fire," said Scooter, unfazed. "You watching the sunset?"

"Hey, where did you get the green hood?" I asked accusingly, recognizing the hooded sweatshirt she wore.

"Millie lent it to me," she said proudly. "I'm Robin Hood!"

"How . . . butch," I observed through a clenched jaw. Scooter was unbearably pleased with herself. She flexed her skinny legs clad in green tights and executed some jazzy maneuvers in front of the full-length mirror that decorated Millie's living room. I searched my brain for a caustic line I could deliver, but Millie handed me a mug of hot cider just as Scooter returned expecting some obligatory comment on her dance. I gulped the cider, and the rum ignited my esophagus.

"Are you hungry?" Millie let me kiss her, while I kept an eye on the green monster.

"I've been taking a jazz class," we heard Scooter say.

"I'll eat anything. Quick, before I hit somebody," I pleaded.

"You won't hit anybody," Millie assured me with caramel eyes and a hand in the back pocket of my jeans.

"Milliekins, what's in the cider?" Scooter followed us to the kitchen.

"Puerto Rican rum," said Millie, slipping a piece of quiche in my mouth.

"Wow, is that the stuff with the worm in it?" persisted Scooter.

"That's *tequila*, stupid!" responded Millie, since my mouth was full.

Fleetwood Mac's "Rhiannon" was blasting on the stereo while we danced and everyone sang along to the chorus, all except me because I can never figure out lyrics. Scooter showed off her jazz moves, circling three other witches dressed in black besides Millie. Shelley and Beth, the two math majors who had been together ever since high school, had been about as successful with their costumes as I had been in my George Sand outfit. And then I knew I'd have a good time when Tina arrived, dressed in blue as Billie Holiday and extremely self-conscious because none of us had ever seen her in a dress. We hugged, and I took full advantage of the situation to tease her. Tina shoved me away. Her sister, Natalie, the only one who wasn't gay, came as a football player.

"You look stunning!" Millie complimented Tina, while I hugged Natalie.

"You have real shoulder pads here, Nat. Where'd you get 'em?"

"I went all the way, girl, to the costume store. Millie, you said you made rum punch?"

"This way, Natalie!"

"Erica, you look ridiculous—"

"Shut up, Tina!"

"What are you, some Victorian lesbian?"

"Radclyffe Hall, to be exact!" put in Scooter.

"And what are you, a grasshopper?"

"I'm Robin Hood!" Scooter protested.

As far as my twenty-first birthday was concerned, it wasn't turning out all bad. Millie had planned this party for me because she knew I was secretly rather sentimental about things like this. I'd told her about when I was growing up and Mami and Nélida always made sure that things would be happy when there was a family celebration. Mami would play her old guitar, and we would sing. Nélida would decorate the apartment with crepe paper roses in bright colors that I loved; this made Mami shake her head, because she liked things more subdued.

"Esto no es carnaval," she would mutter to herself, but she was in a good mood, and I remember she never got sick when it was my birthday or Nélida's.

At ten, Beth declared she was leaving Shelley for one of the witches, and Millie gathered everyone around to watch me blow out the orange candles on the chocolate cake that was as thick as it was gooey, and then I got presents. A date book, a record, a scented candle, and even a box of incense from Scooter. Tina and her sister gave me a hardbound edition of all the poems by Julia de Burgos and thermal long underwear. Millie gave me a plaid flannel shirt and a bottle of massage oil.

With all the attention, I was almost over my jealousy and feeling even charitable toward Scooter as Millie and I danced. It was a slow ballad by Rita Coolidge that everyone loved to wail along with. Beth had decided to stay with Shelley forever, and Millie had her arms around my neck. I was holding her as close as I could, remembering the first day I saw her at the library where I used to work.

"Meet me in front of the library," I whispered to her, making her laugh.

"You still remember that?"

"Of course. It was the first thing you ever said to me," I reminded her.

"I don't know whatever got into me that day. I was trying to tell you about the rally by the lake, but I guess I thought you were cute," she admitted.

"Oh, you guess so!"

Millie wriggled in my arms in a way that I loved, as she nestled herself perfectly in place. I would have made everybody disappear right then, if I was really a witch on Halloween. But that's precisely when Millie contrived to have her nonmonogamous urges. As we swayed to the first strains of a Cris Williamson song, she let go of me and dragged Scooter in to dance a sort of lesbian minuet with the three of us. *Let's burn together all through the night,* sang Cris Williamson, and Scooter sang along, inspired, taking my hand. I swore I would die before I did any such thing, even to please Millie. Thankfully, Tina caught my eye at the turntable, where she nixed Cris Williamson in the middle of *Oh, oh, my land is all on fire!* and replaced the record with Carlos Santana. "Oooh, Santana!" cried the Andrew sisters and Natalie, and we danced earnestly until it was time for me to leave.

I told Millie that one of the women from my ward was in the intensive care unit at the hospital, hoping that the seriousness in my voice would bring her attention back to me.

"You know I love you, don't you?" Millie cooed into my ear. I forgave her instantly. She spent long, affectionate minutes helping me with my coat and bundling me with my scarf.

"Is it Christina, the blind woman?" she asked.

"Yeah, she's not doing too well," I held Millie's hands around my neck.

"Listen, I'm going home this weekend—" she reminded me.

"Damn, it's my days off! Why are you going to New Jersey again?"

"For my cousin's wedding, but I'm not leaving till Friday night. I'll come to wake you up before I leave." We hugged until one of the Andrew Sisters came to get her coat; it was Shelley, who was leaving Beth.

On my third night at the hospital, my muscles were so stiff I had to take frequent walks in the hallway to loosen up. Christina was still on the respirator, but the nurses told me that she was on only at night. During the day, she could breathe almost normally.

Her hands felt limp, like a doll's. I tried to imagine what it

11

would feel like to be in her place. If I were retarded, blind, ill, in a hospital with people doing unexplainable, painful things to me. Would I understand any of it, would I trust the people around me? I took a look at the chart at the foot of the bed. On it, Christina's temperature, pulse, and respiration were listed at regular intervals. The familiar list of medications reminded me that Christina was also epileptic. At least she hadn't had any seizures since she'd been in the hospital.

Nurse Ramírez came in (her first name was Gloria—I had decided) to do the hourly checkup. Christina didn't stir. Nurse Ramírez was very gentle with Christina. I looked on, thinking that if this nurse couldn't cure Christina with her smooth hands, nobody could.

"What's your name, dear?" she surprised me out of my reverie.

"Me? Oh, Erica," I stammered.

"Erica, get me that pillow, would you?" The nurse raised Christina's head slightly and removed the tube from her nostrils. When Christina coughed, the nurse quickly got a sterile catheter and suctioned her throat. Christina breathed evenly.

"She doesn't need the draining tube in her mouth anymore?" I asked.

"She pulled that out herself today, didn't you, chica?" She stroked Christina's forehead. I was amazed and proud of Christina.

The nurse went out of the room with her quick step and returned with a pile of washcloths and towels. She washed Christina's face, arms, and back, with my help. I was glad to have something to do, and Christina seemed revived, a slight flush on her cheeks. It seemed she liked having us talk to her, and then suddenly, she spoke in a hoarse voice: "I . . . want to go . . . to the . . . bathroom." Nurse Ramírez and I looked at each other in surprise.

"It's okay, chica, we've got little tubes for you to use. You don't have to get up—"

"I-want-to-go-to-the-bathroom," came the low voice. I had a lump in my throat.

"Christina," I said, "You've got tubes now, but tomorrow you can go, okay?" I took her hand, and she squeezed mine. The nurse adjusted the intravenous needle in Christina's arm.

"Gina!" A blonde nurse with a pony tail popped her head in the doorway and called out to Nurse Ramírez, "You eat pepperoni?"

So, Gina, not Gloria, wrinkled her nose, trying to decide. "I'm sick of pizza, you know?" she waved at me as she left the room.

I moved my chair next to Christina's bed and talked to her about the school, the other women, about the time when she and Mrs. Morse, the senior aide, sang "Oh, My Darling Clementine" together.

"I wanna go to the . . . bathroom," said Christina. There was nothing I could do but imagine how uncomfortable she must feel.

"I'm sorry," I told her, "try not to think about it."

After a little while, she fell asleep, and I went to get a cup of coffee. I felt chilled. Around four every morning my body temperature dropped, and I could never seem to warm up. I was glad at least for the sandwich, which I'd eaten more for the novelty of it than for the taste. At the Training School, all we got were stale bran muffins or cinnamon rolls without enough icing on them. It was better to have something in my stomach. Remembering Millie's party, I thought about her crackling fireplace, the food, the rum punch. I stood by the nurses' station watching the activity, catching an earful of gossip now and then. They passed a dish of Halloween candy around.

A whole week without Millie, just so she could help her cousin pick out flowers for the reception and outfits for the honeymoon. I wished I had a cousin who was my age. The shift changed, and the nurses came and went. Young doctors in residency began their rounds. The sun was rising, and the light was strong on Christina's face. I went around the bed and closed the blinds a little. By seven-thirty, I realized that there was no one to relieve me yet. When a new nurse came in to check on Christina, I went to call the School for another aide. While I waited, I talked to Christina and explained that I had three nights off.

"But, I'll come see you tomorrow morning . . . and bring you roses, so you can smell them," I promised her. She moved her cool fingers in my hand.

The first cat came to my yard the next day and sat facing the tall weeds that overflowed onto the cement walk. She sat there, with her tail flat against the ground, like Toti used to sit. I looked at the last leaves on the pear tree.

That morning I found out that Christina had died. The nurses told me when I went to visit her, and I didn't want to believe it. It hurt so much that she died alone, after two weeks in the hospital. Her heart just stopped.

The second cat was yellow. After I brought the water bowl inside the house, he came around and sniffed the spot where it had been. I figured they knew there were no more animals in this house.

I felt surrounded by spirits and turned away from the window. My cup of tea was on top of the desk, steaming among the papers. Bluish light shone through the window. It was getting cold in the evenings, and that light would soon mean gray skies and dead weeds and no more Toti prancing in the yard among the weeds, staking out her territory. *It's not that I'm sad she's gone.* The cat was old and lived a happy life. Toti used to walk slowly, almost floating on her orange, bushy paws with her tail up in the air, stiff and coy, and sit by the weeds under the pear tree. Sometimes her

14

slow movements seemed magical to me, as though she were in a trance. An old cat, listening.

Cats get old and die. I know that.

That day my house was empty. Toti was too old. I brought the water bowl inside and washed it, kept it under the sink to remember her. At the ward, someone would remove Christina's name from her bed and from the checklist. They'd throw her toothbrush away, and someone else would inherit her institution sneakers. Slowly, she'd disappear from all the lists.

For three nights, I performed the 3 A.M. bed check with my heart in my mouth, or in my hand, as I touched each woman's shoulder to reassure myself that her breathing was even. This is how people are found dead in their sleep—someone has to find them—but I didn't want it to be me. The thought terrified me.

Darlene, one of the younger women, usually slept on her back, with her legs on top of her in perfect lotus position. She was cuddled up like a newborn, with her legs tucked under her and completely covered by the blankets. Since she's so slight, I thought she wasn't there at first, and my pulse raced. Then, I saw she was there. I asked Mrs. Morse to help me coax Darlene, who is blind and deaf, to sleep with her head out in the air. But she would fold up her limber body and insist on covering up completely. It was odd, because on other nights, she would refuse to be covered at all and her thin arms would end up icy in the morning.

The label was still there on Christina's bed, only Eva Nathan had hopped in and was chewing the corner of the blanket as usual, and staring at me with her big green eyes. I didn't know which was worse, seeing it or not seeing it. I said, "Come on, Eva, let's go to your bed!" and she responded with her favorite sentence: "Eva-get-up-and-pee!" I tucked her in and stroked her gray hair. Nobody knows who taught her how to say that, but she blurts it out almost every day.

When I got to Rosie, she was already wet and was sleeping at the foot of the bed, shivering. Mrs. Morse came in to help me with Rosie, because somehow she never yells when Mrs. Morse is there.

One night, Rosie woke up crying, and there was nothing I could do for her. She screeched until I brought her wheelchair and took her to the day hall. She can't walk, but she can crawl pretty fast and grab at people's legs with her strong arms. Mrs. Morse likes Rosie; I would like her more if I weren't so afraid of her sudden blows.

By the time we finished, it was three-thirty. I was annoyed, trying to stuff the wet sheets quickly in the laundry bag, their edges flapping against my jeans, and I was certain that they smelled of Rosie's strong urine. As for Rosie, she sat in a chair in the bathroom, wearing a clean yellow nightgown while Mrs. Morse changed her bed.

At the little bathroom next to the office, I washed up to my elbows with foaming betadine, then tried sponging my jeans, leaving the door open to keep an eye on Rosie.

"Forget it, Kid," admonished Mrs. Morse on her way back from the dorm. "The smell of pee won't come off till you go home and do your laundry—might as well come in the office and have us a cup of coffee."

"I don't want to stay like this the rest of the night, though—"

"Then, you best learn to wear your apron all the time, hadn't you?"

There was no arguing with her solid grandmotherly logic. Mrs. Morse went to get us coffee and came back to sit in the office with me. I rather liked being assigned to C side to work with her and all the ambulatory clients on this part of the ward. We worked fast and kept moving all night, me and the kindly, white-haired and blue-eyed Mrs. Morse from Maine, who calls me "kid" and treats me like a daughter. I don't mind staying in the office and skipping the break room now and then, where Fran and all the aides gossip and cackle at their own jokes.

Mrs. Morse had been around longer than some of the other aides, but somehow being a veteran of the place hadn't turned her hard-edged and wisecracking, like Fran or the aides in Bentley North, who handled their bedridden clients with the precision of drill sergeants. Mrs. Morse could be as agile as I was, and she could shake up the clients with a firm hand if she needed to, but I'd never seen her be cruel, and even though she knew their tricks inside and out, she would never say a mean thing about "her kids."

If she was in the mood to chat, she'd tell me some story about living on a farm in Maine during World War II or about the ward in the old days.

I was curious about Madeleine Mallard, a resident who slept way at the back of the dorm on C side. I told Mrs. Morse about my first encounter with the large, redheaded Madeleine, during my inservice training. She'd just had a bath and had come running toward me, naked, her skin all blotchy pink and dripping wet. I thought she might slip on the tiled bathroom floor, so I put my hands out to steady her, but Madeleine grabbed both my wrists tightly, giving me plenty of time to practice breaking off the "wrist-hold," a maneuver we had just learned. I pretended not to be afraid and smiled stupidly while I struggled to release my wrists from her hands. She smiled too, showing two missing front teeth and a glint in her eye that was chilling.

"Madeleine is a good kid," Mrs. Morse was saying. "I don't care if she is retarded, she has her own sense of humor." I sat back with my coffee and got ready to enjoy a good yarn. Mrs. Morse adjusted her glasses, smoothed her apron, and crossed her hands over her stomach.

"When she was first sent to this ward, I used to work C side alone. They locked you in, so's nobody would run out while you was doing your chores." Mrs. Morse relished my astonishment.

"But, what if there was an emergency?"

"Then, there was always the phone in the office, and you could call the building supervisor. But, nothing happened that night," she continued. "In the morning, I was pretty busy with the dressing and the toileting, you know, and I forgot all about Madeleine Mallard. Well, she got up about seven and went right to the corner of the dorm and peed on the floor!" laughed Mrs. Morse.

I shook my head and laughed along with her while she told me about the size of this puddle and other housekeeping details that would interest no one but those of us who worked there. I wondered if I would lose my grasp of reality if I stayed too long.

"Well, now, we also had to make the beds," Mrs. Morse was tapping my knee with her fingertips and really getting into her story. "And first shift was already in, checking their list and asking questions, not helping at all, you know how they are. So, when I was done cleaning the mess, I started on the beds, stripping sheets and bagging them as fast as I could. The last bed was nice and smooth when the dorm door opens and in comes Madeleine Mallard, back from breakfast with cereal all over her gown . . ." I closed my eyes at the scene. Mrs. Morse was on a roll.

"How old is Madeleine now, about thirty? Well, she was fifteen then, and she started hopping with those long legs of hers, from one bed to the next, messing up everything and dragging the wet sheets with her as she went, quick as a deer!"

I was more appalled by the story than amused, since I was usually dead tired in the mornings and could barely drag myself out to the car. But Mrs. Morse thought it was hysterical and got me laughing by imitating Madeleine, round, innocent eyes like saucers and a Jack Nicholson grin.

"Lighten up, Kid. How're you gonna stand up when you have kids of your own?" She punched my shoulder.

"I'm not having any, that's how!" I punched her back, gently.

After our break, we went to do the laundry, and Mrs. Morse told me about the time the second-shift aides took all the residents in C side on a trip to Friendly's for milk shakes. I couldn't imagine just three aides managing to keep track of everyone, since most of the women had some peculiarity that was difficult to handle. But Mrs. Morse told me about the precautions the aides took: The Kiniry twins, who hated clothes and stripped naked several times a day, were dressed in jumpsuits with tie-strings around their waists—also to keep them from wandering away; Eva Nathan had her sneakers laced all the way up to her knees so she wouldn't pull them off; Agnes had mittens on, so she wouldn't scratch herself or anyone else.

"But you can't plan everything, Kid," Mrs. Morse shook her head, an indulgent smile on her face. "See, the milk shakes were slow in coming, and Madeleine Mallard stripped her dress off in protest. While one aide put her arm back into one sleeve, Madeleine would be grabbing at someone else's milk shake, pulling her arm out of her other sleeve. You best believe the parking lot at Friendly's cleared fast."

Mrs. Morse thoroughly enjoyed the memory, and it was me who shook my head in disbelief, my sense of order challenged. But I laughed, too, gratefully realizing that my pain over Christina's loss was leaving me.

2

Something about the sun hitting the windshield dead on as I headed home in the mornings made me almost fall asleep driving, watching the mist just breaking up over the bare hills. But on my first day off I was always reluctant to go to sleep when I got home, suddenly wide awake and excited by the prospect of three days all to myself. I began by making the bed, watering the plants, and dusting off the windowsills where the dry leaves from my neglected begonias had fallen, and lining up the five books I had been waiting to read. Then, abandoning this plan, I spread a map of New England on the floor and traced a route to follow on a camping trip. If I couldn't convince Millie to get away with me, maybe Tina would go. I decided to call her at the campus bookstore.

"Stockroom."

"Tina! I'm so glad I got you, listen—"

"Hello?" I could hear Tina's voice in a din of many other voices. I raised mine.

"Tina, it's Erica, can you hear me?"

"Hey, what are you up to, you home? It's loud in here, we're having a used book sale, so you gotta yell," Tina shouted.

"Listen, I got a great idea, wanna go camping in Rhode Island?"

"And freeze to death? You're crazy—is Millie going?"

"I haven't asked her—"

"What? I can't hear you!"

"I said I haven't asked her, I'm not sure she'll want to go in the cold. Unless a whole bunch of us go. What do you think?"

"Well, I think she's the one you want to cuddle up with in your sleeping bag, so don't ask anyone else. But I'll be your back-up, after I finish up all these school interviews—we have to hang out together more, like in the old days!"

"I know! You want to go to the woods with me tomorrow morning?"

"Oh, I can't, tomorrow's my last day at this stupid job—but do you want to meet afterwards for dinner at the Campus Restaurant?"

"Yeah, meet you at six?" The noise was getting horrendous.

"What?"

"At six, I said!"

"Perfect! Hey, we got all these books in Spanish we're throwing out, you want me to save them for you?"

"Hell, yes! I love you, Tina!"

"I know, I'm adorable. Bye!" Tina hung up, and suddenly I felt the quiet.

Three-thirty in the afternoon, and I was regretting not having slept. I felt disoriented, with a dry feeling in the back of my throat and twinkling spots in front of my eyes. I took a hot bath to calm down, trying to find the daytime equivalent of what people do at night, before they go to sleep. Sitting on the floor, I placed my mother's old guitar on my lap and plucked the strings. For a while I became engrossed in removing the dust around the tuning pegs. Finally, I took my calendar to bed, looked at the Japanese peonies on the border, and counted days off and holidays, figuring I'd better find a way to get Millie to spend time alone with me. I fell asleep just as the sun paled and left long shadows across my windows.

This time I remembered a dream. When I was a kid, I used to have dreams I could never grasp hold of, something vague about floating, about some place where I had never been but that was all around me just the same. In this dream, I chased the old cat Toti among the weeds in a field, trying to find her before the first snow fell. She eluded me, sometimes poking her orange head behind milkweed and staring at me with a human look in her feline eyes; then she disappeared. I seemed to feel anguish and the detachment of dreams at the same time. I remember half awakening with my mouth desperately dry. Drifting back into exhausting sleep, I dreamt Darlene was dying of thirst because she'd been slumped over for so long. I was crying, trying to get to her, but some work that had to be done always prevented me. In the end, I was mopping an interminable red floor, surrounded by the residents in nightgowns walking across it. Darlene was pulling my arm as she usually did, only she wasn't blind anymore.

I woke up, thinking I understood something that disappeared with my dream. I sat up in the dark for a while, trying to grasp that something. The loneliness of the ward, the residents, and my distance from them. It was as if I was feeling all this for the first time.

To chase away the mood, I took a walk in the cold night. The narrow main street of Willimantic was quiet. I headed south and crossed the metal bridge that connects the old factory districts left over from the growth spurt of the 1940s with the rest of the city.

The river below was a soothing sight, reflecting stars and street lights, although I knew that during the day it was shallow and dirty.

❖

Out in these farming towns, the beginning of November is a deceptive time. The colors of the countryside have softened considerably, and the fields are covered with the leaves that have fallen and the remains of the summer's corn. Everything seems quiet, but underneath that blanket of leaves, there are scurrying field mice with sharp little teeth, worms, crickets, tardy moths that fly up in small, fading circles once in a while. These signs were important to me, because I tried to pay attention to the changes in the woods, and the rhythms that never touched me when I was growing up in New Britain. I didn't always understand the logic of fields and migrating birds, but I wanted to belong to all of it, even if it wasn't my birthplace. I wanted to belong.

In the morning, after a good night's sleep, I was anxious to go out in the woods and get to my favorite place by the pond in Gurleyville. It isn't difficult to get out of Willimantic. Any road one takes leads out into the country, and eventually, toward some other small town.

The day was cloudy, and by the change in the wind, I realized it might rain. I felt strangely exhilarated by the muted colors, the shifting wind. My old car raced over the bumps and took the turns easily, speeding through the little section of Storrs called Gurleyville, until I steered into the hidden road that leads to a large field by the Fenton River. This was the place where Tina and I would go walking when we lived in the dorm together. Since I'd moved out, it had become mostly my place, but either she or Millie would join me there sometimes.

When I got there, there were two men fishing, knee-deep in the water. We ignored each other by way of acknowledgment, as everyone does who comes to this secluded spot. The wind pushed away some clouds, revealing a light patch of sky. I confirmed to myself the things I knew about the country here. *This is the color of the November sky*, and *now is when the air smells spicy from the pine needles*. I crossed the field, figuring I'd better prepare myself for a cold season. Three squirrels crossed the narrow path in front of me and darted into the woods. Was that the same anxiety that I recognized before the cold comes?

I took a deep breath, contemplating with pleasure the walk ahead—about half a mile along a path by a little stream. A lulling effect usually took hold of me, my feet falling easily into a rhythm that allowed me to think or not to think at all. The leaves crunched under my feet. The path took its turns over the stream bed—through familiar pines, rocks, small branches snapping back with a dry sound after my intrusion. November sunlight filtered onto ferns now yellowed and covered with spores. My boots stirred the smell of moist earth and pine needles.

Soon I was thinking about the ward, about the residents there and about my coworkers, about whether I'd ever go back to school, about what I was doing with my life. I had left school after two and a half years, when my scholarship had run out and I couldn't take out a student loan by myself. And I hadn't wanted to bother Nélida with all that. So I gave up my work-study at the library in January, and I started doing as many odd jobs as I could. But perhaps I'd left because I wanted to explore the world around me, and because I didn't want to go back home to New Britain after graduation, to memories of my mother and her illness, to my sister and all her expectations. The job at the Training School had saved me. Working at a gas station, pulling weeds and mowing lawns, and all the work I could find just wasn't enough, and by April I was busted broke. This was my first real job.

But it came with an odd mixture of feelings. Nélida was angry with me because she didn't want me to do the same thing she had done all through high school, working in a hospital as a nurse's aide, not even a candy striper, complete with the cute little uniform like the girls who volunteered after school. I could tell she was proud of me, though, for supporting myself. I wished Mami could have seen me, going to work at night, getting a paycheck, and joining the credit union.

The paperwork necessary to become an employee of the State took two days. The in-service training period was about ten days and so thorough that sometimes I thought they would own me, body and soul. Only the hardiest of us would make it, we were told, to begin an even more demanding job. For a week, I studied several manuals along with fifteen other prospective employees. I read many pages on the human rights of retarded citizens, on physical restraint, on drug therapy, on institutional innovations, and on behavior modification theories. Then, we practiced tying each other's wrists to learn the correct restraining procedure. This is when I felt like a traitor to my generation. What was I doing? This was 1977, the post-Nixon era, and I could just as well have been joining the FBI.

We were given white terry-cloth squares and denim strips about a yard long, called "tie-strings." The terry cloth went around the wrist first, to protect the person's arm from chafing. Then, the tie-string was fastened on with a square knot, leaving it loose enough to place two of the aide's fingers under the terry cloth. If it was too tight, circulation would be cut off. Slip knots were prohibited, because a person in restraints would naturally pull on them and tighten the knots. After we learned this procedure, we discussed how violent clients in any of the wards could be restrained and tied to their beds for no longer than three hours, checked periodically to make sure they were not hurt. Besides this precaution, a "restraint order" would be obtained by calling the doctor on duty at the central administration building.

The part of me that listened with a cynical ear to these instructions resisted believing that these trainers, some of them therapists and nurses, could possibly have the best interests of retarded people at heart and still discuss coldly the best way to tie them down against their will. But another part of me was frightened. What if I had to become violent to defend myself? I felt small compared to the men, even the women aides. I was being trained to control people who had no awareness of hurting themselves or others, who would be under the influence of psychotropic drugs. I paid careful attention when we practiced grabbing one another's wrists, arms, or clothing, and learned how to break away from different holds.

On the fourth day of orientation, the instructors took us on a tour of the grounds. Our group had already diminished to twelve, and though I don't remember anyone else, two trainees made an impression on me. One was a woman about my age, with long, coppery hair in a ponytail and blue eyes ringed with black liner every day, who looked too frail to fly a kite, much less take on the job of a direct-care aide. I expected her to quit early on in the training, but she hung on. The other was a little man who burped to make a point and bragged daily about having been a sergeant in the army.

On our tour, we visited the "worst" buildings first. "If the smell don't getcha, the screamin' will—" boasted the gross little sergeant, who seemed to know a lot about the place. We walked through the buildings for older residents, for residents using wheelchairs only, for young men only. We saw half-clothed and naked men walking aimlessly in the day halls, shouting or singing, drooling, having epileptic seizures, or banging their heads against tiled walls. Some wore leather helmets, others didn't, and I was amazed they didn't crack their heads open. If it hadn't been for the war stories my sister brought home from the hospital when I was a kid, I would have turned around and left, but the effect was intense, just the same. The smell of feces and urine was overpowering at times, but I was determined to ignore it and make it to the end. The ex-sergeant hoped he would be sent to the violent wards to work with the male clients. I thought the trainers would realize that this man intended to violate people's rights and he wouldn't be hired, but he was. The trainers seemed to appreciate his commitment to keeping things under control.

When we visited the building for the blind, the layout of the place was different, less like the institution we were in. Small, friendly people came to look at us, to touch us, at the doorways where we stood. The ones who could talk greeted us as though we were space travelers landing on their planet. In a ward where almost everyone was blind, the walls were colorful, and the rooms were even cheerful. A small man propelled his wheelchair toward us eagerly and offered to show us around the ward. Some of my group went with him. The rest of us were led away by a blind woman who knew exactly where I stood and how tall I was. She took my arm and motioned the other trainees to follow as she showed us the women's section of the ward. She touched the textured marker on each door and told us something about the client who lived there. At the end of the tour, she squeezed my hand and told me she hoped "they" would send me to her building.

Walking back to our classroom, some of the trainees in the group talked a lot about the weird behavior they had witnessed. Two were very pale. The rest of us were trying to act as naturally as we could. I felt embarrassed. Kelly, the woman with the eyeliner, said she'd put in a special requisition to work in the building for the blind. "At least they pee in the toilet in that ward," she reasoned. Of course, the only ones who had been acting *normal*, were the clients. I didn't realize that then. That day was exhausting; I felt the strain of appearing unaffected by anything or anyone I saw.

On the last day of in-service training, we were sent to our assigned buildings to work all morning. I met my women for the first time at Bentley South. They were severely and profoundly retarded women of all ages who were divided into two sections. Section C was known as the trouble side because most of the women could walk on their own. The women on D side used wheelchairs for the most part, or moved very slowly, so this section was considered to be an easier assignment.

We mostly gave baths that morning, in the huge bathroom that was the same in every building: pink tiled walls, gang showers, six stalls with toilets, and next to them, an area with six sinks under large mirrors and two steel tubs that looked like big sinks with a place to slide into the water. The women got washed with white washcloths and pink soap. We used strawberry shampoo that didn't irritate their eyes. Toothbrushing was a game of tag, since most of them simply made off with their toothbrushes to eat the toothpaste and then threw the brushes on the floor.

There was a short coffee break, but so much work to do that I didn't stop moving all morning. There was little time to think about what was happening. I got scratched by a woman with small brown eyes, her face gaunt, who refused to take a bath and looked scared, but she made it a point to stay close enough to try to grab the tube of toothpaste and scratch us. The rest of the time, she kept her thin arms folded underneath her blue-and-yellow-flowered dress. It was then that Madeleine Mallard grabbed my wrists and scared me so much. After we went a couple of rounds with the wrist grabbing and breaking away, I managed to put a dress on her, comb her red hair, and find a pair of sneakers labelled with her name. She watched me patiently while I laced them up with new laces, put them on her feet, and tied them neatly in a bow. She sighed and took them off quickly, before running out into the fenced porch beyond the day hall.

My scratches bled a little and got itchy immediately. I was shown how to wash with a thick solution of betadine. During the afternoon lecture on first aid and self-defense, I got terribly discouraged. I was sure I could still smell that indescribable stench of feces and disinfectant. I could smell it even in the watered-down coffee I was drinking, in my hair, and in my clothes.

Behind me, the ex-sergeant entertained his neighbor with horribly cruel stories about the retarded, which had been told to him by former aides who had retired. Some of these things had happened in the very building where we were, before the Department of Health condemned it as a ward, and it was used for offices and classrooms.

I was at the pond, touching the small ripples at the water's edge with my boots. My thoughts still revolved around the training school, six months earlier. "*The Tiger*," the ex-sergeant had said—"They called her 'the Tiger' because she was like a wild animal, attacking people. The social workers found her locked up in a basement when she was thirteen, and that's when they brought her to the School . . ." There was nobody like that anymore, at least not in my building, but every time I remembered that story, I couldn't help thinking it must have been an exaggeration. Nobody could be made to suffer that much, it would be inhuman. Squatting by the water, I watched small perch jumping out of the smooth surface, at the deepest part of the pond, where the water looked like black glass, expanding in circles.

Millie came over early on Sunday, my second day off. As usual, we spent the first fifteen minutes arguing about my job, my rotating schedule, and her relatives. When Millie and I had first started seeing each other our third year at school, I couldn't go away with her or even for a beer at the Huskies Pub because I never had any extra money. But when I started working, I thought I was doing pretty good with a full-time job, a car, and an apartment of my own, until Millie started looking soulfully at me. In this, she could be worse than my sister, which was the reason I didn't go back to New Britain half as often as she went back to New Jersey to see her family.

But at least Millie complained because she thought my job kept me away from her. She wanted me to be a student again, have the same schedule she did, have weekends off, see foreign movies at the Art School, and stay out late with the rest of the women we knew. When I thought of it that way, it didn't bother me. She had come straight over to my apartment, which was a few storefronts away from the bus station on Main Street. Her books, her knapsack, and her bag stuffed full of leftovers from her mother's house lay on the floor at the foot of my bed, while Millie sat on her heels and looked at me. I had stopped arguing and lay back against the wall, watching her face.

"What . . . ?" Millie realized I wasn't talking and wanted to know what I was thinking.

"Your mouth gets red when you're excited. And your hair frames your beautiful face," I told her, watching her blush.

"Oh. I thought you were going to tell me I'd gotten fat."

"What!?" Then it was me who had trouble following her thinking. But I followed her off the bed where she had scrambled to open the food containers.

"What's this?" I pointed to some pastry in a blue tin.

"Apricot rugelah. Does it remind you of something?" She broke a piece of it and put it in my mouth.

"Mh? No, but I like it. It's buttery and fruity."

"Yeah, no kidding. Something your grandmother made, or your mom?"

"Nope."

"Erica?"

"What?"

"You never talk about her."

"Who?"

"Your mother!"

"Oh, Millie. You want some coffee?" I asked her, getting up to make it.

Millie pushed the tin into my hands. "Keep the rugelah. It has about a thousand calories a bite. And here, let's put the fish in the refrigerator. It's smoked, so it will last."

"Well, thanks, but you should keep some of it," I said guiltily, since my own refrigerator was empty, and we would have had to eat at the diner across the street.

"Here's some chicken and look! Real bagels!" In the small kitchen area we stashed away containers of this and that, Millie already deciding that the richest food would stay with me, and she would start dieting on Monday.

I made us some café Bustelo, strong and sweet, with hot milk, and coaxed Millie to cuddle in bed. She loved the way I prepared coffee, and she leaned comfortably against me, loosening her jeans.

"I must have gained ten pounds," she declared with her eyes closed. "My mother would love to feed you, you're so thin."

We spent some time sipping coffee and undressing, comparing our body structures. I reassured Millie that her hips were no wider than mine, but then she moved on to the size of her thighs.

"Wait," I said, stroking the offending limbs, "shouldn't we, as feminists, be perfectly delighted with the size of our bodies?"

"I'll let you know when I can fit into my size-five jeans!"

"Why do they have to be size five?"

"Well. Because I'm five-one, and that's what I should wear. How tall are you?"

"I don't know exactly, five-two or -three," I told her.

"Let me measure you," she said, and she slid her body on top of mine.

It was Monday night, I had dropped Millie off at her house, and I was back at work. I walked into the ward in a bad mood, bored by the same work, cleaning floors that never get clean enough. The clients were asleep when we got there at 11:30, and they would sleep through our cleaning routines until 6 A.M. or so. I wondered what it would feel like to sleep through the banging of wheelchairs and squeaky mop buckets.

One of the older clients was awake, Angelina, a woman in her sixties with white hair and tired eyes. She was in a bad mood, too. She grumbled something at me. I grumbled back.

"Bad mood tonight, hey, Kid?" Mrs. Morse tapped me on the shoulder in greeting. If there were other aides working, they didn't talk to me very often, and although sometimes I wondered what they thought of me, tonight wasn't one of them. Fran, the third-shift charge, thought I was *okay-for-a-college-kid*, and she pulled me into the office when I worked on D side, to discuss her philosophy of life.

Angelina, for her part, wanted some attention, and she kept walking through the wet floor, getting clean nightgowns from the laundry room and folding them. I kept thinking about my languorous day with Millie, feeding each other a cold supper in bed, planning a winter weekend at a women's inn in Maine that I had no idea how we could afford. She had nixed the idea of camping, beach or no beach.

"We can take my car," Millie had said. "It's got better tires, but you drive."

"Okay, but how much do the rooms cost? I've never been to a hotel—"

"You worry too much, and it's not a hotel. It's just like a guest house. We'll figure it out. Now lie still," she ordered me, as she continued to calculate my height, her belly button against my belly button, her hips on a level with mine.

"Mmmh."

"Shhh."

"Ooh."

"Wait, Erica!"

"What?"

"You're leading again—"

"Are we dancing?" I asked in a gasping whisper.

"Yes, in a way we are, aren't we?"

"And I should slow down."

"Yeah."

"But, you're on top. Aren't you leading?"

"Well, somehow you manage to lead from the bottom—"

"I'm not making a move—I'm all yours."

"That's better," she whispered and took me at my word.

But Angelina was winning me away from my reverie. From time to time, she shot me a knowing glance because I wasn't stopping her from building up her cache of nightgowns. Fran had heard that Angelina wasn't retarded, that she had become "institutionalized" through her life-placement at the school. It was a frightening thought.

"I want another nightgown," Angelina stood with her hands folded on her belly, pouting.

"You've got at least three on your bed."

"I don't like them, *Mary*, not those colors—" she called us all "Mary."

"That's all we have. Are you getting some sleep tonight, Angelina?" I said, hopeful.

"No!" she screamed. "Sally Mayo's up! Sally Mayo's up! She don't let me sleep, no she don't!" Angelina walked back into the laundry room, yelling and gesticulating like an imitation of someone who was supposed to be very angry.

Angelina and the other women did the most outrageous things sometimes. We laughed at them, and they seemed to laugh at us trying to keep things in order. But there were moments that struck me like a joke on the world. Like Angelina, fretting and sputtering the way any old woman would when she's annoyed in her own bedroom, fussing with her nightgown and her bedclothes. Only there were strangers all around in her house, mopping the floors and keeping her awake. I went to investigate and told Fran on the way.

"She says Sally Mayo is up," I told her, poking my head into the Plexiglas office between the bathroom and the dormitory. Fran put out her cigarette and followed me into the dorm with a flashlight. We walked right out when we saw Sally Mayo coming toward us, swinging her big arms back and forth.

"No!!!" Sally bellowed with determination, looking much taller than the two of us, which she was, certainly heftier, her white hair whiter against her sallow complexion, her thin lips settling back into their perpetual frown. Fran and I scrambled to put some distance between Sally and ourselves, running from the bathroom to the day hall, while Sally took large, lumbering steps, going right past us to sit in the last bathroom stall.

Fran locked the day-hall door quickly. Through the top of the door, which was double glass with wire mesh in between, we could see Sally sitting on the toilet as though it were a chair, her legs crossed, her right hand supporting her chin.

"Go lock the bathroom door, and get Mrs. Morse," Fran told me in a low voice. Inside the bathroom, Sally murmured "Nooo," like an engine revving up. She was beginning to look scary.

I locked the door, ran across the hall, and explained the matter to Mrs. Morse, taking some pleasure, I admit, in being the bearer of such exciting news. Mrs. Morse gave the other aide some instructions and followed me to join Fran, who was standing outside of the bathroom door, by the utility sinks still full of laundry and surrounded by mops and buckets and cleaning supplies. Inside the bathroom, Sally had gotten up and walked in long, dragging steps, sometimes swinging her arms and whacking the aluminum stalls or the Plexiglas surrounding the office.

"Talk to her, Mrs. Morse," said Fran, without taking her eyes off Sally.

"What shall I say, Fran?" asked Mrs. Morse, grinning a little. Behind us, three aides from Bentley North were standing on tiptoes, trying to get a look at what was happening.

"Who do you have in there, Fran?" said their charge, joining the group. Their part of the building was now entirely without supervision.

"Did you forget to tell your clients a bedtime story, Fran?" another Bentley North aide chimed in.

"You all shut up! Go ahead, Mrs. Morse."

Mrs. Morse unlocked the door slowly, returned her keys to the pocket of her apron, and walked in with the assurance of a grandmother. Sally was now lounging in one of the wheelchairs, looking very tired. Mrs. Morse put an arm over Sally's shoulder.

"Come on, Sally, let's sing a song with Grandma." Sally arched her eyebrows at Mrs. Morse, but a few seconds later, a faint smile dimpled one of her cheeks. The crowd by the door started to relax and occupy the entrance to the bathroom.

"Old Mac Donald had a farm," from Grandma Morse.

"Ee i, ee i, oh!" Sally bared her gums in delight.

"And on this farm he had some pigs," sang Mrs. Morse, joined by the Bentley North crew.

"Pigs!" Sally clapped her hands and rocked her torso in the wheelchair. Mrs. Morse sat on the steel tub next to Sally and kept a grandmotherly arm on her shoulder. Fran, sensing the calm wouldn't last long, joined the chorus of "Old Mac Donald" and strutted her four-foot-eleven frame over to Sally and took her arm.

"Let's go to bed, Sally," said Fran as she and Mrs. Morse helped Sally up out of the wheelchair. Sally stood up, seemingly to obey, and walked with them halfway toward the dormitory, but then she let out one of her sonorous "NO's!" and flung Fran against the office door, which she quickly opened and locked behind herself.

From the office to the doorway outside the bathroom where I stood, time slowed to a crawl. Mrs. Morse took long strides back to my side, Fran picked up the phone and looked up, letting us know she would call for emergency help. Angelina came from the laundry room and hugged me. The Bentley North aides dispersed silently, or almost silently, a murmur surrounding them like bees. Inside the bathroom, Sally Mayo picked up a wheelchair and let it fall in front of her, bringing us all back to real time with its crash.

Fran hung up the phone in the office and nodded. Someone was coming. She lit up a cigarette and stood in her characteristic pose, one arm crossed under the elbow, smoking slowly, her dark eyes narrowed. She must have seen many episodes of clients losing control like Sally Mayo. Mrs. Morse and I waited also, with complete confidence in Fran's ability to handle the situation. In the tiled bathroom, Sally sat on one of the toilets and talked to herself. "Pigs? He had some pigs!" We could hear a low ripple of a laugh. Angelina, meanwhile, insisted on keeping one arm around me, saying, "She's a bad one, that Sally!" probably repeating what the aides had been saying for years about Sally Mayo.

Mrs. Morse was about to say something to me, when a loud bang and a cry from C side indicated that Rosie was awake. I transferred Angelina's arm to Mrs. Morse and offered to go take care of her. It was time that I learned to handle the more difficult clients all by myself. Fortunately, Rosie wasn't in too much of a bad mood, and she allowed me to help her into a wheelchair, taking only feeble swipes at me with her strong arms. The other aide, Abby, stayed in the office and ignored me. Finding a gown that was short enough for Rosie was a problem. She generally sat with her legs tucked under her. If the gown was too long, it interfered with her crawling and she would just rip it to pieces. I found a small pink gown that Rosie liked, and she was soon washed and dressed, sitting in the day-hall by herself.

"You think you might go back to sleep, Rosie?" I asked, just to make conversation, since I'd much rather have been across the hall watching the action.

"These black kids are the worst," commented Abby from the doorway to the day hall, where she had perched herself to watch us.

"Rosie's forty-three, Abby, she ain't no kid—"

"Taka-taka-taka!" screamed Rosie, as if to underscore the point.

"I hate slow nights like this," continued Abby on another tack. "There's nothing to do!"

"Well, if you're done with your cigarette," I jumped at the opening she provided. "I'm going to check the laundry and keep an eye across the hall, in case they need me. Okay?"

"I don't care," Abby adjusted her pink plastic headband, and I made for the laundry room. The dryers were buzzing already, so I began to unload them. In the hallway, a door creaked open and slammed shut. I leaned out to see who it was.

A nurse came running into the building, carrying a black leather bag. He first turned toward Bentley North, where the four aides told him to come down the hallway in our direction, calling after him with warnings about Sally. I escorted him to D side.

"Good evening," he said to us as we made way for him to look at Sally through the bathroom door. Something military in his bearing made me think about the ex-sergeant from my training days, except this man was black, his hair parted to the side in a sort of old-fashioned style, and he had a very gentle voice.

"She's sitting in the stall," Mrs. Morse told him, but she didn't need to, because at that moment, Sally leaned out of the stall and looked at us, her eyes bulging out, and, baring her gums in an absolutely crazy smile, squealed, "Pigs!"

The nurse, who had started to open the door, slammed it shut again and confronted us in a quick half-turn, clicking his heels together, "Why didn't you tell me this client was dangerous?" We all jumped at the crash we heard and leaned over to watch Fran go running by the fallen wheelchair thrown by Sally, through the day-hall door, around to join us.

"Fran Bernaud," said Fran, almost saluting, but then shaking the nurse's hand quickly. Not waiting to hear his response, she stretched her frame to reach almost to his chin. "Now, look. That kid is gonna hurt herself or somebody else if the rest of the residents start waking up and coming into the bathroom. That's why we called you!"

"Very well," he answered, opening his bag and taking out a hypodermic syringe, which he quickly loaded with the solution from two different bottles. "Open the door," he said to me.

As he walked over to Sally, we all piled up against the window to watch him. But somehow, our expectations of a big showdown were not fulfilled. When Sally saw the nurse coming, she walked over to the wheelchairs and sat down on one, as if she were finally getting a seat on a crowded bus. The nurse gave her the shot without a struggle, then walked quickly out and handed Fran a form to sign while he washed his hands at the utility sink.

"Roger Sinclair," he said to us, clicking his heels again. "Call me if you have any more problems with her. A physician will examine her in the morning."

Roger left, and Sally stayed up the rest of the night, pacing back and forth, muttering to herself. Fran sent me to C side to work with Mrs. Morse, who gratefully traded me for the sulking Abby. I took the opportunity to ask her what kind of a shot the nurse had given Sally.

"Thorazine," she told me. "A lot of it, by the look of her."

Toward morning, Sally was really dragging her feet and walking as though her arms weighed a ton. She sat down from time to time on one of the day-hall chairs or the toilets, with her arms folded and her legs crossed. It was funny to me that a toilet or a chair was all the same to Sally, she could be lounging in her living room with such an attitude of abandon. But she never yawned or gave signs of being as sleepy as she should have been.

D side was quiet, except for Sally, so Fran had no trouble teaching Abby the different little tricks to get the women up. Angelina, though, went grumbling back to bed. On C side, the women seemed to feel the tension, and they gave Mrs. Morse and me a hell of a time that morning. Rosie grabbed Diane's legs, who in turn kicked Judy, who was very unsteady on her feet and fell down. Before I could get to her, Elaine got very upset and started smacking her own head—this usually meant she was close to biting someone—so I went to calm her down. Mrs. Morse put Rosie back to bed until she calmed down, but this didn't last long. Frances took advantage of the situation to pull Judy's hair since she couldn't get up. While I ran to rescue Judy from Frances, Diane started kicking again, which made Agnes cry and begin to scratch everyone within reach. This was the kind of chain reaction we tried to prevent, like a game of strategy, but the catch was that we had to keep washing, dressing, brushing teeth and hair, and mopping floors and stripping beds at the same time. I imagined my grandmother in the Bronx in the 1940s, chasing after seven children all born a year apart, with no sisters or aunts to lend her a hand. It was clear why my mother was so glad to have only my sister and me.

"Daydreaming again, Kid?" Mrs. Morse's voice brought me back to the ward, so I could isolate Agnes by making her stand in the shower, and then run in the office to call in a restraint order for Diane. "Better make it a double!" called out Mrs. Morse, as she whisked Rosie away from the shower, where she had toppled

Agnes with one swing of a left hook. The aides from first shift marched in like the school principal and the homeroom teacher patrolling the girls' bathroom. Everybody was quiet, except for Rosie, who picked that precise moment to let out one of her formidable wails and staccato screams. For a novice aide, the screams were blood-chilling, but we were seasoned and determined. Still, it took three of us to tie her to the bed. Poor Rosie! In the tangle of several pairs of brown and pink women's arms, her own were as big as a man's three times her size and just as strong. Straining to hold her down while the other aides tied the restraints to the bed, I felt a kind of shame ripping through me. In Rosie's eyes, in her tightly furrowed brow, there was determination. I looked at the shock of gray hair, the lips pressed together. I began to feel dizzy, with the thought of tying down a forty-three-year-old retarded woman who couldn't walk. There was no time to feel sick. We had to strap Diane to the restraint chair next, before she really hurt someone with her kicks, separate Agnes and Elaine, and restore some semblance of order before breakfast.

"Poor Sally, her face is gray like cement," Mrs. Morse was saying on our way out of the building.

"It's the Cogentin that made her flip out like that," Fran had learned from the first-shift nurse and told Mrs. Morse and me in the parking lot.

"So, what's the Cogentin for?" I asked Fran as she started up her red Ford Pinto.

"You know that shuffle some of the kids get and the way they tilt their head to one side or the other? That tardy-something they get with the Thorazine."

"You mean tardive dyskinesia?"

"That's it, to counteract the side effects, only with Cogentin you get something else after a while. They don't usually prescribe it for more than ten days," answered Fran through the smoke of her Marlboro 100's.

"'Course, Sally's been on Thorazine for at least ten years," Mrs. Morse said, half to herself from her gold Pontiac.

"But wait, Sally's had the Cogentin on her chart ever since I've been here—since April!" I looked at both of them. Fran was putting on her gloves. Mrs. Morse looked back at me.

"She's been on it ever since I can remember, Kid," she answered.

"I mean, it's criminal!" I protested.

The engines idling in the cold morning air sent clouds of steam and blue exhaust around me.

"She's too deep for me, Fran!" said Mrs. Morse, backing up slowly.

"It's that college education—" put in Fran, throwing her car into reverse, "do it to ya every time!"

"All right, make fun of me!" I shouted after them. "And, change your oil before your valves freeze up!"

Going home, the sun rising high above the hills steeped in mist, I felt like I was keeping a dirty secret. I tried to find a name for myself. *An accomplice of the State*, I thought. Fran and Mrs. Morse had stopped fighting it, perhaps never felt they could. I remembered Diane's leg suddenly shooting out while we were strapping her down in the chair and missing my face by a fraction of an inch. I didn't know what I was supposed to do at the ward. How I could help, how I could make things better for the residents? Then again, I wasn't even sure how to make things better for myself, other than to keep things under control.

3

The first time I kissed Millie, we were at a protest rally on campus. She'd seen me working at the library earlier that day and had given me a flyer about the event. But first, she'd asked a whole lot of questions about the reference room and then about a women's newspaper she wanted. Her mouth struck me right away; then her eyes, amber; her hair, dark curls around a lovely face.

"Hm?" She pursed her lips waiting for me to answer, and I was enchanted.

"That's in periodicals. I can get it for you if you want." I knew I was going to do whatever it took to find out her name, where her dorm was, and whether her heart beat as fast as mine did at the moment.

"No, please don't bother, I'll get it." She placed her hand on mine to stop me from pushing the wooden partition door that swung out. I stayed behind it, immobile. She didn't want me to get the issue of *Commonwoman*, Fall 1976. It was in the periodicals room, and I didn't work there. What was I going to do?

But she didn't go. She waited, hung around, watched me work, when I could finally move. She was small, about my height, had small hands, had a pink scarf. I couldn't see the rest of her things, but I wanted to know every detail about her. The library clock ticked, the smell of books returned, I felt the green index cards of the reference catalog under my fingers. Suddenly, Millie was back at my cubicle, and her beautiful mouth was moving.

"Meet me in front of the library, for the march—" She handed me a flyer, and she was gone. She had grabbed her books, her pink scarf, and whatever else she had, and she was gone.

That's how we ended up together that evening, protesting against the administration for not responding sooner to the rash of rapes and attacks on campus. It was a sad night. There had been speeches, chanting, calls to action, the usual things. But for the first time, I had felt solidarity with other women in that public way and also realized that a lot of what I was feeling came from despair, from knowing this was a long road we were on, a long, long fight. I walked Millie to her dorm on the other side of Mirror Lake, holding hands. Everyone had held hands, the thousand or so students who had shown up to protest. I remember standing by the lake, holding hands in circles and circles of women—Tina, who had come from her drama class, on one side, Millie on the other.

I can't remember much else about that night because at times it seemed unreal and hazy. It was the night of the first day Millie and I met, the first time we kissed, and the first time we made love. And neither of us could explain how it happened.

There was a calm that took us over, I had never felt so close to anyone before, and I was quiet, looking at her, answering her questions about this or that, until I was kissing her. We were sitting on her bed, and the woman with the heart-shaped mouth was kissing me back. Then, she stopped.

"Don't stop," I pleaded, my lips still brushing hers.

"I was taking a breath," she said, and we laughed, sort of sighing.

Music had been playing, I don't know by whom or even what kind, and then the record ended. I remember we were lying down on the bed, my shirt half off and my jeans in a pile. Millie was struggling out of her white bra, the last item of clothing that remained on her body, when her roommate banged on the door.

"Go away!" Millie yelled, and the bra flew across the room to land on the stereo, shaking the turntable enough to make the arm jump and skid across the record. It started to play again.

"You're supposed to put a sign on the door when you have a guy in there!" her roommate yelled back, and I could hear other girls giggling in the hallway as they all walked away.

"Millie, we can wait," I whispered half-heartedly, rolling off her body.

"No, we can't," she whispered back, getting me back on top of her again.

We kissed for a long time, because it seemed there was always one more kiss to be given or taken, one more soft word, one more chance to gaze into each other's eyes in the candlelight, and then, kiss again. Until I was kissing Millie, stroking the underside of her lip with my tongue, over and over because I couldn't get enough, but so insistently my whole body was embracing hers, and I felt Millie start to come, just from kissing.

"Don't stop," she breathed and managed to slip her hand under me, slipping her fingers in my labia so gently that I didn't realize they were moving until I was gasping for air. And talking into her neck—

"Harder, a little harder," and when Millie pressed harder, she asked, "Erica?" in my ear, but I didn't answer because as she pressed she sighed, and I was becoming a lake, a mountain, an eagle, expanding, a sun.

"Fire! Fire!" cried Betty Dumond with the French inflection that accompanied her limited vocabulary.

"Okay, Betty, fire drill's over," Mrs. Morse assured our newest addition to C side. We quickly put everybody back to bed as unceremoniously as we had roused them out of it.

"Burn, burn, burn," Betty chanted in a deep voice, lulling herself back to sleep, then opening her playful black eyes. "Keess me!" She pursed her lips at me.

"Good night, Betty Dumond," I was trying to be affectionate but efficient, and I was being ridiculous. The truth is, I felt distracted and just wanted to sit in a corner and brood. All day I'd been steeped in thought, remembering how it had been the first few months with Millie. I couldn't understand why we couldn't get the sweetness back.

"Eva Nathan! That's not your blanket. Here." Mrs. Morse attempted for the umpteenth time to tuck the thin yellow blanket around Eva's shoulders, so she would stay in bed.

"Eva-get-up-and-pee!" mimicked Eva, giggling softly under the covers.

"And they say these women are retarded," commented Mrs. Morse. "Crazy is more like it!" I nodded in agreement. She tucked the disobedient lock of gray hair back in her bandana and fixed her apron. I fixed my apron and turned out the light. In the twilight, I counted twenty-eight women back in their beds, all covered with pink, blue, or yellow blankets.

We joined Fran in the hallway, as she contemplated the aftermath of a well-planned fire drill.

"Four and a half minutes on section D— what about C side?"

"Seven minutes, Fran," answered Mrs. Morse calmly.

"Seven minutes!? Your side burned, Morse!" Satisfaction was etched on Fran's smile.

"That's what Betty Dumond said," I put in, dragging perpetually wet sheets to the laundry chute. I watched her smile freeze.

"What if we hadn't been tipped off about the drill—" challenged Fran, then realized she was saying too much. "We would have really 'burned'!"

"Smoke inhalation, right Fran?" Mrs. Morse loved to test Fran's volatile temper. Fran rose to her full height and glared at Mrs. Morse with sharp, black eyes. One felt compelled to obey.

At the coffeepot, Mrs. Morse chattered on.

"She was a lazy aide, Fran was, but she got her charge's rating in two years. It's what she does best, I imagine—"

"Mrs. Morse," I entreated, "let's figure out why it took us so long . . ."

"It doesn't matter. If it ain't one thing, it's another. You never know who's gonna decide to have a seizure during a fire drill." It hadn't been a bad one, but Eva Nathan's series of petit mal seizures did slow us down. Still, I wasn't satisfied.

"But D side finished in four and a half minutes, and Fran's got thirty-two women over there," I reminded her.

"So, we've got thirty-one when everybody's back from the Clinic. Fran knows those kids, and she's got two aides besides. She sent for an extra one because she knew there'd be a fire drill tonight." Mrs. Morse looked at me over the silver of her wire-rim glasses.

"Then I don't know our kids—" I conceded. "I didn't know Rosie could be so cooperative or that Betty Dumond would walk out of her wheelchair—hell, I didn't know she could walk!"

"She can sing in French, too," was Mrs. Morse's attempt at humor.

"See what I mean?" I persisted.

"Well, it was nothing you did, Kid. We've got the ambulatory side, and they're not gonna stay by the fire exit when you tell them to. Over on D side, you put your wheelchairs by the door, and they stay there." She enhanced her explanation with a tap on my knee.

I was quiet.

"Maybe you oughta go on first shift, Kid," suggested Mrs. Morse. "If you wanna know these women, that's the way to do it."

I sipped my coffee, nodding for her to go on, because she might just have hit on how I could do better.

"I was on second shift for three years. They're very different during the day—"

"I can imagine," I interrupted. "For one thing, they wear clothes and shoes, right?"

"But not for long. You spend a lot of time putting them back on or trying to!"

"What about the Kiniry twins?" I asked, remembering the trials of my orientation.

"They go naked," she assured me.

"All day!?"

"Most of the day. Now, I remember when I requested a few of those gray jumpsuits for the Kinirys, and they liked them for about an hour." I was disappointed that there was nothing beyond what I had already seen of their behavior, but Mrs. Morse leaned back in her chair and placed her hands on her lap. She was headed for a good yarn. I stared at the clock that ticked by four-thirty and settled back in my own chair.

"When I was on second shift, I met their mother and their uncle who came to visit them once. They brought them toys, candy, and other presents that the girls enjoyed for a while, but of course, we had to put them away later. This was over ten years ago, when the twins were younger and they remembered their family."

"Hm," I interjected.

"What?"

"Well, how are they supposed to remember anybody if they don't come back for ten years!" I exclaimed, a little rattled by the idea.

"Good point," said Mrs. Morse. "But, you know, people get old and tired on the outside, too."

"I guess."

"Anyway," she continued, "the mother just got to talking, telling me about the girls before they were brought here, how she made jumpsuits for them so's they wouldn't run naked out the front door. See, they all lived out in the country at her father's house, and somebody had to watch them every minute, 'cause they was always climbing over everything, taking off their clothes, and undoing all the locks in the house. The grandfather built a playground in the yard with a fence, so's the twins could play and not get hurt, like if they ran out into the road. When the twins were eleven, it got so they could open that lock, too, and nothing worked . . ."

I looked at Mrs. Morse, who was nodding to herself a little, thinking perhaps she had convinced me of something with her story.

"And that's when they brought them here," I proposed, with the bit of arrogance that she picked up on, just as I expected. Mrs. Morse leaned back, closed her bright blue eyes behind her glasses and folded her veined hands over her belly.

"Well, what would you have done, Kid?" she challenged me, opening her eyes again. "What are you gonna do when your Mama gets old and maybe you got a husband to take care of, and some kids . . ."

"Ah, well, that's just it, I'm not getting married, and besides—" I told her. Then, I felt a little guilty for speaking so harshly to Mrs. Morse and a little confused.

"Besides?" Mrs. Morse sat there, sort of watching my thoughts. I didn't want to tell her about my mother.

"Besides, my Mama's not around anymore. But, how do you feel about getting old, are you just going to pack up and head for a nursing home? What about your son, won't he take care of you?"

"My son," said Mrs. Morse, crossing and uncrossing her fingers. "No, I guess I'm just gonna stay in my trailer with my dogs 'til I die. Why, going to a nursing home is just like coming to this place," Mrs. Morse jutted her chin toward the dorm, and I agreed with her. But there was more she wanted to say, so I waited for her.

"He's like you, you know," she finally finished, and I swallowed a whole lot of air just to keep quiet and let her talk. "He's gay, but he's too busy, always going to parties and traveling with his friends. Has about three cars, keeps 'em in top shape, not like our cars out there . . ." We shared a weak chuckle about the state of our cars, and then she continued, "No, he's not like you, he's a man, too many parties; I guess I'm gonna be fine in my trailer with the dogs."

The clock ticked by five-fifteen. It was one of those moments when I felt I understood everything in the universe, but couldn't say what I understood. Someone woke up in the dorm; we heard the shuffle of bare feet going toward the bathroom. I put my coffee down on the desk and followed Donna to the day hall where she found her way without any trouble. Mrs. Morse had told me once that when Donna was first admitted, the aides didn't know she was deaf. They could see she was blind, but they yelled at her a lot to stop lying down on the floor, until someone clapped her hands in front of Donna's face, and Donna didn't even flinch.

I stood in the day hall, close to the bathroom door, and watched the night dissipate into the first touch of daylight outside. I turned off the lights and let the day begin to drift through the tall windows. It felt like somebody's huge, empty house in there. Mrs. Morse joined me. Donna lay down on the floor near the opposite corner of the day hall, and we both probably considered getting her a blanket, but we knew she wouldn't want one. She may have been retarded, but she had definite ideas about what she liked and didn't like.

"Take Donna, for example," Mrs. Morse was still talking to me about transferring to first shift. "She's a lot wilder during the day, and you can't keep shoes on her more than five minutes."

"Come on," I challenged. "I've never seen her act up or even heard her talk. She just likes to lie down on the floor and, you know, rock!" Mrs. Morse and I smiled at each other a bit self-consciously, while Donna, her round face smiling beatifically, rocked on her side, her legs locked together, until she climaxed and giggled, the way she did every morning, three or four times. But it was very early, so after a few minutes I walked over to Donna and talked to her as though she could hear me. I took her dark hand in mine and made her stand up. Her nails were long and perfectly shaped, as though manicured.

"Let's go back to bed, Donna, you've still got a couple of hours worth of sleep—" but Donna dug her smooth, oval nails into my palm and emitted a sharp refusal. She pulled away from me and started walking in circles. I was startled; Mrs. Morse looked amused.

"Don't bother, she's up now. You would be, too, after a fire drill," she reminded me.

"But it's not even six, and it's cold in here," I tried taking Donna's hand gently.

"Doesn't matter to her, does it," put in Mrs Morse.

"Aah! Aah!" screamed Donna, stomping her bare feet on the floor. "Aah!!" She bit her hands furiously, groaning.

"What do I do, Mrs. Morse?" I asked, bewildered.

"I'd get her some socks," she said, walking to the laundry room. "It's cold on these floors."

By 6 A.M. half the ward was awake, so Mrs. Morse and I began the toileting and dressing routine. Donna had been the first one, and then the usual crew woke up. I kept an eye on Donna as we continued with the morning's work. Some women got their period, so I recorded it in the book. Just out of curiosity, I leafed back to the previous month and didn't see Donna's name until I went back to October. It said, "October 20 Menses: Eva Nathan and Donna Scott." So she had missed November. Could she be having cramps now? I walked over to the day-hall and sat down next to her, she in an orange plastic chair, me in a yellow one. Her brown feet grazed the red tile as she swung them back and forth, and the white socks were in a heap next to her. She held her hands in her lap while her face looked up, her eyelids closed.

Looking at her face, knowing she couldn't look back, felt like an intrusion. I took her left hand, and she let me hold it. She hurt, there was no doubt in my mind, but I didn't know how to comfort her. So I took her pulse; it was rapid, but she didn't appear to have a temperature. "Mrs. Morse!" I called. "Donna's got cramps!"

"The nurse won't give her an aspirin, though, until after her period comes," pronounced Mrs. Morse.

"Well, what do I do?! If it were me, I'd be climbing the walls!"

"See if she wants to go back to bed," suggested Mrs. Morse, struggling with Agnes, who was on a scratching rampage. Fortunately, Donna took my hand and let me put her back to bed, where I gave her an extra blanket and a pillow to hold against her belly.

While I was in the dorm, I woke the Kiniry twins up and took them both by the hand to the bathroom. Like clockwork, they both started their period. "It's got to be a full moon," I said to

Mrs. Morse, who took in my bit of lesbian theory without question.

"I bet you'll be next, Kid, by the time you get home!"

"And you're so relieved you don't have to go through this anymore, right, Mrs. Morse?"

"You said it!" We worked as an efficient team, dressing the Kiniry twins with sanitary pads and jumpsuits tied at the waist with Mrs. Morse's square knots. "That oughta hold them 'til breakfast," she patted the twins affectionately and sent them into the day hall. We finished at the stroke of 7:30, just when the buzzer rang in the office and the first shift walked in. I answered the telephone, knowing it was for me.

"Hi, baby!" Millie's endearment brought me back to who I was.

"Hey, love—what are you doing up?"

"Your sister . . ." yawned Millie, "called me from New Britain—"

"Oh-my-god, who died?"

"Nobody!" Millie laughed, since she was well aware of the strained relationship between me and my sister. "There's a snow-storm, and she asked me why you weren't home. I told her, because you were working, and she said you should move back to New Britain because your car will never make it in this weather—"

"There's her wonderful logic for you—"

"And, she said if you don't go back, maybe you should get married. She's better than my Aunt Barbara!"

"Thanks, Millie, I'll call her."

"I miss you," yawned Millie.

"You think we should get married?"

"Not 'til June, anyway," she tossed back. "I'd have nothing to wear for a winter wedding. But I think you should drive to my house and stay on Route 32, then 275 should be clear when you turn. Park at the corner and walk up to the lake—your sister is right, you'll never make it to Willimantic in this stuff."

"Okay, see you soon . . ." I whispered, while the first-shift charge came in to shuffle papers on the desk, and her ears strained to catch something meaningful out of my conversation. It had been snowing for the past couple of hours, and even on 32, I'd probably slide from side to side, maneuvering my old Valiant on bald tires.

At the utility sink I took off my red apron and stuffed it in my knapsack. Mrs. Morse and I scrubbed our hands with betadine like a couple of surgeons.

"Looks like a foot of snow out there," she jutted her chin toward the windows. The meal truck backed against the building while the dining room supervisor motioned the driver to get closer to the ramp. An argument of sharp gestures and hand motions ensued, but the driver won and started unloading the huge trays of steaming hot cereal, the steam rising into the flurries, the old man up to his knees in cushy mounds of snow.

Snow blew into my car in large flakes because the old convertible top could no longer be fastened. I'd bought the car from a mechanic in Willimantic who warned me not to put the top down, or the rusty hinges would never allow me to roll it back again. Of course, that was during the summer, and the first thing Millie and I did was to put it down, dangle some beads from the rearview mirror and head for Moonstone Beach in Rhode Island. Those had been such glorious days in the sun; even the nights when the sudden summer rain would send me cursing outside to roll the top back before the Valiant got flooded. In the mornings, Millie would wake me with pastries and delicacies for our late breakfasts in bed and then complain that being in love was making her fat.

Back and forth, the beads swayed from the mirror with every slow curve of the snowy road to Millie's house. The last thing Mrs. Morse and I talked about was how many of the women in the ward were "on the pill." We usually sat in the parking lot for a bit, while our cars idled, and if there was a problem, I helped her start hers. This time, she sat with me while I rocked the Valiant out of the snow ridge the plow had left, while I carried on about how unfair it was to prescribe birth control pills for all the women clients who had "difficult" or irregular periods.

Mrs. Morse agreed, but I couldn't get her to go with me and present a complaint to the human rights commission for retarded persons. She thought they'd never take it seriously, but she didn't try to discourage me from writing my observations down in the log. The only advice she gave me was not to write anything *feminist*.

As I drove, I worked myself up to confront the administration: I had no idea where to start. Realizing I'd lost all traction, I had to stop that and concentrate on the road. The defroster was worthless, my sleeve wasn't wiping the condensation off the windshield anymore, and a set of yellow headlights was suddenly pointed right at my hood. Another car had skidded and was sliding sideways across the right lane. With a sudden swerve of the steering wheel, I avoided a crash but ended up in a snowbank while the other car rolled safely away.

Once the wipers stopped moving, all I heard was the hum of the stalled motor, and all I could see, with a curtain of snowflakes enveloping my car on all sides, was the alternator light flashing red on the dashboard. It couldn't be dead—*I would be dead if anything happened to my car*—I was scared. Suddenly, for no reason I knew, I conjured up images of my sister watching the "Lucy Show" and laughing like crazy. She knew my car wouldn't make it. I couldn't be angry, this actually was funny. I decided to become Ricky Ricardo and let loose my frustration inside my snowbound car. I swore in Spanish and made spurious references to the other driver's paternal and maternal relations. I felt better. But it was eight-thirty in the morning, and I was stuck in a snowbank five miles from Millie's house. More snow drifted in through the convertible top, the spot that always came undone no matter how many times I banged on the latch. I banged on it with my fist, and miraculously it stayed secured. Feeling more encouraged, I abandoned Ricky Ricardo and searched my cluttered backseat for the shovel tangled up in the jumper cables.

Outside, the scene was breathtaking. Not another car for miles, the trees along the road dusted with snow, smoke curling up from the chimneys of the only two visible houses. I shoveled all around the car in a few minutes, trying to imagine glowing fireplaces and the smell of something hot on the stove. A sudden gust of wind uncovered the north side of a monumental pine, brushing clean the lush branches swaying dark green against the gray sky. Unexplainably beautiful. Unexplainable, too, the image that crossed my eyes of a bewildered Eva Nathan exhausted between seizures, staring at me with vacant green eyes. Getting back in and rocking the car, I got most of the way out onto the road, until the right wheel began to spin fruitlessly and to dig into the gravel and the ice. I prepared to push with the door open and jump in on the run, feeling exhilarated, hardly aware of the cold. *How can I be enjoying this?*—I wondered. I figured it was hypothermia setting in.

I had just begun pushing when I saw headlights through my frozen eyelashes. A faded blue Saab came coasting over to a stop. Millie. She ran out and pressed her hands against my cheeks.

"I've got to be dreaming," I told her. I kissed her, and she stuck her tongue in my mouth. "Hey, cut it out!" I protested, laughing, and still holding on to her.

"You're being rescued!" She pushed away from me and went to look at the back wheel stuck in the snow. We studied the situation.

"Give me a good shove with the Saab so I can get this thing outta here!"

I began to wake up, my teeth suddenly chattering with the cold. But it only took one shove on my rear bumper with Millie's car, and I was sliding merrily down the slick road. At the bottom of the hill, I put the car in gear, knowing there was little chance of this working on an automatic transmission, but it kicked in and started up. Then I tried the brakes and kept right on sliding on my bald tires. I prayed for luck to make the turn at the intersection, and I did. By revving all eight cylinders to a scream, I managed to fishtail into a sort of parking space around the corner from Millie's house and then jumped into the chortling, lifesaving old Saab.

"H'about a hot bath with me in it?" Millie suggested. She could take my breath away in a second. The sun made her dark hair glow red, her mouth was redder still, and I was dying to kiss her.

"You oughta rescue me more often," was all I could think of to tell her, but it was enough.

Waking up at dusk had a terrible effect on me. I was still tired, my body ached in every tight muscle, and when I saw it was five o'clock, I rose and deliberately stepped under a cloud of ill temper.

"I've wasted the day already," I announced to Millie.

"You didn't seem so tired this morning," she winked.

"I was hypothermic."

"Well, now you'll be rested for your days off," she consoled me.

I sat at the round wooden table and watched Millie plucking dead leaves from under a huge spider plant that hung over the kitchen sink. All the plants in Millie's house thrived under her care. I wanted to trade my existence for that of one of the happy ferns in her bathroom and give up all my worries.

"I'm working overtime three nights so I can get tires for the Valiant," I decided. Millie looked alarmed.

"But you won't get that money for two weeks," she reminded me. "And by that time the snow will be gone," she tried.

"And my tires will be flat," I countered. Millie clicked her tongue in exasperation and turned to remove a glorious eggplant parmesan from the oven. I got up to get dishes and forks, wishing she'd try again to convince me not to work. I hated the idea of working during my pass days, but plenty of people did it routinely at the Training School, to get new cars or to pay old bills. Why shouldn't I strive to get my old Valiant outfitted with new tires? "Besides, I thought I would keep an eye on Donna and the other women at the ward." Millie kept silent.

I served squared portions of the eggplant onto the blue-rimmed plates and regretted being difficult. I was anxious about more than just the car, but I didn't know quite what was bothering me. Whatever it was, I had a feeling I should get lost in my work and forget it. Millie slid an empty blue glass on the table with the tips of her fingers toward me.

"I suppose you can't have any wine, then." She sat next to me, in jeans and a pink sweater, her eyes teasing me. I hugged her and buried my face in her hair.

"I'd love some wine," I mumbled into her curls. "I don't know what's bothering me—"

"Eat," she said, pushing me gently away. She poured red wine into our glasses while I had the first bite. We were silent for a long time. It was a luminous night, and the moon was just waning.

"Guess what?" asked Millie. "The street got plowed, and the Saab is buried up to the windows in snow. I can't drive you in now."

"That's okay, babe. There are emergency rides I can call." Millie's face was blank, but I kept on, "Nurses and aides can get a break in snowstorms, but I'll help you dig the Saab out tomorrow, Millie."

"So you're determined, aren't you?"

"I need snow tires—" I felt I had to convince both of us.

"That job gets you depressed, not to mention . . . cranky."

"It was the full moon, I'm probably getting my period," I said, hitting on the first sane explanation for how I'd felt.

"But look at you, you're as sallow as . . . a vampire!" She indicated the little mirror framed by two planters overflowing with ivy. "And you're no fun during the day, and can't ever stay late at parties . . ."

That got to me. While Millie piled the dishes in the sink, I did go take a look at my face. I was pale, with puffy eyes, no spark in them.

"Millie, I think I want to change my major to Sociology and go back to school. Once I get new tires for the car, I can save up to start part-time. Do you know that at the Training School practically all the women on my ward are on contraceptives to regulate their periods? Can you imagine what the incidence of cancer could be for retarded women? I'm going to organize a protest, and I might even join the union."

"You sound like my grandfather in Russia, except you're a feminist. Why don't you get a loan from Nélida to go back to school? Sit down, have some more wine."

"I don't want any more wine, and Nélida doesn't have that kind of money. And what do you mean I'm boring?"

"I didn't say you were boring, I said you're no fun . . ."

"During the day, I know. Well, I'm putting in for a transfer to first shift, then I can be normal, and you can love me again."

"Oh." Millie didn't look very happy.

"Didn't you hear? I'll work during the day and sleep at night, when you sleep!"

Millie hugged me, smiling indulgently, and I pulled away. "Now, what?" she complained.

"I thought my plans to be a normal person would make you happy. I know it's stupid, but—"

"It's not stupid! Really. Look, do you want to make me happy?"

"Of course. You know I do."

"Then you can move in with me and save money on rent and get your tires, and we can go away tomorrow for the weekend!"

This sounded very odd to me, but I didn't want to think—I didn't know if that's what I wanted, but I didn't want it to happen like that, on an economic basis. I wanted love, I wanted . . . "What do you mean—for the weekend?"

"Everybody's going up to Vermont, to Scooter's parents' cabin. We'll go skiing."

"Millie." She had started to work on another plant, and I couldn't see her face through the leaves.

"What?" She plunged her fingers in the dirt. I took one of her hands and wiped the dirt off. She bit her lower lip a little.

"I thought we were going to that guest house in Maine, just you and me."

"But this is easier and closer, and we'll be with friends up there!"

"I don't know what's up with you and Scooter, but if you're interested in me, I can't just switch schedules when it's convenient. I have to put in for it, wait, get my evaluation . . ."

"Why not?"

"That's how the State works, there are a lot of people working there . . ."

"Then take a vacation!" She brightened with the thought.

"I have to put in for that, too."

Millie took her hand back and attacked the potting soil again. "You sound like a factory worker. What's the big deal!"

My face fell, and Millie sighed. I got up to go look for something in the other room. Millie followed me, and I turned to her before she could speak.

"I *am* a factory worker. I'm a direct-care *aide*, you know? My father was a factory worker and my mother. And my sister was an aide like me until she made it to nursing school—you didn't know that all this time?"

"I'm sorry." Her voice was a trickle. I was looking for the emergency number in my knapsack. Millie's bedroom was dark, and I couldn't see a thing despite the moon. The silhouette of plants on the windowsill was a sinister play of shadow puppets. Millie turned the light on.

"You know," I told her, knowing that the words would sting, but not wanting to admit how rejected I had felt. "It's a good thing I'm not moving in. Scooter warned us about the evils of lesbian merging and bourgeois expectations. Her grandfather must have come from Russia, too."

"No, Erica, you're wrong!" Suddenly, Millie was crying.

"He's not from Russia—?" I felt stupid, like the whole conversation was stupid.

"No, I mean, about Scooter. She doesn't mean anything to me. I love you. *You*, not her!"

"Okay." Millie and I stood across from each other. I didn't know what to do.

"She's just a waspy rich girl, and I like hanging around because things are easy for her, okay? Is that what you wanted me to say?"

"No, Millie. I wanted you to say you love me."

4

I run on the bathroom floor using my well-worn sneakers to slide across the smooth tile. Tonight I've been assigned to D side because Mrs. Morse has two new aides to help her. It seems the snowstorm brought quantities of loyal aides out of their snug houses to make sure there would be enough coverage, especially in the larger wards. Things are fairly quiet, and I like it fine, although I hate cleaning the wheelchairs. It's monotonous work; the wheels have urine and food stuck on them, and sometimes it turns my stomach. (I focus on my work, it's my work, and I can play at it just as well as I can do it seriously. Millie is constantly in the back of my mind.)

Now that they're all clean, I line them up by the old gang shower that never gets used, and I run as I push them, sliding across the floor. Fran is in the office, writing in the files, smoking a cigarette, and watching me from time to time. I know she thinks I'm a little strange, different from the other aides, because she watches me with her piercing black eyes while I try to amuse myself, and she doesn't say anything.

Next is the huge day-hall floor with its dull red tile. I find the least squeaky mop pail and fill it with hot water and a long squirt of bleach and detergent. Last week, Fran and another supervisor had a fight over what to use on the floor—some people use ammonia, some use bleach because it removes the scuff marks from the chairs sliding all over the day hall. As a result, one sometimes gets a wicked whiff of ammonia and chlorine vapor, and the stringy mops fall apart in a few weeks. This particular incident was controversial because somebody got the bright idea of using a pine cleaner on the floor. It certainly smelled better, but the first time a client peed on the floor, the oil from the cleaner had everybody skating. (Are these things really important? Do I go home and remember them just like all the other aides? Is there a life for me beyond the ward and my paycheck twice a month?)

I submerge the cotton mop in the dark brown water and push the pail on wheels to the day hall. Every door is locked for security, so it's quite an accomplishment to be able to lock and unlock the heavy doors with one hand.

Invariably, the first time I squeeze the water out by pulling the mop through the rollers, strings get caught in them, sometimes in the wheels, and I have to yank the filthy strings out of the hinges. The mop smells, it's never clean enough. I wash the floor pretending it's the deck of a ship, seeing the imaginary sunburn on my rugged hands, my sailor's cap askew on my head, then I start marking out geometric shapes to make it more interesting. A sudden noise startles me, and I look up to see Fran staring at me, hands on her hips. She has snapped me out of my game.

"You want to be here all night, Erica?" She reached for the mop. I figured she'd given up trying to say my last name correctly. She showed me again how to wash the floor in wide, efficient swirls that methodically cover ground in even rows. I followed her, pushing the pail with my foot, row after row, until the floor was done. She's shorter than I am, about fifty, with short black hair, has a dynamic slim figure, and wears sporty coordinated outfits. Her white Keds are always clean, a fact that baffles me.

"Come have coffee with me in the office," she said finally, handing me the mop. I thanked her. There were more strings stuck around the wheels, and the pail wouldn't roll in a straight line anymore. I dumped out the dirty water and decided to leave the strings there for the next person. A squirt of betadine in my hands made abundant lather, up to my forearms.

With a paper cup full of Maxwell House, I followed Fran to the office from which we surveyed the ward at night. The control tower encased in Plexiglas.

"You're quiet tonight," she began.

"I'm on overtime," I explained. "Five nights is really the limit for me, but I need snow tires—" She eyed me in her offhand way, yet I could tell something else was on her mind.

"You go around with boys?" She got right to the point.

"Nah," I shrugged, and drank some coffee.

"You're better off," she assured me, leaving nothing further for me to explain.

The last swirls dried on the day-hall floor. Sitting comfortably inside the office I stared at my completed task. The floor looked as dull as ever, with the same bleached stains here and there, the plastic bucket chairs lined up against the pink-tiled wall. It occurred to me that the purpose of the large, ugly hall was to evoke, for our residents, an ordinary living room. The console TV sat eight feet high, braced on metal brackets attached to shiny walls. I communicated my despair to Fran.

"Nobody ever watches that old TV. Why don't we ask for a basketball hoop?" She cracked a smile.

"Maybe you need a vacation," she prescribed.

"What about you, Fran? After eleven years, you should take a month off," I pointed out.

"Oh, vacations never last in this place," she shook her head, took another extra-long Marlboro out of the pack, and for some reason, I lit it for her.

"They never last. You always come back to this, and this is the same thing, day in and day out. You know what I mean?" She stared intently at me, wanting me to understand—"You know. . . ?"

"I think I know." I tried to understand or to tell her what I thought. "You mean, this work is so constant that everything else seems temporary?" I asked. She looked puzzled.

"No. It's just that we're here more than anywhere else!" She turned her palms up, cigarette smoke rising between her fingers, annoyed that I didn't seem to get it. We were silent. I felt distant from the scene at that moment. After just a few months of working there, I became *existential*. I was the Cortázar of the institution, seeing the irony nobody questioned, working with older people, getting worked up about the injustices I saw. Or maybe I was the Emma Goldman of the state wards. I had to laugh at my own pretensions.

"Look at these *kids*," Fran said, pointing with her cigarette toward the dormitory where the women residents slept. "All they've got to live for is some stranger coming to them every day, saying, *Put your footsie in this sock; sit on the toilet.* Every day the same thing." She sighed. I sighed. Then she got a bright idea.

"The Bentley North supervisor was talking about washing the walls last night," she said with an inspired look I feared, "but we've already done ours!"

"That's right, Fran," I agreed, hoping she would forget any notion of spectacular cleanings in order to show up her rival from Bentley North, in a match of domestic fury.

"So tonight, since we've got all this extra help—look, it's just 2 A.M. now, and you've got all your work done. We can wax our end of the hallway," she put her cigarette down with finality. I cursed my luck. Why now? I've always hated cleaning sprees.

Growing up, I felt terribly inadequate whenever Mami and Nélida would be smitten by the desire to set the world to rights. There was no escape. My inexperienced pair of hands would be immediately drafted into a kind of ritual that promised to purify in its wake every shred of indolence manifested in me, for the sheer coincidence of being female. I deeply resented this fact as I was lost forever in a melee of hot water, rags, and hard wax.

I followed Fran obediently to the dispensary in search of the electric buffer. I felt my stomach knotting up, my palms beginning to sweat, becoming positively phobic as Fran unlocked the door, and the smell of wax and industrial cleaners assaulted my nose. The phone rang in the center office, and Fran went to answer it while I struggled with the heavy buffer. I wondered at my violent reactions—could the other women, presumably straight, tell that I felt so alien as they bustled about, filling buckets, fetching assorted scrubbery, even my buddy, Mrs. Morse? I figured that's how she knew I was a lesbian, though she was the only person at the school who'd ever brought it up. I'd wanted to hear more about her son, but she wasn't going to say any more about that. I managed to untangle the cord from the push brooms and mops in the closet. There were mouse turds in there, too.

"*Gracia!*" Fran called suddenly from the office. "Never mind the buffer, I'll do that." The eyes of all the night staff were on me.

"*Garcia*, Fran," I corrected her. "What's up?"

"They need a wagon driver tonight. Seems there are practically no men on overtime, so they asked for anyone who could drive in the snow." Fran seemed at once concerned and proud to be able to provide the third-shift administration with a suitable driver, even if it wasn't a man.

"You're a hot rod, aren't you, Kid?" said Mrs. Morse, ambling up the hallway to the utility closet.

"She'd have to be, with that blue wreck she drives," joined

Fran, making the other aides snicker. I shot her a look. "No offense, *Gar-cía*," she said finally.

The administration building looked curiously like a college dorm from the outside. I walked up to it following deep tracks in the snow and sort of slid into the front door, where the coming and going of many feet had made the surface slick. I stamped my feet against the stone steps and shook off my cap. With one hand, I brushed my hair back and had the odd sensation of waking myself up, feeling solid again after playing at not feeling anything. *If I can just keep going, one foot in front of the other* . . . who'd said that. My mother? Nélida?

Inside, the building consisted of endless narrow corridors and cluttered small offices, much like the small offices of the Humanities Building at school. At night, only one floor was lighted. The hallway was cut in slices of yellow light from the open doors. I walked into room 302 and was greeted laconically by the man at the books.

"Wagon driver?" he asked, without looking up.

"Right," I answered. He handed me keys, mileage chart, and a Night Shift Destination Log on a clipboard.

"Pick it up at Tennessee Hall, return it to the garage behind the Laundry at 7:23 A.M. Any problem, write it down."

"Right," it seemed like the best thing to say.

Tennessee Hall was one of the oldest buildings on grounds, where the "senior" residents were housed. Rumor had it that many of these people were *normal,* but that they had become "institutionalized" from living there since they were young. These were the *misfits* of the '30s and '40s, the wayward teenagers, the pregnant girls from the working class, very often the children of "mixed-race" marriages between blacks and whites.

I located the brown station wagon in the parking lot and

started to get in, only to be scared out of my wits by the little man who sat in the passenger's seat, chanting in a husky voice:

"Jerry-to-the-hospital! Hello-Jerry-hello-Jerry!"

I took a deep breath and adjusted my cap. "Tennessee Hall, Jerry Fournier, Clinic," read the log. It was signed by the previous wagon driver who apparently had gone home sick. Poor Jerry must have been waiting patiently for the past half hour. I turned the heater on full blast.

"Why do you have to go to the Clinic, Jerry?"

"Hello-Jerry-hello-Jerry," came the response.

"Right, Jerry," I said, just to keep my end up.

The snow had covered the swings and slides in the fenced yards, and left the grounds looking quiet and manageable. Neatly plowed roads, fresh mountains of the stuff surrounded by brick buildings. I drove the oversized wagon confidently, feeling oddly exhilarated. There I was, entering the tough buildings, the violent wards where only the men work, talking face-to-face with those cigar-chewing supervisors, earning the respect of the older women in my building because I can drive like a man. *Better than a man*, I thought, shifting into low to make it up the hill.

I drove up to the Clinic door and went around to help Jerry out of the wagon.

"Go-to-clinic-Jerry-go-to-clinic," babbled Jerry incessantly.

"Here we are, Jerry, let's go in." I took his arm, but he stayed glued to his seat.

"Go-Jerry-go-to-clinic-go-to-the-clinic!" He rocked stiffly back and forth, his hands in the pockets of his parka, his gray hair covering his eyes. The more agitated Jerry became, the faster he rattled off his sentences. I didn't want to scare him, he already looked frightened enough, with his red-rimmed, watery gray eyes, and his ashen white skin. Then I thought, there must be something he responds to, a key prompt, a code word. In his regimented life things must happen the same way every day, even the

Clinic visits must have become routine, so that they were part of his vocabulary.

"Jerry, give me a hint," I leaned into the car again.

"Hello-Jerry-hello," he responded, rocking faster.

"Jerry, come on, what's the password?" I asked.

"Hello-Jerry-to-the-clinic!" He yelled.

"Jerry," I said very softly, "don't you want to see the doctor?"

"Doctor-Levin-yes-doctor-Levin," said Jerry, getting obediently out of the wagon.

"I don't believe it," I took his arm and led him to the Clinic door. I saw then that his left foot was bandaged and barely fit in a brown slipper. Jerry and I walked slowly on the icy sidewalk. A nurse opened the door, taking the log sheet from me and greeting Jerry.

"Hello, Jerry, is Dr. Levin going to look at your leg?"

"Yes-doctor-yes-doctor-Levin!" responded Jerry, a smile on his thin, wrinkled face. Driving away from the Clinic, I was thinking that everybody on grounds must have known the secret to make Jerry move. Nice of them to tell me.

Between 2 and 3 A.M., I covered half the buildings on grounds, delivering manila envelopes and picking up messages. In each building, the charge aide asked if I wanted coffee and the other aides eyed me suspiciously. At Eaton West, two aides were sleeping in the plastic bucket chairs, while another kept watch and folded laundry.

"Quiet night," I said to him. The other two men jumped out of their chairs.

"Want some coffee?" he said sheepishly. I handed him an envelope and a package from the Clinic.

"No, thanks. Which ward is this?" I asked.

"Violent males," answered the youngest aide. "But they sleep good at night," he assured me.

"I see. Well, good night," they watched me leave, probably wondering whether I'd squeal about them catching some sleep between the hourly phone checks. One group of buildings had to call the supervisors on the half hour, and the rest, on the hour. If they missed their call, a supervisor would be visiting the building within ten minutes to check on them.

At 3:45, I picked up Jerry at the Clinic, three packages of special meds, and took him back to Tennessee Hall. Jerry was in a festive mood after receiving some personal attention, and he sang "Jingle Bells" in his husky tones, but perfectly in tune. I whistled along with him until we arrived at his ward. He stepped carefully on the snow with his newly bandaged foot. A young woman came out to meet us.

"Are you the floater?" she asked, hopefully.

"See-the-doctor-jinglebells!" burst out Jerry.

"Shh! Jerry!" she half-whispered. "Let's get you to bed!"

"I'm just the wagon driver," I told her, while she helped Jerry with his coat. "What's the matter?"

"We're short one aide, and everyone's waking up," she told me.

"Hello-Jerry-go-to-clinic," called Jerry from the office.

"Jerry, what are you doing there?" she raced after him, but it was too late. Jerry had finished the cup of coffee that was sitting on the desk and was now devouring an ashtray full of cigarette butts.

"Gross, Jerry, cut it out!" We both attempted to get Jerry to spit out the butts. "You're disgusting," she admonished him. Ashes fell all over the papers, and Jerry stank of nicotine. I said sharply, "Jerry, *Doctor* Levin wants you in bed resting that leg—now!"

The man's face quivered, and he wiped the ashes from his mouth, his startled gray eyes acknowledging the order, and moving his entire body like a mechanical doll, he rushed off to the dorm murmuring Dr. Levin's orders over and over. I immediately regretted showing off and offered to radio administration to remind them to send another aide to Tennessee Hall.

"Thanks, they already know," the young woman told me, as she escorted me back out through the laundry room.

Toward morning, I was exhausted but wired from the coffee. Every errand took longer than I expected, so I didn't stop to eat anything. I went back twice to the Clinic, once to bring fresh ground coffee from another building, and once to pick up a nurse who was needed at Eaton West because one of the "kids" had put his fist through a bathroom window.

My last envelope was delivered at the Morrison Building where I'd gone during my orientation and had met all the blind clients. It was after seven, everyone was seated at the breakfast tables. Brown and mostly pale faces, young and old women and men, their hair neatly combed, their eyes closed or staring fixedly, their hands crossed on the table, and in front of each person, a steaming bowl of oatmeal.

Giddy from lack of sleep, I leaned on the door jamb, observing the people. There was a hush when the morning supervisor entered the room; a plump brown girl stood up carefully, her hands still clasped together in front of her, and she began to sing, her head thrown back, her lids tightly shut, like Christina's had been. All at once, a harmony rose out of every person seated there, music so vibrant and perfect it had no words I could hear, only melodious tones that reverberated inside me until tears came to my eyes.

The singing ended as suddenly as it had begun, the girl sat down, and everyone started on their breakfast.

"You the wagon driver?" the supervisor said, taking the envelope from my hands.

"Do they do that every day?" I asked, stumbling out of the dining room after her.

"Beautiful, isn't it? Yes, every day for the past fifteen years, they sing grace before each meal. Which building do you work?" she asked.

"Bentley South," I answered, still dazed.

"Ah, one of Fran's girls. Tell her I said hello," she signed my log sheet and watched me while I put my brown leather cap back on.

Outside, the sun was pale behind the clouds, the winds blew cold, carrying flecks of snow that stuck to my face. All I'd been thinking of was how to make things right again with Millie and feeling too damn sorry for myself. But she was going on that ski trip, and I was a fool because I didn't know how to let her love me. This, I decided, was the trouble with our relationship. I didn't want surprises, I wanted to know what was coming, so I never let my guard down, trying to stay on top of every moment. I was a double fool.

I returned the wagon to the garage, then walked on the crunchy snow through the sidewalks by the administration building. Inwardly, I tried to decipher the mystery of the difference between night and day. The same building at night had seemed ominous, now it was drab, ordinary. Noticing a bulletin board in the lobby, I went in and scanned a few of the job openings. They were for the Cottages, but on third shift. Nothing for first. I took one of the notices with me anyway and read it as I walked out to the main road.

The wind whistled even under my cap, and I pulled it down to my ears. I wasn't sure I wanted to work at the Cottages. According to Fran, that was for lazy people. There was a certain loyalty in staying at the large buildings.

I stuck out my thumb and hoped for an uneventful ride back

home. It might be days before I could get my car out; it was probably buried in snow by the lake at Millie's.

For the next two nights, I was called to drive the wagon, which was fine with me. I escaped waxing and polishing at my building and joined the night crews on grounds, trying to keep up with the snow that never stopped falling. The men shoveling and pushing snow with small tractors waved to me as I drove the wagon; the aides, sending laundry bags, ground coffee, or extra sheets from building to building, got to know me by sight. The young aide at Tennessee Hall saved me a blueberry muffin, and Jerry greeted me with a cheerful, if monotonous, "Hello-doctor-Levin-hello!" I complimented him on his much improved left foot, on which he wore a bright red sneaker only a couple of sizes too big for him.

I had no problems getting rides to work and back, and all the activity kept my mind safely away from thoughts of Millie. The last morning the snow stopped, and I hitched a ride with a sociology professor in graduate studies. With an English accent, he asked me what I did at the Training School. "Forgotten souls, aren't they?" he commented about my clients.

He dropped me off right in front of my apartment, and I went to sleep thinking about how someone would manage to get to graduate school. It was very unsettling, since I couldn't even think about how I would finish my B.A.

Minutes later, it seemed, the telephone woke me.

"Hey, baby, I hate to tell you this, but the Valiant's been towed," said Millie, somewhere between my dreams and a headache.

"Hi, love, when did you get back?"

"Just now. What are you going to do about the car?"

"I'm going to die," I mumbled, seeking comfort under my quilt.

"No, you won't," she assured me. "It's probably just on Main Street, at the Mobil station—"

"Of all the ungrateful things to do!" I clamored, wrapping the quilt around my flannel pajamas. "I spend all three of my pass days working to get it new shoes, and it gets its worthless chrome ass hauled away while I sleep."

"Are you okay?" Millie asked softly.

"Yes, it's just cold in here, I'm going to freeze on the way to the bathroom."

"Oh, god, I forgot—"

"What?" The conversation was beginning to take on its familiar comfort.

"Your bathroom," Millie sighed. "I forgot yours is out in the hallway. Listen, I feel so bad."

"Why? It's not out in the snow or anything, and it's private. Nobody else on this floor can use it," I added with some pique.

"I know, I meant about the other night," Millie appeased. "I spent the whole time at Scooter's thinking about you. I'm sorry I was insensitive. I missed you."

"Do you know what time it is?" I asked quickly.

"Yes," Millie said expectantly, "do you?"

"Well, if it's before five, will you come with me to collect my wayward vehicle? Meet me there, we need to talk."

"It's three-thirty."

"I'll see you at the Mobil at four, then I'll treat you to dinner at the veggie restaurant."

Millie agreed, and I ran down the hall to take a hot shower. Making faces in the mirror, I acknowledged a couple of things to myself. One, circles under my eyes did not look good on me, and perhaps the cottages were one way to get on first shift a little faster. I had to give it a try. Two, Millie probably felt worse about *being insensitive* to me than I felt about being left out of the skiing weekend. I should get over it and have a good time with my girlfriend, now that she was back. I dressed in flannel-lined jeans, my favorite flannel shirt and black turtleneck, my navy pea coat, and the hiking boots that I bought cheap at a men's store that carried small sizes. I felt insulated against anything that came my way, except the boots were still a little stiff, and I had a hard time going down the stairs. Calculating my overtime check, I headed for the Mobil.

The Valiant sat in the parking lot at the gas station with two feet of snow on its sagging roof. Out of the corner of my eye, I saw Millie walking over, wearing her blue down parka and her pink scarf. The snow was melting and dripping into the backseat, so I began to take chunks of snow off with my hands. The rear bumper was visibly bent in the middle.

"The payloader bumped into it," explained Jack, the mechanic. He looked about 35, with a mass of reddish hair escaping from under a greasy red cap, crowning his brown face. "We didn't know what could be under all that snow," he pointed out in congenial tones.

"I guess not," I said.

"Sorry about the dent," said Jack.

"You bet," I said, just as friendly; after all, I had abandoned my car in a snowstorm.

"Hey, how does that thing run? It's gotta be over ten years old—"

"Fourteen," I told him, turning the key in the ignition. The faithful engine turned over and roared.

"A V-8?" said Jack, slightly impressed.

"Take a look," I offered.

Millie grinned at me while I went around to pop open the hood. Wiping his hands on an oily rag, Jack chipped at the ice on the latch with a screwdriver. Gas and oil fumes rose from the carburetor.

"Automatic transmission," noted Jack.

"Push-button," I said coolly.

Millie got a broom from the garage and pushed the rest of the snow off the roof, while Jack charged me only five dollars for the tow, considering the dent in the rear bumper of such a classic old car.

The name of the restaurant was "Erehwon," like the bread, which was supposed to be nowhere spelled backward. The bread was only sold in special places like the health food store on campus. Tina told me about the natural toothpaste I like. It tastes like fennel and mint, and reminds me of a vegetable my mother brought once from the bodega; it was called "hinojo," and I never saw it again. Anyway, Millie hated the toothpaste, but she loved to go have dinner at Erehwon. She claimed that if she could cook like they did, she'd be thin forever.

Sitting at our favorite booth by the window, we took off our coats, and Millie leaned over and kissed my cheek. I felt a little tense because it's not a gay place, though several gay people we knew usually went there. I wasn't sure if it was even a feminist place. I *was* sure that it wasn't very friendly.

"What do you mean, it's not friendly here?" Millie was already deep into the menu, even though she knew it by heart and she always ordered the same thing.

"You know, like it's the customers who've got to prove something by coming here and paying six dollars for a spinach sandwich."

Millie was about to say something, but she caught the eye of the waitress, and she smiled at her at the same time that she asked me with her eyes if I was ready to order. I knew I was going to get their version of arroz con gandules, so I nodded. Then it happened. It was almost as if the woman was going to help me prove my point. She stood there in her Indian print skirt and Mexican peasant blouse until we sat back to wait for her to come over. Just at that point, she picked up her notepad and went over to the next table to talk to the two blond-blue-eyed-bearded men who had just come in. She waited until they were ready, adjusting her hair, playing with her Indonesian earrings, smiling at everything the men said.

"You see, darling," I said to Millie loud enough so that the waiter in the thick socks and Birkenstocks standing next to us could hear, "next door at the greasy spoon we can have a full meal for $2.95, including apple pie and no attitude. What do you think?"

Millie giggled and started to put her coat back on, so I followed her, laughing as she took most of the whole-wheat bread from the basket and stuffed it in her pockets. "It's the bread I really come for, you know," she confessed as we ran over to Pearl's Diner, where you could smell the gravy half a block away.

By the time we were settled at the diner, I had forgotten what I wanted to talk about. So had Millie. Looking around at the clientele, she was self-conscious when she could have just been herself. The truckers and the rednecks and the housewives and the hookers, they didn't care who came in there. People went to Pearl's to eat, not to have somebody look down on their polyester or their wrinkled dollar bills. I started to regret bringing her there, because what made me at ease made her nervous, so I took her hand under the table. She sat closer to me in the booth while we looked at the menu. We ordered.

"You know that journal you gave me for my birthday?" She asked softly, without looking up. No one in the place seemed to notice how close we were to one another. "I finished it already."

"Wow, you write a lot, Mill."

"Well, I liked it so much, sometimes I would jot down my psychology notes in it, too—"

"I can get you another one for New Year's Eve—"

"No, they're too extravagant! Just get me a nice notebook?"

"Okay, a nice one. Hey, look. They have arroz con leche on the menu now." I pointed to the hand-lettered addition.

"What's arroz con leche?"

"It's almost like rice pudding. Nélida tried to make it once when she was taking home ec in high school, and Mami yelled at her—"

"Why? That's mean!"

"Well, I guess, but we burned the milk and sugar in the pot, and it never came off. And it was my fault, anyway, because I was supposed to watch it while Nélida looked for the rice, but I spaced out. My sister took the rap for me." I laughed at the memory, because Nélida and I had really gotten into some scrapes together when we were young and made our mother crazy. I tried to tell Millie about this, chuckling myself, but she looked horrified.

"Don't look like that, you should have seen what a couple of stooges we were, messing up Mami's kitchen. But things always worked out okay. Like that night, Mami made us the best arroz con leche she'd ever made. And the three of us ended up laughing and kidding around. I loved those days!"

Millie smiled and hugged me. I reached for her and kissed her, first gently, and then her lips stayed on mine for an extra beat. We ate in silence, watching each other. I loved to see the changes in Millie's face, the deepening of the color in her eyes, the delicate furrow in her forehead while she was thinking. I wanted to tell her all this, it seemed I never told her everything I felt. Pearl came over and refilled our water glasses, asked me if I wanted some coffee the way I usually ended a meal, but I said, "No, Pearl, do you have any herb tea? My friend wants some."

"No," protested Millie, "Nothing special for me! Make it two coffees, please."

After Pearl had walked away, Millie turned to me, her eyes flashing, mouthing, *I want you.* But the intimacy seemed broken, and I skidded on some icy plain.

"Listen, Millie, I'd like to tell you . . ."

"And I'm trying to tell you that you excite me so much when you're like this."

"Like, how?"

"Like this, spontaneous."

"I'm always spontaneous. I don't know how to think before I do something."

"Yes, you do! You're always thinking, trying to plan things so they'll always come out right. Well, they don't always, so why don't you just follow my lead for once?" She rarely said that much that fast. Pearl came back with two coffees and gave me a look that almost said: *Yeah, I know how it is, honey, trouble with your squeeze.*

"Well, I guess you're right," I told her.

"Okay," Millie conceded, "what were you trying to say?"

"That I . . . it's about how much . . . I don't know, I think we're always pulling away from each other just when one of us wants to get close. I mean, I think I just did that to you, and I'm sorry."

"Do they have Sweet 'n Low here?"

"Millie."

"Okay. Now, you're right. I don't know what to do. I'm afraid of the commitment."

"Then don't give me double messages!" That hurt more than I'd thought. I drank half the coffee in a gulp. "I mean, don't ask me to live with you when you're still lusting after that broomstick, Scooter!"

Millie looked shocked. She put two sugars and cream in her coffee and stirred conscientiously. "I, I," she began.

"What?"

"I don't lust after her, she's just . . . "

"Familiar?"

"How the hell do you know these things?"

"I don't know, I'm asking you. What . . . happened with you and her?" It was so hard to say, to ask. I wasn't sure I wanted to know anymore.

"We didn't sleep together. But we got close again, and we talked a lot. I guess I needed that."

"Oh—"

"I mean, you might think Scooter is kind of stiff, but with me . . . she just really opens up." Millie looked at me, her beautiful eyes wanting me to see what she saw. I couldn't.

"Okay—" I whispered.

"I need her too, Erica, can you understand?"

For the rest of the evening, Millie's question had just sort of hovered in the air. Because I didn't know, and I didn't want to understand, and the pain of suddenly being pushed into knowing was too much.

The streets had been cleared, but Willimantic looked small, a toy town of brick buildings and old-fashioned streetlights glowing over the neat rows of snow from the storm, piled four feet deep. Toy people from a greeting card slid among the snow walks with shopping bags, and here and there, a little evergreen was hoisted onto a pickup truck, destined for Christmas. I followed Millie out to the lake, driving carefully and avoiding the icy patches so I wouldn't get stuck again.

When I pulled into Millie's driveway, she'd already gone inside and turned all the lights on. I lingered by the front door, shaking the snow off my boots.

"Come on in where it's warm! I'm making some mint tea!" she shouted from the kitchen. There I was, in a blue mood while

Millie clinked cups and reached for the joy in my heart. "You want chocolate chip cookies?"

"Uhm, yes, but, Millie?"

"Hm?"

"Would you still go to Nélida's with me on the 25th?" I braced myself.

"Of course! What do you mean, *still?*" She looked puzzled.

"Oh, that's great, thanks! I just thought—I mean . . . never mind, thanks, Millie."

"Erica, hold me?" She reached for me, and I held her as tightly as I could. Then we stood, leaning against the kitchen counter, my arms about her shoulders and hers around my waist.

"You'll be off New Year's Day?"

"Yes," I told her.

"So, you'll be with me?"

"Yes."

"If the storm is over, do you want to drive to the beach?"

"Yes, if you want to, Millie."

"Erica—"

"Hm?"

"I just want you to be happy."

5

I returned to the ward that night by 11:15, feeling tired but victorious after working eight nights in a row. I hung my pea coat in the locker in the break room and turned to see Angelina in her pink nightgown, standing barefoot on the red tile, staring.

"Hi, Mary," she greeted me with her generic name for the aides.

"Hi, Angelina." She looked at her feet and pouted. This was her way of indicating something was wrong. "What's bothering you?" I asked, still not taking my mind off my own concerns. I looked for the big coffeepot to set it up. By midnight, I was going to be ready for that first cup.

"I've already started the coffee," said Abby, walking in. She seemed to be accruing brownie points, I thought, uncharitably.

"Oh, good," I abandoned my search and put on my aide's apron with the big pockets in the front. Angelina helped me tie it in the back.

"Clients-aren't-allowed-in-the-break-room," Abby chanted to me, as though Angelina weren't there.

"You tell her that," I smiled at Angelina. Abby was annoyed, and I was glad. I was taking out my frustrations on someone who'd done nothing to me, just because I was tired and out of sorts. But I wasn't going to stop. Angelina followed me out of the break room to the ward, sticking close to me in her exaggerated way of showing allegiance to one aide or another.

"I don't like her, Mary, no I don't," pouted Angelina.

"Will you help me with the laundry tonight?" I asked her.

"Yes, Mary," she said in her "good girl" voice.

"Clients-aren't-supposed-to-do-the-aides'-chores,"chanted Abby behind us. I wondered if she carried a rule book with her.

In the office, Mrs. Morse was on the phone to Administration, and I didn't see Mona anywhere, the relief charge who took over when Fran was off.

"We're only three tonight," Mrs. Morse was saying, "and after the accident, we really should have someone else."

"What accident?" I asked Abby, who pretended not to hear me. She was busy trying to send Angelina back to bed.

"No, Mary, I can't sleep!" protested Angelina. "She'll take my eyes out too, Mary!"

"She's on the other side, Angelina, now go to bed!"

"No!"

"Who's on the other side?"

"Shh!" said Mrs Morse from the office.

"What is going on?!" I insisted.

"Myra Jenkins got the *eyes*, Mary," whined Angelina, and then she ran to sit in one of the bathroom stalls.

"All right, what happened?" I demanded from Abby.

"You know how Myra goes around saying, *eyes, eyes?*"

"Yeah, about once a month."

"Well, last night she really got into it, she said it all over the place, and then she scratched Joan Kiniry's and Rosie's eyes."

I shivered, not wanting to imagine anything, but immediately I visualized Myra Jenkins in the evil act.

"Rosie hit her, Mary," put in Angelina from the stall.

"That's right," said Abby. "Myra just scratched her below the right eye, and Rosie woke up and smacked her."

"Is Joanie in the hospital?" I was afraid to know.

"Black and blue, Mary, she can't sleep, no she can't!" cried Angelina from the stall.

"Shh, quiet!" from Mrs. Morse.

"Angelina, you go to bed now!" yelled Abby.

"No!" Angelina shook her white hair and got away from Abby, walking around in circles past the stalls, waving her hands, and denouncing Myra and Abby together. Still stunned, I just watched them.

"She's a bad one, Mary! I don't like you, bitch!"

Mrs. Morse hung up the phone and came out of the office. Abby took hold of Angelina's arm and tried to pull her to the dorm, but the old woman, only about four feet tall, refused to go and sat down on the floor.

"Let her stay up," I said belatedly.

"Abby!" called Mrs. Morse. "Go on C side and relieve second shift. What's all this commotion?" She turned to Angelina, who pouted her best pout.

"But Mrs. Morse," began Abby.

"C side, Abby," said Mrs. Morse.

Abby went across the hall, and I picked up the log book to read the particulars.

"As for you, Angelina, if you sit quietly in the day hall, you can have some coffee later," promised Mrs. Morse.

"Okay, Mary," mumbled Angelina on the way to sit down in one of the stalls instead, crossing her legs. Mrs. Morse shook her head. Her usually pleasant face looked tired and worried. She cleaned her glasses on her blue apron.

"I'm playing charge tonight, Kid. Fran's off, and Mona called in sick. I don't blame her."

Having read the account in the log book, I wanted to get it from Mrs. Morse, so I asked her how it happened.

"I was in the break room, about 3:30, when I heard Mona scream. I guess she heard Rosie crying and hitting Myra Jenkins. I went running in and separated them two. Rosie's face was bleeding a little under the right eye. Meanwhile, Mona saw Joanie and she almost passed out on me—"

"You mean, Joanie wasn't screaming?"

"Nope. She was standing by her bed, very quiet, she had blood running all down her face. I was so scared, I couldn't tell what Myra had done!"

Mrs. Morse rubbed her temples. The scene became very clear to me: Myra Jenkins, walking on her toes because she can't step flatly on her feet, making her way around the beds, hissing *eyes, eyes* to herself.

"Mrs. Morse, it says in the book that Joanie might lose her eye?"

"No, that poor child was so lucky; the doctor said she would heal completely."

"Ay, Dios mío," I whispered to myself, cringing at the thought of the pain. "Is Myra still on the other side?"

"Yup, she's gonna have a partition all around her bed, like a little room. It'll be locked from the outside," explained Mrs. Morse, smoothing her apron.

"You sure you don't want me on the other side?"

"No, we'll be getting two more aides. Things will be quiet over there tonight. Rosie's sedated. In the morning you can go over to help Abby get the kids up. That girl drives me crazy . . ."

"She's a bad one, Mary," said Angelina, standing at the doorway of the office. Mrs. Morse laughed.

"What do you know about this, Angelina?"

"Myra's got the *eyes*, Mary, they're gonna lock her up!"

"Right, Angelina, let's go do the laundry," I put my arm around her, and we went to the laundry room where Angelina would try on some new dresses, fold a couple of nightgowns, and eventually decide to go to bed.

Once there, I tried to forget where I was. I took the bundles of clothes out of the dryer and gave myself entirely to the routine task of folding them. Angelina put on two new nightgowns over the one she was already wearing. I folded three stacks of towels and started another load of wash. Abby came by to let me know the coffee was ready, and Angelina was lured away. I folded all the gowns and paired up the socks.

I still felt full from my dinner at Pearl's, even a little nauseous, thinking about the blood on Rosie's face, and Joanie's. Mostly I wanted to be alone with my thoughts. What the hell was the point of my job? I listened to the wind outside, the washing machines on both sides, the clinking of sneakers inside the dryers, and an occasional wail from Bentley North.

The laundry rooms of both sides were lined up all around the walls with metal shelves that reached to the ceiling. There were metal cabinets and a clothes rack where we put the special outfits the clients would wear on occasion. On the shelves there were labels that read "sneakers," "gowns," "tops," "pants," "towels." There was a box marked "shoelaces" that contained a quarter, two elastic bands, and an old Bic lighter. I threw the lighter away and decided to bag the trash. When the dryer stopped, I took out gobs of gray lint from the filter. I realized that I loved the Kiniry twins when I thought of Joanie, with her eye nearly gouged out of her face, standing by her bed, not even crying, her head tilted to the right because of the Thorazine, and her thin arm raised as if sheltering herself against another blow coming at her, her face bleeding. I'd told Tina about how I'd like to change things around at the School, in all the institutions like this, when I'd gone to help her type her applications for graduate school. She'd looked at me with her quizzical face.

"What? Why are you looking at me like that?"

"You know, I think you're in the wrong line of work. You oughta be an urban planner or something like that."

"Okay, if I ever go back—" I smirked.

"You will. And where did you learn to type?"

"My sister taught me, said it'd come in handy someday."

"Hm, all my sister ever taught me was not to type, so nobody would make me, just because I was a woman."

"Well, she's probably right. That's why my mother never taught me how to cook, so I wouldn't get stuck inside the house, she said. Okay, this is finished. You're going to Yale!"

"Let's pray!"

And now this had happened. Could an urban planner, whatever the hell that was, could they have foreseen Myra Jenkins flipping out? A psychiatrist? A behavioral therapist?

I folded the last blue gown, thick cotton with red-and-yellow flowers. I supposed it made sense to have stacks and stacks of them. Rosie made a habit of ripping hers in two before breakfast. Angelina copied her sometimes. And Jean, Joanie's sister, wouldn't even wear one of them for more than a minute. That's why we had the gray jumpsuits, although they didn't last for very long, either.

At three, Mrs. Morse sent me to the break room. She said I was brooding. The women from Bentley North were always in a lively mood. They had baked brownies, and Ivonne, the youngest one, insisted that I have one even though I told her I felt queasy.

"Uh, oh!—" she said meaningfully, laughing loudly. "You're not pregnant, are you?"

"No chance, Ivonne," I told her just as meaningfully.

"Have some more brownies, then!" she grinned and pushed the tray toward me.

"Wait a minute," said Marie, the charge from Bentley West, charging into the break room. "Where is the tablecloth?" She waved her arms, faking alarm. The "tablecloth" consisted of a sheet folded in two and placed neatly on the formica table.

"Fran's not here tonight!" said Ivonne in her booming voice. "We don't have to get fancy!" The two women laughed and carried on, gossiping about Fran and teasing me about squealing on them. Another aide came in, and the conversation soon turned to a common subject—home decorating.

I sat quietly and visualized my small apartment. Since the storm I had merely gone home to sleep, avoiding my life, and postponing decisions I felt compelled to make when I was home alone. I felt ready to go back and clean up my desk, water the few plants I had left, perhaps fill out a new financial aid application for school.

"What are you doing for Christmas?" asked Marie.

"Huh?" She took me by surprise.

"Oh, leave her alone! They had an accident over there with the fat crazy girl," Ivonne came to my defense.

"Wadda-you-mean, I'm fat-and-crazy!?" exclaimed Marie, and the two launched into another chorus of wild laughter and knee slapping. The other aide joined in, the three of them went off in a bout of comic relief.

I didn't like Marie. Even though she came from the same town in Maine where Ivonne was born, she insisted that she didn't speak anything but English. Ivonne, on the other hand, spoke French-Canadian freely and often traded stories with Mrs. Morse, whose Irish family had picked potatoes at the same farms where Ivonne grew up. Ivonne was tall and muscular, had an easy smile and a hearty way about her. Marie seemed to me to be looking for something she could hold against people. That's why I stayed away from her, but she always managed to try to get me involved in her conversations. Tonight, the subject was her recent divorce and redecorating her kitchen.

"I hate blue and green together, don't you, Erica?" Since the other two agreed with her immediately, I said, "I kinda like those two colors together."

A door slammed out in the hall, and Ivonne went to see who it was. Soon we could hear her laughing in the hallway, and we knew she must be joking around with the wagon driver, now that it was back to being a man's job. Marie and I were left in an uncomfortable silence. The other aide ate all the little pieces of brownie cake that lined the pan. Abby walked in and broke the silence.

"They sent two—well, colored girls to C side," she announced. I bit the edge of my coffee cup, because whatever she meant by that, I decided I didn't like it. Marie handed her a cup.

Abby helped herself to some coffee, shuffling over to the table since she never bothered to pick up her feet. My older sister would have made her walk right. The other reason for my petty dislike was that she had the kind of thin, light brown hair that just sat there, held back with a pink plastic band that never fell out of place, no matter what she did, even if it rained. What every Puerto Rican girl in New Britain wouldn't have given for hair that didn't fight back.

"I told them to wash the walls," said Abby.

"The walls? What the hell for?" I asked her.

"Told who?" asked Marie. The rest of us looked at each other, trying to confirm what we thought Abby had done.

"Figured, might as well take advantage of them—" Abby continued.

"Abby—" Ivonne started to speak and blinked rapidly, not knowing what to say.

"Abby, you're sick!" I threw my cup in the wastebasket, making Abby jump.

"Well, they're not lazy or anything—" stammered Abby. "They got right to it, they didn't mind!"

I stood up, shaking.

"You can't take advantage of a new aide," Ivonne told her.

"Besides, you already did your walls," added Marie irrelevantly.

"Abby," I told her curtly, "tell those women to come out on break right now, and I'll be in to relieve you in ten minutes. I'm going to speak to Mrs. Morse." Her lip quivered a little, but she put her cup down and headed down the hall. I ran past her and into D side to lay it all out to Mrs. Morse.

I waited until I saw the two new aides go by on their way to the break room before I went to C side to relieve Abby. Mrs. Morse went with them, friendly and grandmotherly as usual. I didn't want these women to think I was like the others, but they would. I was always "passing." I couldn't help wondering, even about Fran and Mrs. Morse, how did they see me? They always remarked how "nice-and-dark" I was. Did they talk about how I wasn't "lazy" either? I went to get a bucket of clean water out of the utility sink. From the hallway I could hear Ivonne, now flirting with some other man, the laundry driver perhaps.

It was after four. Abby came walking sheepishly in. I dipped a sponge in a bucket of water and betadine. I washed all the bucket chairs in the day hall, top and bottom.

I didn't stop working when I got home. There were small cobwebs behind my desk, next to the tall windows with the wide sills where I stationed my plants. The front windows looked out on Main Street and were always dusty. The side windows faced the little patch of grass and weeds below, now frozen with mounds of icy snow, bunching the weeds together like matted hair on a brown dog.

I swept and washed and cleared the mirror-top table of magazines, letters, and little piles of incense ashes. Underneath I could see the cracked yellow paint around the glass on my second-hand find from the antique store downstairs. I bought little things there—a silver cup, a glass, heart-shaped ashtray—because the older woman who owned the store seemed to me like a lesbian. And she was; I found that out when she came up to have coffee with me one day, but she was so used to never talking about her personal life that she never told me any of the fascinating stories I wanted to hear about gay people on Main Street Willimantic. So much for my romanticizing the dreary street and its denizens. I scraped the old purple candle wax from the wood on a windowsill, trying to remember when it dripped there.

The sun shone strong through the windows at noon, guiding the particles of incense to the mirror, mixing with the fragrance of some old potpourri. Satisfied, I made an omelet with three eggs and a lot of cheese, which I was barely able to finish before falling asleep.

When I opened my eyes it was ten o'clock and very dark. I had not awakened once all day, probably hadn't moved, either. In the shadows by the windows, some of my dreams still played on. It was Joanie, her face black and blue like Angelina had said, and Elaine, Frances, Eva, Judy, and Donna. They all walked slowly across the day hall, the floor was shiny, and Joanie bent down to touch it. She was wearing a red dress with a yellow rose, one I used to have when I was twelve. I remarked on how small Joanie was and saw her bruises were gone.

"I'm really thirty-seven," she said.

I sat up in bed and remembered how glad I was that she could talk. In my dream, it seemed like she had always talked.

"Do you know you're retarded?"

"Yes, but my sister doesn't," said Joanie.

I was crying in my dream, so relieved that now they would be free, they could talk.

"Where do you want to go, Joanie?"

"To live with Mrs. Morse," she answered, moving away.

"And your parents?" I asked in the darkness.

"We don't remember them anymore," said her voice.

Clouds moved in the sky and moonlight came through the dusty windows, outlining the begonias in their little clay pots. Joanie was gone.

It was good to have my old car back. As I pulled out onto Main Street, I noticed there was a fight at the bar on the corner of Walnut Street. One guy knocked the other on the sidewalk, and their red faces glowed under the street lamp from the strain and the alcohol. Turning on my AM radio, I listened to the Beatles singing "I'm So Tired."

At work, things had settled down considerably. Mona was back, and Abby was off. Fran would be coming back the next night, and we would be having a party with Bentley North. Mona was a touch more nervous than usual, smoking Marlboro Lights in short puffs. She was about forty-eight, wore her hair long and red, applied dark eye shadow, and had very long nails. Fran thought she should leave her bum of a husband because he beat her, although she probably wouldn't say so to Mona. Sometimes I thought that if Fran had just told her to, Mona would have left him and been very happy. But there must be an unwritten rule about not wanting to be responsible for a woman leaving her husband, even if he is a bum.

I spent a great deal of time thinking in the next few days before my days off. While I thought about Millie and what to do about our relationship, some interesting developments were taking shape in the office. Mrs. Morse kept me informed, but she didn't say much else to me, since she knew I needed to be quiet for a while.

Mona, always wanting to impress Fran, had gotten together with Ivonne and had collected a supply of holiday decorations which we obediently put up all along the windows and walls, out of the reach of the clients. All except in the bathroom, near the steel tubs. I was working with a part-time aide when Jean Kiniry got up and jumped on top of one of the tubs and ripped off the red garland that was taped there. When I turned to look at Jean, Agnes grabbed the toothpaste and ran with it. I started to laugh. The aide looked at me for a clue.

"Look," I said, laughing still, "you'd better get that from her."

"Why?" she looked a little uncertain as to how to do that.

"Well, she's going to eat it, or something!" I explained, one hand on Agnes's arm as she tried to squirt the toothpaste. The aide rushed after Jean.

I took Agnes to one of the sinks and got the toothpaste away. At that moment, Linda walked out of the dorm, crying and slapping everyone.

"Catch her!" warned Mrs. Morse. "She's got her period—"

I let go of Agnes who, for some miraculous reason, stayed where she was, and grabbed Linda's arm.

"No, no!" bawled Linda with knitted brows and clenched fists.

"Come on, honey," I coaxed Linda, who eyed me suspiciously. She could easily push me out of her way when she got her swing going. I stroked her hair, pushing the tangles out of her eyes. She calmed down enough to stay on the toilet.

"That's a good girl, Linda," I praised her, hating the words, but knowing it worked.

She leaned against me and whimpered, hitting me softly with her large hands. No one should be angry with her, but I had been, more than once when she threw chairs around the day hall, and I'd pushed her away roughly. Would I be able to stand eight hours of this behavior on day shift? I managed to wash her, get her a clean gown and cotton underwear. She even allowed me to set her up with a couple of pads on a brand new sanitary belt. I combed her hair and took her to the day hall, where I tied a fabric belt around her and her chair. A certain part of me performed these tasks with appalling calm, another part watched the action in amazement. Linda, for her part, dug her nails into my arm, still whimpering softly. She could untie the belt anytime she wanted, but she seemed to feel better having it around her. Agnes preferred it, too, and she liked to put her arms inside her gown, only taking them out to eat or to scratch somebody. A lot of the women liked the "tie-strings," as these cloth belts were called, because they had spent so many years in straitjackets. They felt insecure without them.

Agnes sat in her chair and rocked, humming to herself. The part-timer showed me part of the garland she had rescued from Jean.

"She peed on the rest of it," she said, pointing to Jean, who stood next to her puddle, snickering, the garland all wet on the floor.

"Jeanie," I called her name to acknowledge her. She covered her face and giggled. She quickly slipped out of her jumpsuit, which Mrs. Morse had carefully tied on the back. Jean just snapped the knots. I walked over, and she handed me the wet suit.

"Would you bring me the mop bucket?" I asked the aide, while I collected all the socks, gowns, and shirts that were being thrown around already by the usual crowd. I surprised Frances with her hands on Judy's hair, and she slapped her own head, pretending she had no intention of pulling out another handful. I threw the wet clothes in the big plastic hamper and came back with another stack of clean clothes. Diane went running by and took Elaine's ball. Elaine, as if answering a summons, stood in the middle of the day hall and smacked her head.

I got the sense of watching a jerky ballet, where every human being was part of a perpetual motion machine. But I had to stop watching and move myself before things got completely out of control. Out of the corner of my eye, I could see Mrs. Morse shaking Jeanie and forcing her to step into a clean jumpsuit, but Jeanie refused. Jeanie could try everybody's patience, even Mrs. Morse's, but I hated to see her lose her temper. If I stepped into this dance, it became a play somewhere, outside the reality of the ward, and it sometimes threatened to take me away. So, I ignored the feeling and kept moving.

"Elaine, you big baby," I chided, and she stopped the head-slapping. I gave her back the ball, which Diane had solicitously returned to me as if nothing had happened.

"Are-you-cold?" asked Elaine rhetorically, since she only spoke two or three sentences.

"Are you?" I responded.

"Well!" said Elaine, laughing contentedly. After she delivered her lines, she was very pleased with herself. The aide looked at me, expecting an explanation. Jean Kiniry laughed, scratched her crotch, and stretched, yawning. She looked so much like her sister Joanie in my dream. Frances pulled Judy's hair. The aide mopped the floor.

"Is that all she says?" she asked me about Elaine.

"Sure. Sometimes we can get her to say 'hair,' but not very often," I walked over to Elaine and patted her shoulder. She hugged me and repeated, "Are-you-c-c-old?"

"Are you?"

"Well!" she laughed. The aide shook her head. I took Jean Kiniry to the sinks and washed her before putting a clean gown on her and a pair of socks. I thought then, as though for the first time, that these women had no privacy. They had to do everything in front of us, innocently, without knowing what we thought of them, or having any control over it anyway. Although, sometimes it seemed that they knew. Jeanie put both her socks on the left foot.

Mrs. Morse came out of the dorm dragging a couple of laundry bags, so I ran to help her. As we passed the stalls in the bathroom, she jutted her chin and made me look at Mary Ann Kopeski, who sat like a yogi on the toilet seat.

"Meditating, I suppose," said Mrs. Morse.

Mary Ann sat very still, the soles of her bare feet touching, her hands resting on her knees with thumb and forefinger pressed together, her head thrown back, humming.

"She's blind from birth, Mrs. Morse, what could make her sit like that?" I pondered as we dragged the laundry away. As we pushed the bags down the chute, the first-shift women filed into the day hall. I heard the visiting aide scream.

"For Pete's sake, Jean, give me your foot!" Mrs. Morse and I ran into the day hall, where the aide had managed to sit Jean down and was busy pulling wet socks off her foot. Jeanie giggled and allowed her to remove one sock after the other, her foot looking as swollen with white socks as if she had a cast on it. Of course, Jeanie had gone around and collected the socks off the other women in the day hall and put them on her own foot. I thought, this makes the perfect closing number for this ballet, and I could only laugh. The other aide watched me.

The next night Fran was back and commented on Mona's decoration of the ward.

"Bentley North even frosted their windows," she added, squinting at the smoke from her Marlboro extra-long. Mona fluttered her eyelashes.

Fran put me and Mona on C side and moved the party to Wednesday night. This finished upsetting Mona, who took great pride in covering the ward while Fran was off.

"Of course, you wouldn't know anything about it, Mona, but I've been tipped off about a visit from Administration. We'll clean and wax the floors in the laundry room tonight," ordered Fran, and Mona praised the wisdom of this decision.

While we were deep in old clothes, stacks of regulation underwear, and nightgowns, Mrs. Ferguson, the third-shift supervisor, showed up to have a look at Myra Jenkins's new partitioned room. It had been put in during the day, and there were strict rules to be observed.

"She has to be the last one to get up in the morning and the first one to go to bed," Fran walked ahead of the tall Mrs. Ferguson, took the keys out of her sky blue sweatshirt, and opened the door with easy authority.

"An aide keeps an eye on her at all times," Fran relocked the door behind us. Mrs. Ferguson immediately noticed the seasonal garlands taped well out of reach of the clients and complimented Fran.

"I'm glad you didn't frost your windows, Mrs. Bernaud. It's very hard to get that substance off Plexiglas."

"Thank you, Mrs. Ferguson," Fran responded as if she knew this all along. Mona went to sit in the office, pretending to nurse a weak cough.

"So, you must be Erica García," Mrs. Ferguson's blue eyes fixed on me, and I just nodded.

"This is it," Fran pointed to the door of the partitioned room where Myra slept. Fran flicked off her flashlight, but it was light enough to see the formica walls and the slide lock on the outside of the little room. All the women were asleep. I wondered why Eva Nathan never got up singing and slipping off her nightgown when there was a nurse or a supervisor around.

"Very clever," whispered Mrs. Ferguson, who could lean right over the partition and look at Myra sleeping. I had to stand on tiptoe, and Fran was not quite as tall as the five-foot wall.

"Does she know how to work the lock?"

"Why—" whispered Fran, "it's on the outside."

"She can climb on this nightstand, lean over, and open it," Mrs. Ferguson whispered back.

"No way," Fran began to lead the way out of the dorm. I turned and saw Eva Nathan's green eyes smiling at us. "Myra would never manage to get on top of that table. Besides, she walks on her toes, and you could knock her over with your pinky."

"Does she have special shoes?" asked the supervisor, surveying the ward.

"She has a pair with braces on them," I told her, "but the other women still take them off her. See, it's not as if they're always scared of her, even though she can be dangerous . . ." Both women were listening to me, but I stopped talking as I felt their curiosity. Was it that I talked too much?

Mrs. Ferguson chuckled, chin in hand, and Fran picked up the thread of my story and continued talking about Myra. I knew she enjoyed discussing the things that happened in the ward, but when a supervisor was around it seemed that she preferred to do the talking. She invited Mrs. Ferguson back to the office on D side for a cup of coffee, and I went to finish the work in the laundry room.

Just when I had gotten used to the idea that maybe it was time to get another job, that nobody would ever pay attention to me or my ideas at the wards, Mrs. Ferguson walked in. I was sitting on the floor trying to pair off a whole box of orphan sneakers, and the supervisor looked taller and younger under the overhead light.

When I stood up, the lines around her eyes were again deep, and the gray in her blond curls was evident. She pushed aside a bunch of socks on the folding table and sat on it, making room for me to sit with her.

"I've had a conversation with Mrs. Bernaud about you."

"You have?"

"She says you and Abby Goodwin are in competition for the next charge's rating in the ward."

"What? Fran wouldn't say that. She knows I couldn't care less one way or the other."

"So, maybe it's Abby who's in competition with you."

"Maybe, but I don't see why."

"Mrs. Fournier says you're so efficient, you even saved two new girls from getting stuck cleaning the walls." At this, she smiled slightly, and I was puzzled as hell.

"Mrs.—you mean Marie? From Bentley North? Mrs. Ferguson—forgive me for being so direct, but what is this about?"

"We've had an opening at the Cottages," she took a breath. "Third shift, though." I followed her gaze as she looked at the shelves packed with towels and clothes. Then I remembered the request I had submitted, for transfer to first shift.

"You mean my request was processed already? But what's this got to do with—"

"You can start in January, right after your pass days, and this automatically carries a promotion to Aide II—you'll be in charge."

I sat there, thinking about it, dangling my legs off the table. She didn't want to tell me about Abby or about Marie, but I wasn't getting punished, either. What the hell was she getting at?

"Look, García, I know you wanted days, but this will get you in line for the first opening back at the wards. You do want to come back to the wards, don't you?"

"Yeah, I do. I want to work with the clients, maybe even

become part of one of the therapy teams, and help with their programming!"

"For the low-functioning kids—you mean, here?"

"Yeah, why not? You should see these women in the morning—" I started, but Mrs. Ferguson began looking for her cigarettes, and I knew she was going to say she had to go.

"Oh, I have to go! I have to see the wards across the road before 5 A.M." She shook my hand. "And, let's keep the other matter between us, you know."

"Well, but Mrs. Ferguson—" I began.

"García, I can't get into it. Anything having to do with a possible race situation, I have to keep the peace."

"Are you trying to tell me I did something wrong?"

"No, I just can't give the impression of giving preferential treatment. You're a good worker. Stay that way." She avoided looking at me. I walked her to the side door as she gave me instructions and a pat on the back. She waved as she got in the black station wagon with the State seal on the door and drove off.

Stupid Abby. She was pissed because I'd gone over her head; she didn't care at all about whether what she did was wrong or not. How did Marie come into this? The Cottages. What a strange thing to happen. I went back into the dorm on C side for a 3 A.M. check. Almost everyone was asleep; I could hear Eva Nathan humming to herself, and Madeleine was snoring a bit too loud. I heard something to my left and turned, a sudden chill down my spine.

"Mommy," she said, barely moving her thin lips. "Mommy home." Myra Jenkins was staring over the partition of her room. She looked bizarre, either grinning or pouting; I couldn't move at first.

I walked over and unlocked her door, leading her by the arm to her bed. "Okay, Myra, you'll see your mother on Saturday." She got into bed, breathing with difficulty. The acrid smell of her sweat, altered by Thorazine and barbiturates, repelled me further, and it was something else to make me dislike Myra. I knew she wasn't responsible for what she did, but I couldn't find a kind word for the woman who rolled over and lay her head on the pillow, her eyes still open.

"Good night," I said, efficiently, tucking in the blanket, locking the door, rushing to get out of there and away from her.

On my way out of the dorm, Fran came to talk to me.

"So, you'll be going to the Cottages."

"Mm-hm," I unlocked the small bathroom across from the office and washed my hands while Fran watched me critically, narrowing her dark eyes. I wanted to know if she was going to say anything about Abby or Marie.

"You'll do all right. It's one way to get your charge's rating—you'll be all by yourself at night!"

"Fran, if you recommended me for the job so I wouldn't fight with Abby, you didn't have to. I wasn't going to fight with her. She took advantage of those two women, and I blew the whistle on her. If I was braver, I would have punched her out—" I sat in the office and put my feet up on the desk. I grinned at her. She smiled indulgently and lit a cigarette, always handy, never lost in the depths of a bulging handbag, like Mona's.

"Nothing to do with it. Abby's a sniveling fool."

"Well, I'm grateful to you because I'm coming back to the ward on first shift. Going to the cottages is only so I can be on the waiting list, you know? And, how did Marie Fournier get involved in this?"

"Marie's a jealous old bat!" She pushed my feet off the desk.
"Oh—"

"Well, García, you'd better learn to give orders," smoke rose from her nostrils, "or Madeleine Mallard is going to pee from one end of that cottage to the other."

"What! She's going with me?" I couldn't believe it; why not Joanie or Elaine, even? Someone who was verbal.

"Let's go to the break room, Kid, and we'll celebrate your good luck. I'll be off between Christmas and New Year's, so I won't see you. The inspection's over, so we might as well have a party every night. Mona! Come and relieve García over on C side!"

I don't know how the time passed. I slept little and spent the rest of the day doing errands that seemed crucial. I even went to the biggest automotive junkyard on Route 32 and looked among the wrecks for another '63 Valiant with an intact taillight to replace my broken one. Later, I ran into "The Other Brother," the bookshop on Main Street, and got my niece a book of nonsexist fairy tales. For my sister, I rummaged through the antique silver at "With a Wink and a Smile" and bought her a ring with a pale yellow stone, which I knew she would like. Millie and I had agreed to give each other presents only on our birthdays, but I did want to give her something like that ring, something she'd want to keep with her. Then I remembered the party at the ward, so I got Italian pastry on the way to work.

"Why didn't you cook something Spanish?" complained Ivonne when I put my contribution on the break-room table.

"I don't cook." Ivonne laughed expansively while she placed an elaborate casserole next to the pastry. "I'm serious."

Ivonne arranged the napkins in a fan design. "What do you live on, then?"

"Omelets—"

"You're a lazy bum!"

"Yeah, and I don't have to wash dishes all day."

"You gotta cook at the Cottages, you know. Can you pour milk on cereal?" She cracked up at her own joke and left to get the large coffeepot.

I caught sight of my reflection in the window—jeans, my red apron over blue-checkered shirt, short hair—besides jeans and shirts, I had nothing to wear to Nélida's. And, why did I care? Didn't I tell her every year that I didn't care?

"You admiring yourself?" Ivonne returned with the coffeepot full of water. "Look, Fran, she's getting ready to be the charge over at the Cottages."

"I've got to visit my family on Sunday," I explained, blushing.

Fran, dressed in dark wool slacks and an impeccable gray angora sweater, placed a fruit salad in a glass bowl next to Ivonne's casserole. "I thought you were going to cook something Spanish," Fran registered her complaint. Annoyed, I announced I would go check the wards. Karen, the part-timer, would be helping me on C side.

"Wait, Erica," called Fran. "We're going to put the table in the hallway, that way we can keep an eye on the whole place."

"Pretty brave, aren't you, Fran?" Marie came in balancing two bowls and a brown grocery bag. I stared at her, and she turned away.

"They do it at Eaton and Tennessee Hall every night," replied Fran.

"But they don't have the kind of kids you have, Fran," Ivonne put in.

"No, worse," countered Fran, causing another wave of laughter and knee slapping.

"So, you're going to the Cottages," accused Marie.

"Right now, I'm going to the ward."

"Yeah," persisted Marie, placing her hands judiciously atop her stomach, "They always send you there if you've been to college."

"Well, Marie, you've been to college. Didn't your old man peel potatos in one?"

"Shut up, Ivonne, you ain't never been to high school!" Hoots of laughter from the three of them reverberated down the tiled hallway. I sat down in defeat and ate the cream off one of the pastries. Fran lit a cigarette while Ivonne and Marie carried on. I couldn't understand Ivonne, she was generally sincere and steady, but in combination with Marie, she lost her head. They quickly turned their jokes to Marie's favorite subject: sex. And the laughter became unbearable. Suddenly, the heavy storm door in the hallway opened, and everyone stiffened, fearing an Administration spy. Instead, the wagon driver came in with a message—a young man about twenty, tall and dark, good-looking and shy. Marie and Ivonne looked like they would have him for a snack and lost no time in luring him into the break room by offering to share their casseroles as suggestively as they could. Fran just sat smoking, observing them quizzically.

I went back to the ward and busied myself until about three-thirty when the table was moved to the hallway, and we all stuffed ourselves. When Angelina woke up, she was allowed to sit next to Fran and partake of the feast.

At five, Jean Kiniry woke up screaming, followed by Rosie, who, having wet her bed, was in a terrible mood. She crawled on Donna's bed and pulled the blanket off her; I put the blanket back on Donna and coaxed Rosie to sit on her blanket while I pulled it into the bathroom. Rosie enjoyed the ride, and I was in time to see the new aide chasing Jean Kiniry around the day hall. She had dressed her prematurely, and now Jean was running around with a wet jumpsuit.

"Ka-da-ka-da-ka-da-ka-da-daka!" yelled Rosie with delight as she bounced on her bent legs. Her eyes were closed; she let me wash her and change her pajamas while she bounced and chanted her happy syllables.

But it didn't take long before everyone was awake and carrying on. Karen didn't know the routine on C side, of course, and although I tried to tell her who to attend to first, things got out of hand. The worst was discovering that Agnes had diarrhea and had situated herself from her shooting position in a bathroom stall. I scooted her into the shower as soon as I could, avoiding her projectiles while she screamed bloody murder. I told Karen to keep everyone busy in the day hall, and I managed the bathroom. I thought about the outside world, the beach, going back to school, getting a new top for the Valiant, and somehow got things cleaned up. Then Karen told me about the mess Agnes had left in the dorm.

"Please don't make me stay in the day hall anymore," Karen pleaded. "Just go in there, and I'll clean up the shit."

I wanted to laugh, but it made sense. The women settled down as soon as they saw my familiar face. For about a minute. Jean Kiniry started stealing socks, Rosie went around on her knees and whacked everybody she could reach on the head, Myra plopped in a chair and chanted over and over, "mommy-home."

First shift came in like the cavalry, two aides and their supervisor, Jaycee Travers, the woman who had blamed Fran for the pine cleaner incident.

"Can you stay for overtime?" Jaycee's peremptory tones echoed in the bathroom, her ponytail and her horn-rim glasses made her a cartoon.

"No chance, Ma'am" I drawled. "I'm on vacation."

"We'll see about that!" She turned on her heels and headed back to D side to speak to Fran about me, but one of her aides called her back.

"Jaycee-oh-my-god!!"

Karen and I ran behind Jaycee to see what the problem was. Fran came from across the hall, and we all converged by the laundry chute where Jaycee's aide was pointing down to the basement.

"For godsakes, girl, we thought somethin' was wrong!"

"But there is—those sheets got diarrhea and the laundry truck won't take 'em."

"It's 7:45," I said to Karen. "Get your coat, we're outta here." If I'd learned anything about the ward, it was to let the veterans fight it out.

"What are you yakking about!" Fran elbowed her way past Jaycee to look down at the offending sheets. The other aides all crowded precariously around the opening, as if the sheets would get up and walk, diarrhea and all. Karen looked as guilty as she was, but she went to get her coat in a hurry.

"Somebody hold this door, it's heavy!"

"Fran, those are soiled sheets down there!"

"They smell, too!" Fran agreed.

"I'll call you from the Cottages, Fran!"

"Nobody leaves—" yelled Jaycee. "Whose sheets are those?"

"Not mine—"

"Well, my girls didn't put them there, your girls can go get them!"

"My girls are off duty, Travers, them sheets belong to first shift now—"

"Like hell! You there, go check who had diarrhea on third shift!"

"You were supposed to rinse them first and then bag them—" I yelled to Karen as we ran to the parking lot.

"But they were covered with shit!" she protested, as she scraped the snow off her windshield. I jumped in the Valiant and waved at her, turning on my powerful engine and letting my windshield wipers do the work. I didn't have heat, but I had a V-8 under the hood. Karen was lucky Fran felt like a fight just then, any other day she would have had this girl on her hands and knees, mopping every inch of that filthy basement floor.

6

The second-shift charge had described my duties and warned me about Gloria and her fits of temper, which had resulted in two holes in the wall of her bedroom so far.

"If she wakes up in the middle of the night, don't try to deal with her yourself, call the guy at the next cottage."

"Right."

"You're pretty small for this job."

"Yup."

"Either Gloria or Madeleine could send you flying across the room," her close-set eyes seemed to twinkle as though she relished the thought.

"I've dealt with Madeleine before."

"Well, Gloria's worse."

"Okay."

I wasn't supposed to like anybody from the Cottages, and it was easy enough. There was an unwritten rivalry between the aides at the older wards, where the real work was done, and the folks at the newer cottages, where work was a vacation. The second-shift charge and I stared at each other and held our ground.

Finally, she and her aide, a mousy girl who reminded me of Abby, left at 11:45, after showing me around the kitchen, the office, and Gloria's bedroom, where there were two large patches of plaster on a blue wall. The mouse made some crack about the urine smell in Madeleine's room and how *the kids* from the wards were hopeless. Then the charge took one last pass through the kitchen and told me what I should make for breakfast in the morning. I could hear the two of them cackling out in the parking lot.

Aggrieved, I sank down in one of the vinyl cushioned chairs, watching the "Tonight Show" at low volume on the black-and-white set. I consoled myself with the thought that I was on my way to a job where I could make a difference, and the stupid jealousies of the ward were only helping me get there faster. And I had to laugh at the aides at the cottage for trying to scare me. After all, I could run faster than any muscle-bound Gloria or ill-tempered Madeleine. Of course, I'd have to unlock the door first. Or I could lock myself in the office. Ridiculous, I was being ridiculous. It was the strangeness of the place. It looked just like an apartment with four bedrooms, a dining room with French doors, varnished pine furniture, and two bathrooms with doors on them. The thought of washing floors and doing laundry in this place made it feel just like cleaning in my mother's house. My old allergy to housework flared up. Besides, being in a living room made it more obvious that I was up all night, working, while other people were asleep.

I considered calling Mrs. Morse and having a good laugh with her about anything. It was easier working with her at the ward, where the office really seemed like a safe, Plexiglassed island (with a phone) where we could take refuge before the hectic morning rush of the women waking up and the battle to communicate our wishes to them, "Go to the bathroom, put your footsie in this sock, give me back the toothpaste, and stop smacking yourself on the head." Just like Fran said.

Turning my attention back to the TV, I watched Joan Rivers trying to get some secret tidbit from a female guest who laughed incessantly and wouldn't reveal a thing.

What was it that the cottage changed, that suddenly made me self-conscious about the people I had become used to? The cottage was almost like a home. Only two people shared a bedroom, and their clothes were folded in individual bureaus, not all stacked up in piles in the huge laundry room. At the ward, the only client with her "own room" was Myra Jenkins. At the cottage, the women seemed . . . like women. That's what it was, I felt the distance between me and them receding.

On the tube, Joan Rivers sat back triumphantly. She had probably learned what she needed to know from her bleached blonde, big-bosomed guest. Now I knew something else about myself: I was just like all the other aides. It was time to get my work done.

Waking up after my first night at the cottage, my bed felt so smooth that I didn't recognize it at first. Then I remembered all the cleaning I'd done after the holidays, and the reason my small apartment still looked decent. A fading afternoon light colored my windows barely gold. I longed for the sultry, endless days in the middle of the summer, going to the beach on that cold New Year's day with Millie had only made me ache for it more. I wanted warmth, delight, *feeling* in me. I wanted my work to mean something. The night might be good for a poet; it only turned me into an ogre.

It was two-thirty. Time enough for an invigorating walk in the woods to my favorite spot. I dressed in a hurry and stomped down the stairs with my stiff boots still unlaced. Outside, the wind howled down Main Street toward the old footbridge. I scraped the windows enough to see ahead, and rummaged under the seat of the car for a screwdriver to open the trunk to throw the jumper cables in. I'd had to use them over Christmas because Nélida's car never started around me. She seemed to be challenging me to see if there was something I couldn't fix, so she could tell me to go back to school. It was her logic, not mine.

Within minutes, I had driven to the edge of the large field, now completely covered with snow except for a clump of yellow foxtail grass here and there. Since I had the field to myself, I pranced all around, admired my snow tires, tied my boots tight, even considered whistling had it not been so cold. I couldn't get my lips to purse. Straight across the field there were horse tracks, small footprints, rocks glistening in the sharp light, but not much else.

I walked as quickly as I could to the path by the evergreens that would lead me to the pond. Here, the Fenton River was a stream snarling around rocks and icy branches, cracking the thin ice that had formed closer to the edge where the moss remained, cushiony and dark with moisture. I passed by the fallen tree, the little bridge, the thicket where I lost my sunglasses one day, and the small fir with the branch that bent 180 degrees looking for light. From this point, the pond was within view. I adjusted my cap to filter the last pink rays of sun and looked at the reflections of the pines on the water and my own reflection. A woman in a pea coat like mine stood up by the edge of the pond.

"Who's there?" she called out.

"Tina! Tina, it's me, Erica!" I ran toward her. We hugged and sat down on the wooden pier by the ice. Tina told me about spending time with her family in Bridgeport over the holiday, I filled her in on my visit to my sister's house. We sat in silence, watching the gentle colors of the sunset stroking the surface of the deep pond, skimming over the tops of the bare trees. Winter dusk surrounded us.

"Remember when you first showed me this spot?"

"Yeah, you were telling me about the science major you had a crush on."

"Right, and you said science majors would only go for boys," she reminded me.

"Yeah, well, I was wrong. You got her."

"And shortly after that was when you got Millie away from Scooter."

"I wouldn't say I took her away though. Remember, Scooter was still defining her sexuality back then."

"You're cruel! You just don't like that girl because she's white." Tina shoved me. I shoved back.

"That's not true! I don't like her because she's got designs on my girlfriend."

"Still? I thought you said you and Millie had worked that out—"

"We did. Millie's been very sweet to me. If it weren't for her, my sister and I would have ruined my niece's holiday with our arguing. But Nélida and Millie get along. I don't know how."

"She should be a diplomat or a fashion consultant!" Tina howled, and I smacked her in the arm for joking about Millie's concern over clothes. "Hey, look at this—now this is fashion!" Tina removed her wool hat, and her once short hair fluffed up all around, giving her a striking look.

"Far out—are we going back to the sixties?"

"No, you hick—this is my Joan Armatrading look."

"Oh," I considered pretending I knew who that was, but Tina knew I didn't know.

"She's better than Hendrix, and she's beautiful. You've got to come and listen to her, she's got the sexiest voice, and everybody thinks she's got a girlfriend—"

"Okay, okay, I'm sold. When can I come over?"

"Now? It's freezing here, and she's got a voice to melt your heart! You got your car?"

"Yup," we stood up and started walking back.

"So, how is it working at the cottages? Did you start yet?" We were walking in twilight through the bluish snow.

"Last night was my first night there, but it's just until I can work days. I'm sick of the graveyard shift—"

"Tell me about it. My father was a night watchman for GE until he retired last year. He was mighty glad not to have to see the sun come up anymore!"

"Wow, he must be glad to see you get into Yale—"

"Yeah, I think he is, but in The Drama School? He'd be happier if I had your job!"

"Ha! I'm there with one of the clients from the old ward. Madeleine. Remember I told you about her?"

"The crazy redhead?"

"Yeah. I thought she didn't have any sense of, you know, shame or privacy. This morning she proved me wrong—" I was straining to distinguish the path in the dark. "So, I got everyone up at six-thirty, no problem. They went about their business even though they'd never seen me before. Even Gloria—"

"Who's that?"

"A real bruiser of a woman who can put her fist through a wall, that's who."

"Girl—I'm impressed." Tina squinted ahead and tried to make out the path.

"Me too. I had their cereal bowls all laid out on the dining-room table, when Madeleine Mallard comes bounding over to her seat still in her nightgown. I sent her back to the bathroom to wash and dress, and she went without a struggle. I followed her, you know, because I'd never seen her do anything by herself, until she sat on the toilet. Well, she got right up and slammed the door on my face!"

"Hey, she wanted privacy!"

"Which makes me question that whole bathroom routine back in the ward—"

"But, you're going back there as soon as you get on days?"

"Yeah, and maybe get Millie to come back to me full time." I told her, startling myself with my own revelation. Tina looked at me.

"Erica, what's really going on?"

"Well . . . sometimes I think she's trying to say good-bye to me—"

"Damn, you're dramatic."

The Valiant was visible a few yards away, a blue haze in the gray night. I stopped to tie my boot lace, and Tina ran ahead of me. In the stillness I could hear her brushing the snow off the windshield. Reaching with stiff fingers in my pocket for the keys, I heard a muffled shout and looked up to see a shadow push Tina to the ground. I know my heart skipped a beat because there was a second of numbness within me, then my head pounded with every icy breath. I ran in the snow, my feet sinking, the short distance that separated us. I could hear Tina struggle, I could barely see the man attempting to drag her into the woods. My voice finally found me, and I grunted as I kicked him. He turned then, swinging at me with his left arm. I ducked and tackled him while Tina screamed "You, bastard!" but he pushed me away against the trees, and then he grabbed her by the throat, choking her. Remembering the screwdriver in my pocket, I lunged and stabbed at him, anywhere I could distinguish a vulnerable spot, until he let go of Tina. Recovering, I kicked him in the head, and the dry sound of the kick sent him half crawling into the woods with a howl. A dark silence enveloped us so suddenly that I shuddered with fear. An instant later, our breaths came gasping back to us, as we held each other, leaning against the car.

"Are you all right? Did he hurt you?" I managed, finally. Tina rubbed her neck, shaking her head, no, she was fine.

"What's this you got?" she reached for my right hand where I still clutched the screwdriver. "There's no blood on it, is there?"

"I don't know, let's get in the car."

I revved up the motor, and it stalled. Tina's teeth chattered. I started it up again, and flooring the gas, we slid down the narrow road away from the field. I had a sick feeling in my gut, a taste in my mouth like metal, the sensation of having kicked and stabbed was dizzying.

"What if we run into him?"

"I'll break his legs." The fear took me again.

"Nah, just kill him." Tina's teeth sounded clenched.

When the heater began to warm us, we seemed to step out of a nightmare we had survived together.

"Must have thought you were alone—what did he look like?"

"Shit, I don't know. White dude." Tina checked the backseat belatedly, then the road behind us. With a shudder, I adjusted the rearview mirror, which showed me nothing but the tattered plastic of the convertible top.

"Erica!" Tina shook me. "Let's go to the campus police!"

"What, deal with the pigs now? Shouldn't I take you back to the dorm first?"

"No, no, he must have walked in from nearby. The cops got horses and dogs, right? They'll get him."

"Okay, okay." We were silent until we got to the police station.

"Maybe we should come back tomorrow—" Tina held my arm back.

"No, Tina, you were right the first time. All those rapes on campus? The woman that got killed on North Eagleville? . . ."

Tina's round face was quiet, her thoughtful eyes on the brink of tears. "Bastard was fuckin' strong, homegirl . . ." her head shaking in disbelief. "But I feel kinda sick."

"Me, too." I put my forehead against Tina's, and my arms on her shoulders. After a while, we walked into the police station arm-in-arm, scraped the snow off our boots on the welcome mat.

Nights at the cottage were monotonous. The novelty wore off sooner than I expected, and I hadn't expected much. I began a routine consisting of late-night television, coffee, and a phone call to the ward by 4 A.M., having finished all the work in an hour and a half. If there was any time left over, I would spend it daydreaming in the office or staring at the parking lot, waiting for the sun to rise.

Every once in a while, I would read through the clients' day programs and would try to come up with more imaginative behavioral schemes. There were notes in the logbook written in a sort of institutional English that reminded me of police talk. The jargon stretched the simple facts of the women's lives and made clinical episodes out of them: "Kitty has been observed to exhibit self-stimulatory behavior, perseverativeness, and mood swings. Staff reports difficult ambulation and increased falling episodes . . ." Of course, I thought I knew what was wrong with Kitty. She was epileptic, and her period was two weeks late; the Dilantin she was given to control the seizures seemed to affect her more prior to her menses. I had read the logbook and taken note of her cycle because Mrs. Morse had taught me to consider everything that might be affecting the women. "They can't tell you, so's you've got to learn to read the signs. Makes your job easier," she would pat me on the knee, and then add, "and their lives better."

After my first two weeks, the first-shift charge saw me off in the morning. He was a pleasant man, fairly young, but with a receding hairline and tinted glasses, which made him look older.

"I've noticed you always check the backseat before you get into your car."

"Uh-huh," flashing on the episode in the woods, with Tina.

"It's a good idea—lotta weirdos around here."

"Yup." I was getting annoyed. It didn't take much for a man to become a weirdo in my book. Just asking too many questions was placing this one in that category.

"Well," he persisted, "the second-shift charge told me you had an *experience* about a week ago . . ." I revved up the motor. I shouldn't have told her anything, no matter how rattled I was that night. But I would have trusted anybody who'd listen.

"Look," I put on my sunglasses. "I don't want to talk about it, okay?"

"Why? Did he—do anything?" He asked, smiling.

"No. He just said *hello*. In the dark. With his hand over my friend's mouth. Is that enough for you? See you tomorrow." I peeled out of the parking lot, leaving him in a cloud of snow and smoke. In the side-view mirror, I could see him shrug his shoulders and go back in the cottage. He was probably feeling perfectly normal about his obscene interest in my possible misfortune. Adrenaline pumped through my veins. In the cold January morning, with the white sunlight reflecting on the frozen hills and the artificial pond on institution grounds, I was seething hot.

The police had been remarkably polite to us. Tina hadn't said much, at first, limiting her answers to "couldn't see what he looked like," and "white guy about your height," when the cop asked her what the attacker looked like. The cop said to the dispatcher, "caucasian male, about six feet, wearing dark coat, on foot, apparently unarmed." Another cop, an older man, asked us to follow him to an office, where Tina and I told him every detail we could think of. He seemed immensely grateful to us for reporting the attack, asked us three times if we needed a doctor, then gave us hot chocolate and a candy bar each to warm up. When we left, Tina told me she almost felt like a "regular citizen." We'd decided afterward that we would take a self-defense class at the women's center.

The sun felt warm on my face through the windshield. I decided I was too awake to go home and struggle with sleep, so I headed for the Campus Restaurant to indulge in a greasy breakfast of eggs, home fries, and thick toast. Later, I could wait for Millie to come out of the Life Sciences Building along with the other students—her hair billowing about her face and her hat stuffed under her arm with her books. I remembered the excitement of the new courses, the new books—I felt a tinge of desire to go back to school, then, thinking of the fifteen-dollar price tag on most of the books, I squelched it.

How wonderful the rain could be, cold and wicked as it was, raining over dirty snow, ice over ice, copiously and almost gleefully preparing the slippery traps on the country roads, the inclined streets, as soon as it all froze again at dawn. I drove slowly to work almost automatically, thinking melancholy thoughts, admiring the black sky, the shimmering trees in the milky moonlight.

I heard that the first-shift charge had taken the day off. I hoped, to avoid me. I glared at the second-shift charge for blabbing to him about my being attacked in the woods, after I confided in her. She knew I was angry at her and didn't say anything to me. It's amazing how much people know that we never admit to. If we ever decided to come clean, the shock might be so great, it just might put an end to war.

Three in the morning. How many workers were sitting down just about that time every night, having these philosophical thoughts all to themselves. It must be all to themselves because when they talked to each other, all that came out was gossip. No one ever talked about their more useful thoughts, except for Fran and Mrs. Morse, maybe. I walked around in circles for a while, checking through the windows to see if there were any stars out that night, figuring at the same time that the last dryer load would need another ten minutes.

Funny, I couldn't remember Mrs. Morse's first name. Or maybe she never told me. I studied the breakfast menu for Thursdays: bran muffins and scrambled eggs. Suddenly there was a noise, like someone waking up. I stood still for a moment. Nothing. It was a good thing that we weren't expected to make soft-boiled eggs or fried eggs sunny-side-up. The muffins came already baked from the central kitchens.

There was that noise again. I pretended not to feel my heart beating fast, and I went to check on my clients. In the east bedrooms, Jenny and Miranda slept soundly, Carol snored, and Betty grinded her teeth. Carol's hair dryer was still in the box on the bureau. She insisted she must keep the tattered box, that's what kept the dryer new for her. Walking by the kitchen again, I turned the coffee back on. In the west bedrooms, Madeleine and Cindy's room smelled like disinfectant. Next to Madeleine's bed, on the wall, there was a postcard from New Brunswick, her very own postcard that wouldn't have lasted two minutes at the ward. Someone would have eaten it or caused a big commotion trying to eat it. Madeleine slept all curled up, hugging her pillow, her red hair tousled from her undoubtedly active day.

I turned to face Gloria's bedroom, the door always closed, lest some noise wake her prematurely. I pushed the door open just an inch, and looked at Kitty and Gloria sleeping peacefully. Kitty had pink curlers on top of her head. Gloria was completely covered and gave no signs of stirring. I left the door ajar and went to fix myself a cup of coffee. Three-thirty-five; I rushed into the office to make my hourly call.

"Cul-de-sac Two, cottage B, García," I chanted to the other voice.

"Hi. You got extra laundry bags?" the nasal voice was Jeff's, from cottage C, filling in at Administration to help with the hourly check-ins.

"Just two—we got a shortage?"

"Hoarding. It's a war with second shift. Hold the bags, okay?"

"Sure."

I was about to take a sip of my coffe when I heard steps shuffling in the hallway. Grabbing a clipboard to signify authority, I ran out of the office. Gloria was going to the bathroom. When she heard me, she turned and squinted in the light like a child who's just woken.

"Need anything, Gloria?"

Gloria mumbled in the negative, scratching her head. I went into the laundry room and started folding undershirts. Bras. Stretch pants in several dull colors. I heard Gloria going back to her room. Now, that was silly. She was going to the bathroom, that's all. I had succumbed, just like all the other aides, to the preoccupation with "incidents." I should tell Millie about this, she would laugh. A piercing scream from Gloria's room sent me skidding on the tile floor. I flipped the light on, prepared for the worst. Gloria and Kitty were tugging furiously on a thick, blue quilt. Gloria grunted and managed to swat at Kitty, who responded with staccato screams.

"Whadda you think you're doin'?" My sharp tones stopped the action, and Gloria let go of her end of the quilt, from which I deduced it must belong to Kitty.

"Kitty, you take your quilt and get into bed now!" The gaunt, awkward woman pushed her hair away from her face; straight and stringy, it hung back in the same place beneath the rollers. Gloria scratched her belly through her faded flannel nightgown. Her lower lip visibly curled under, she stared at the quilt, her eyes darting, under stiffly-cropped bangs of grayish blonde hair, to study my every move.

"Now, Kitty!" I lowered the pitch of my voice. Kitty sniffled and jumped into bed, but Gloria attempted one last swipe at the quilt and her owner. I deflected her aim by stomping my left foot loudly in her direction. Gloria conceded and dove into bed, the springs twanging under her weight.

"I don't want to see you guys until six-thirty, you got that?" I walked out of their room before they had a chance to respond.

Back in the office, drinking cold coffee, I prepared to wait for the morning. Two more nights before my pass days, and then it would be February. Probably two more months before it was warm enough to go outside without a sweater. Sometimes it seemed as though I ignored what happened in my life between November and March. I only lived for the sun, to see the fields change, to see the river break the ice, and the pond . . . the pond would be like black glass at its deepest point. Would I be afraid to go back there alone, even in daylight? I wouldn't want to give up walking alone just because of that creep who attacked us, though he didn't stand a chance with both of us fighting him. Perhaps I should always carry my screwdriver in my pocket. Why not just get a knife? Tina should. And Millie.

Six A.M., late January. It's time to go to the ocean again, snow and all, just to breathe the salty air, hear the tide, feel the constant movement. Nélida said to me once, "These waters of the Atlantic, they have no color, they're nothing compared to Puerto Rico . . ." and she named beaches with pretty names, like *Buyé, Culebrita, Aguadilla*, that were only words to me. "Don't you remember, Erica? Not like here, just greenish gray." I was only three years old, how could I remember? In fact, I don't think I remember anything about my childhood until I was five, and Mami had a party for my birthday in New Britain. There was sweet food in one room for the children, and arroz con everything in the kitchen for the adults. Nélida gave me a Barbie doll I never played with because it had a fancy dress, and I wasn't supposed to get it dirty. I remember looking out the window at the factories, all the brick buildings, the buses, the smoky trucks, and yearning for something open, some fairy-tale place that smelled clean after the rain. But I don't remember Puerto Rico.

Time. How did I get to be twenty-one? "Nobody drops out during their third year in college, Erica, not with a scholarship." A nasty argument over Christmas, my niece staring at me, wide-eyed, and my sister going on about me being such a disappointment to the family. "Don't yell at me in front of Marisol," I shouted, "what does she need to know about disappointment?" But Millie came to the rescue. "Don't worry, Nélida, she'll go back. I left school for a semester, and I went back." And my sister: "Ay, bendito—but she can't afford to fool around like that, she's Puerto Rican. You're Jewish!"

By the time we left, I felt like a failure again. My sister even brought up Tina as an example of a *smart girl:* "You see, Erica, she's a smart girl, she's black and she's going to Yale!" And this was a concession for my sister, because she never mentioned any of my gay friends, except Millie. Millie at least had long hair and wore lipstick, on occasion.

"So I guess, according to your sister, being a Jew is good for something," Millie whispered to me as we left my sister's house.

"I'm sorry, Millie, did that bother you?"

"Well—no. But, do you think the way she does?" We were standing by the Valiant, it was snowing lightly. Millie was holding the bag with the presents my sister had given both of us, and I was holding the flan. I had no idea what to say, having never considered these things. People were walking by us, on the sidewalks of my childhood, trying not to stare at us as we stood there, looking obviously like a couple having a serious discussion on a holiday. Millie had gone with me on a day that meant nothing to her, just because she loved me. I knew she couldn't bring me home because her mother would be hysterical, and her father would disown her for being a lesbian. All I knew was that I'd been raised to be a model citizen, or people would automatically assume I was a delinquent. Leaving school meant I was headed for a life of crime.

I tried to explain to Millie, as we drove slowly back to Coventry that evening, but it sounded ridiculous when I said it. She thought I had a chip on my shoulder, and I thought she didn't want to see how white people always had more latitude in this country. But we didn't really feel like arguing, we were just happy to be together again, and it felt like we'd just met. I didn't even care anymore about Scooter, as long as Millie was with me. She kept her hand on my knee and leaned on my shoulder. Finally, I put my arm around her and drove with one hand. I remember that, by the time we got to the lake, the windshield was steamed up from our kissing at all the red lights.

The sky grew lighter. I checked the clock to see if it was time to get the women up. I quickly straightened up the office and wrote "Quiet night" in the logbook. When I looked up, Madeleine Mallard was staring at me. Her gown was wet.

"Oh terrific, Madeleine." I took her arm, and we walked back to her room to strip her bed. I gave her a laundry bag and made her put her sheets in it.

"Thanks. That's a big help. Now, let's—cool it, Gloria!" She had come from behind and pulled my hair. I took her arms and held them by the wrists. She leered at me.

"Don't pull hair, Gloria. Let's shake hands and be nice," I said the stupid words evenly, I knew she was testing me. She took my right hand quickly, examining it as though it were a curious object. Madeleine squealed behind me and covered her mouth.

"You got the joke, Madeleine? Okay, everybody get dressed!" I retrieved my hand from Gloria and clapped loudly. Somehow, I had to make Gloria respect me; besides, it had really hurt when she pulled my hair.

Miranda, meanwhile, emerged from the east bedrooms, wet as usual and repeating everything anyone else said. At least she was always in a good mood.

"Hello, Sunshine!" I patted her on the shoulder and led her to the bathroom.

"Hello-Sunshine-hello," she echoed, stripping her nightgown off and handing it to me. She stood there, her large breasts bobbing slightly, her blues eyes wide open.

"Go ahead," I told her, and she sat on the toilet. I stuffed her wet gown in the laundry bag and washed my hands quickly, feeling slightly embarrassed for her sake rather than for mine. I figured she acted the same way with Kenneth, the first-shift guy. It was odd. I was hoping he could see Miranda's innocent eyes as the eyes of a child, before he looked at her body, and I don't know why I'd never thought of this at the ward.

The other women were awake and going about their routines. I handed each one their outfit for the day and made sure they finished dressing before breakfast. Miranda rushed back into her room and waited for me to dress her. I escorted her back into the bathroom and made her take a quick shower, which she seemed to appreciate immensely.

"Hello, Sunshine, hello!" she chanted. While Miranda put on her underwear and pants, Madeleine refused her sneakers, so I negotiated with her to keep her socks on. Miranda handed me her brassiere. I decided right then I would teach her how to put it on herself, so she wouldn't have to ask anyone for help—the men or the women aides. Kitty had gone back to bed and needed some coaxing. I went to get her up again with Miranda sticking to me like bubblegum.

"Hello-Sunshine!"

"Kitty, get up, honey."

"Get-up-honey-get-up-honey."

"Quiet, Miranda!"

"Quiet-Miranda-hello-Sunshine!"

"Shh, come on, Kitty, it's late!" Kitty sat up and slowly began to pull on her slippers. Gloria charged back in the bedroom and pushed Miranda to the floor. Keeping an eye on me, she started thrashing about and throwing things.

"All right! Everybody out except Gloria!" Gloria continued her tantrum while Kitty and Miranda scooted out of the room. I slammed the door shut. Gloria stared at me for a second, which gave me a slight edge on the situation.

"Everybody-out-hello-Sunshine!" mimicked Miranda outside the room.

"Shut up!" from Kitty. I was losing the edge with those two clowns.

"Nooo!" bellowed Gloria, throwing her mattress up in the air. I took two steps toward her. She showed me her teeth.

"Do you know what's for breakfast?" Gloria shook her head, holding her lamp in one hand.

"Good. Then you won't miss it!" I put her mattress back on the bed and made her sit on it. She stuck out her lower lip, almost softening my resolve to discipline her.

"This is time-out, Gloria. Ten minutes, and if you don't cool off, you can have breakfast with second shift." I turned and left her room, leaving the door open just a crack, as I'd been instructed to do. I was shaking mad, and I'd never wanted to smack anybody so much. I even wondered if Gloria would be able to tell on me if I hit her, or if an aide had ever slapped her the way I wanted to right then.

In the dining room, Jenny, Carol, Betty, and Cindy sat obediently at their places, while Madeleine and Miranda had a field day with the clean laundry, spreading it all over the cottage. I began to feel I had crossed some kind of line, where nothing would make me feel better except smacking someone.

"Hello-Sunshine-hello-Sunshine . . ."

"Shut up!" grumbled Kitty from the kitchen, with her mouth full. I ran in to find her eating as many bran muffins as she could hold with both hands.

"Damn it, Kitty!"

"Damn-it-Kitty-damn-it-Kitty," repeated Miranda, helping herself to a few muffins.

"Sit down, all of you. Right now!" I carried the remaining muffins to the dining room, trying at the same time to usher Kitty, Madeleine, and Miranda to their seats.

"Nooo!" yelled Gloria, slamming the door of her bedroom shut. I sat down with the women, determined to keep them at least in the same room, dressed, and eating their breakfast. In a few minutes, the eggs and the muffins were gone and they were all clamoring for their second cup of coffee; taking Madeleine with me to the kitchen for insurance, I turned on the coffeepot and drank a glass of water. Madeleine watched me with her devil eyes.

Just then the sound of a key turning in the lock brought things back into perspective for me. I took Madeleine back into the dining room and made her sit down, while I looked hopefully toward the hallway.

"You're gonna get it!" chanted Kitty, as she smashed butter on Miranda's hair. The relief charge and a female aide walked in to find me trying to wipe Miranda's head with a napkin.

"You're the one who's gonna get it, young lady!" the matronly charge admonished the forty-five-year-old Kitty, who was enjoying the attention. The younger aide started off to get the fresh coffee, and I began to pick up the mess.

"Good morning, I'm sure glad to see you!"

"Good morning, you okay?"

"Oh, yes. Gloria is on time-out, and I'm on burn-out!"

"Oh, don't worry, honey, we were wondering when things would get back to normal around here," she adorned her remark with a belly laugh.

"So, this is normal for them?" The women sat quietly, holding their empty coffee cups, the table a battlefield of muffin wrappers, eggs, napkins, spilled milk. Madeleine clapped her large pink hand on the back of my neck, a sign of affection that nearly knocked me down.

"Sure, you've kept these devils under control somehow, maybe it's your training from the ward. Want some coffee?" The aide was back with a full pot, seven institutional pink cups were raised in unison, and luckily, there was enough left over for us. From Gloria's bedroom we could hear her singing to herself, the springs clanging from her bouncing on the bed—something new for her, they assured me. As if by arrangement, Gloria sang louder, *When the spoon hits yer eye like a big piece a pie, that's amore!*

I filled out the reports for the night in the office, shook hands with my coworkers and walked out of the cottage to the sound of Miranda and Kitty's latest addition to their vocabulary:

"Damn-it-Kitty-hello-Sunshine!"

"Shut up!"

7

March had begun in fog and almost constant rain. The last vestiges of snow had long since melted into the ground, and thirty days later, the rain still battered the playground outside the ward, the grass soaking in pools of mud.

Daytime at the wards had been at once everything and not at all what I had expected. I was feeling a little better, my appetite had returned, but I still felt lost. And I couldn't remember why I expected that working during the day would change me so much. Fix my problems? Cure my soul? That it certainly hadn't done, but getting up at dawn and rushing to be at the ward on time had begun to change the way I looked at things. Like how I found it strange that Millie was just as busy during the days as she used to be when I worked at night. But instead of figuring I'd made a mistake in switching my hours, I figured she was trying to tell me something. I think I even got angry with her and admitted it to myself for the first time.

And work. Work was different. Some mornings I'd come in and think I saw a glimpse of my old self leaving in the breaking light, tired, sleepless. My new self was there, awake, talking in regular voices with other people who were awake, and watching my clients move through their day almost like normal people. I think, at times like these, I would see the School as just a job, one I could leave, and that's when things got confusing. I would drink too much coffee and get a headache.

Thrusting my hands impatiently into my apron, I played with the key ring and the plastic tokens I kept there to give Frances after she had been good for an hour. She could then exchange one for half a cup of coffee. I wondered if she ever got a headache; that is, before she pounded her head.

My mind was in a fog after breakfast. The past five mornings had been closer to chaos than anything I had ever imagined. There had been fights, bruises, cuts, food spilled in the dining room all over everybody's sneakers, and enough restraint orders had been okayed by doctors over the phone to keep everybody tied up for a month, including the aides.

On day shift, I found Kelly again from our in-service training days, who had given up the heavy eyeliner and quickly became my buddy. All my new coworkers had inexhaustible energy. I thought I had been tired at night, but at least there were times when one could rest; during the day, Jennifer, Kelly, and I were in constant motion from 7:30 to 3:30. What kept me fascinated was watching the women I had only known at night, being surprised by their responses, and being so frantically busy that hours could pass without a thought but for the present moment. The Kiniry twins, for example, spent the day trying to open doors and untying knots, and they went through more clothes than anybody. Running a close second were Frances, who could make her clothes disappear, and Belle, a blind woman who could tear her thick cotton dress neatly in half. At night, I hadn't paid much attention to Belle because, being almost nonverbal, she was always quiet.

"Wait till you see what else she can do," said Kelly, the younger of my two coworkers.

"Yeah? And what is that?"

"She smears her shit all over herself—"

"Gross—"

"And she screams like a banshee!" put in Jennifer, on her way to the laundry room.

"I wouldn't have figured Belle would do that, she's always so quiet at night," I told Kelly. She was grinning and performing her routine fixing of her long hair, taking it out of the clip and then slipping the copper brown tresses back in the clip. She was small, wiry—cute, is how I'd described her to Tina, not without a lot of ribbing about how I was shamelessly flirting. I'd appreciated her friendliness. "But you seem to enjoy telling me these horror stories. Why, Kelly?"

"Oh, because, you know . . . 'cause you're always so serious when you work with these kids—I mean women—trying to pretend like what they do isn't funny or weird. And it's pretty damn funny! Look at Elaine over there, she laughs right along with us!"

"But she doesn't know when we're laughing at her—" I protested.

"But we don't do it to be mean, Erica!"

"I know, we egg her on so she'll stop beating herself on the head when she gets into a tantrum." I crossed my arms and looked right at Kelly's eyes behind her tinted glasses. She fought the urge to fix her ponytail again. I could tell I made her nervous.

"So, lighten up," she told me.

It was a draw. But Kelly was right, in a way. I didn't want to treat the women like oddities, and yet, I could understand that sometimes there wasn't any other way to look at the odd things they did. I had to have a sense of humor about it. I just didn't want to get jaded and abusive, like the people I'd met when I first started working there.

I was disappointed, though. What could a bunch of overworked aides do for the clients? On my side, there were twenty-seven women, and generally, three aides. Since all three of us had charge's ratings, it meant we didn't need an additional supervisor. And so, there was almost no time to be gentle or to notice anything that the women may need beyond their physical comfort. Yet, we were supposed to teach something, develop whatever spark of potential each woman had. Even on third shift, it seemed we spent a lot of time obtaining restraint orders, trying to prevent mayhem, trying to keep everyone clean. After my first month, I'd felt like a veteran of the place, a drill sergeant surveying the ward: If everyone had shoes and socks on, my job was done.

By 10:30, bathing was over, and Jennifer had come back from her morning break. She was the motherly one among us. Jennifer was big and muscular, with short red hair, blue eyes, and freckles on her cheeks. She seemed to always be in a good mood, her laughter resonated in the ward all day. With four children of her own at home, she said she had seen everything, and nothing our clients could do would surprise her. She treated Kelly and me like her older daughters, or younger sisters, and even joined us on our daily chin-up contest at the old shower bars.

Now it was my turn to go into the dormitory and finish making the beds. Usually, I would have welcomed the time alone to think, but I had too much on my mind I didn't want to touch. Frances looked at me with her sad, round eyes. I remembered her token and gave it to her. She had kept her hands out of Judy's hair, another black woman whose hair she always wanted to pull, and her dress was still dry. She wrapped her lips around her gums and smiled at me. Still, it seemed as though the veil that clouded her eyes would never leave. With my arm around her, I unlocked the office, where we had kept her lukewarm coffee. Kelly looked up from her notes and feigned surprise.

"Has it been a whole hour, Frances?" Frances held out the yellow token in her hand and gulped the coffee.

"Well, I guess that answers my question. Come on, I'll help with the beds."

"Somehow I don't think this is working." Frances thrust her chin at me where she had dribbled some coffee. I wiped it with my apron, and she showed me the sores on her fingers.

"I'll put lotion on you later, okay?" I dismissed her with the promise of a little attention and walked in the dorm after Kelly.

"Eva Nathan!" came the familiar exclamation.

"Peed-a-peed-a-pee!"

"Scoot now, Eva! You rumpled these beds. What a pain she is." Eva looked at Kelly with her innocent green eyes and twirled her gray hair in a pink hand. Kelly took Eva to the day hall with her quick pace, and Eva let herself be led, walking in her small, dancing steps.

I counted how many beds were still unmade: fifteen, eighteen with the ones Eva had rumpled. I set to pulling sheets and blankets, squaring corners, looking at the sheet of rain against the narrow rectangular windows above the pink-tiled walls. Kelly came back in and tied her brown hair up in a knot. Frances followed her, holding her arthritic hands out to me, to remind me of the lotion I'd promised her. I took a small bottle of lotion hidden in a cabinet and quickly smoothed some on her hands, trying not to betray the slight revulsion I felt touching the ulcerated knuckles she pounded day after day. I was in a hurry to get back to the beds, yet I found myself following Frances with my eyes out of the dormitory with a spasm in my heart; just then I saw Kelly stealing a glance at me. We both tugged a little faster at the corners of the beds.

No sooner had we finished when Jennifer wheeled the cart in

with the eleven o'clock meds in little cups of applesauce into the day hall. We locked the dorm and rushed to help her. I took some of the cups from Jennifer and put the wooden pallets for spoons in my shirt pocket. She dropped the different pills in the applesauce and identified them one by one: "Stelazine, that's the blue one, 25 mg; phenobarbital, 250 mg—that one you know; Thorazine, 100 mg, the brown one; Dulcolax, the laxative, in the capsule. Here you go, Agnes!"

Agnes needed little prompting to come take the applesauce from me. She leaned forward, her hands inside her dress as though it were a straitjacket, and thrust out her tongue.

"The body of Christ . . ." I chanted solemnly, causing a ripple of laughter in Jennifer and Kelly that infected Agnes. She laughed as she ate her laced applesauce eagerly, licking the corners of her dry lips, but then, wheezing her strange giggle, she grabbed an extra cup on the way back to her chair.

"Grab her, she might O.D.!" I took another cup without drugs in it and managed to trade Agnes for it before she swallowed the extra pills. Jennifer sighed thanks as I handed it back to her, the colored coating already dissolving in the applesauce, revealing a hefty Thorazine tablet.

"How much is this?"

"Two hundred and fifty milligrams—for Coral." Hearing her name, Coral got up to swallow her medication.

"Wow—"

"Yeah—"

"Would she have gotten sick?"

"I don't really know. Agnes gets another 200 mg after dinner anyway."

"And Coral?"

"Another 100 mg, plus Dilantin, and phenobarb." Kelly dispensed the rest of the pills and capsules from the plastic envelopes.

"Listen, I read this book about a woman who gets committed to Bellevue, and she is totally out of commission for two days after they give her a shot of Thorazine—and our women take it day and night?"

"Damn—" Kelly was shaking her head. As if by tacit agreement, we turned our thoughts to the lunch hour.

The smell from the cafeteria was overpowering. It smelled like some kind of meat blending with the aroma of spice cake. I pulled out a stack of colorful bibs, some of them as large as a pillowcase, and began calling the women to me—those who would consent to wear one, that is. Standing by the door to the hallway, the large day-hall windows to my right, I could see the sun winning its long battle with the clouds. The light was hazy with pale sunshine. I went to give Rosie a bear hug while she sat in the middle of the day-hall floor staring at the windows. She pushed me away with a strong brown arm but didn't conceal a smile.

"The sun's coming out, Rosie," I told her while I put her bib on. She turned to face me and hopped on her bent legs while clicking a sharp noise with her tongue.

"Ta-ka-ta-ka-ta-ka!" She looked like a child sometimes, except for the intent look in her eyes and the shock of gray hair above her right temple. Elaine came, holding her ball under one arm. She reached down and gave Rosie a wet kiss on one ear, which Rosie wiped off.

"Well!" said Elaine.

"Ta-ka-ta-ka!" yelled Rosie. Having finished with the bibs, I got ready to take the first group to the dining room. The sun came out fully then, brightening the red tile on the day-hall floor. In the hallway, I could hear Jennifer and Kelly arguing about which group Coral should go with. They both had different ideas about what was preferable: a meal with lots of food spilled but relatively quiet or a relatively clean meal with loud and lengthy commotion. I had forgotten to check on Coral, and my pulse raced because I didn't see her at first. A quick look around, and I spotted her, dancing, legs apart, and rotating evenly to the rhythm of the faint radio *Muzak*, her muscular arms wrapped behind her back, her eyes closed, her matted blond hair sticking out of the leather helmet she wore for protection.

All the women were quiet; Joanie Kiniry spinning around, the scar under the eye where Myra Jenkins scratched her gave her face the look of a startled smile; her sister Jean working to slip an extra sock on her left foot, Frances humming, Belle swinging her legs, Eva twisting her dress absently. . . . Was it the warm sun, or was it the drugs? Coral danced in circles, her strong, stiff legs were muscular, a little bruised, her arms gripped tightly behind her. She liked to wrap a shirt or a tie-string tightly around her wrists and twirl like that for almost an hour until we stopped her, and her wrists would be red, her hands swollen. Sometimes, when something angered her, she would stomp hard on the tile floor, her visage darkened under the helmet. She gave me the impression that she struggled against a force that threatened to overtake her. She had a permanently furrowed brow, her coarse features intent on something within her, and suddenly she stopped dancing. She stared past me, walked to one of the bucket chairs and sat down, her knees tucked up under her chin.

A noise called me from the bathroom, and I ran to find Frances banging her head against the Plexiglas above the sinks. Almost by arrangement, Elaine began to pound her head with her hand. I grabbed Frances away from the window and drew Elaine toward me.

"You two are going to drive me crazy!" I admonished them, but almost before the words were out of my mouth, I was thinking, *so, what else are they going to do to get my attention?* Frances had been trying all morning with the business of the hand lotion. Elaine squinted at me with that characteristic way she had of opening her eyes just a crack. But Frances wailed, throwing her head back and opening her toothless mouth wide in anguish.

"What is it?" I studied her eyes; she seemed to be trying to explain, but there was nothing, nothing.

Coral walked toward me unsteadily and pulled me away from Frances. I led her to the sink and gave her a small cup of water. She drank it quickly and held the empty paper cup in her hand as though it hurt to hold it. I took it from her and stuck it back in my apron to prevent someone from eating it. I returned momentarily to my other chores, picking up clothes, mopping the floor, when something made me turn to see Coral balancing unsteadily. I reached for her hand just as she shook, and caught her enough to bring her body down to the bathroom floor, where she began to convulse. I turned her on her side and untied her helmet, keeping her head back to help her breathe. I stared at her and held her a little off the cold floor as she helplessly followed the shocks of her body, some movement alien to her, outside of her, yet impossibly linked to every muscle. She would be exhausted by the grand mal seizure.

The passage of time in the wards refused to be clocked by outside instruments or imposed rituals, yet it left marks, visible imprints on tired hands. Coral's body was heavy, I couldn't move her by myself. I had no idea what was going on in the day hall, it could be peaceful in there or total disaster by now. It had been three minutes; another two and Jennifer would come back from the dining room for the next group. I watched the door to the hallway and visualized her solid figure coming through many times while Coral shook and shuddered in my arms. I thought she might die, and I knew she wouldn't. The spasms calmed down. I realized she was sweating, and so was I. Then the lock turned, and I saw Jennifer, just as I had imagined her.

"Seizure?" She locked the door behind her. She came to help me put Coral in a wheelchair to take her to bed.

"Are-you-cold?" offered Elaine, peering into my face. After the stress, her eternal line sounded outrageously funny.

"No, but Coral is out-cold, Elaine. Help us get her to bed," suggested Jennifer.

"Well," came the expected response, and Elaine pretended to huff and push with us, then planted a wet kiss on Coral's forehead. Coral was hard and heavy as a rock. "Are-you-cold-are-you-c-cold?" repeated Elaine until we came out of the dorm again, and I thought I would wash my hands before recording Coral's seizure. Just then, Diane kicked Jula and sent her flying against the bucket chairs. Jula fell with a crash, but Diane screamed in response. Jennifer went to Diane while I picked Jula up from the strewn chairs where she convulsed in a series of petit mals. I didn't know what to do, her small frame was awfully stiff and heavy, so I leaned her against the wall and held on to her shoulders.

"Knock on the day-hall window, Jennifer! See if D side will give us a hand—" With one hand on Diane's swinging arm, Jennifer tapped her keys on the thick glass reinforced with the wire mesh. Agnes leaped from her chair and delivered a handsome scratch on Diane's arm; Diane kicked her away immediately, sending Agnes crashing in the same place Jula had landed. Agnes, however, didn't collapse, she went into a scratching rage instead.

"Okay, Jula, you'll have to fend for yourself." I sat Jula on a chair and I wrapped two tie-strings across her middle to hold her up and away from possible kicks and scratches. Her seizures continued sporadically.

"Watch her, Elaine," I entreated, while I dragged Agnes into the bathroom and sat her on a toilet. She was so surprised, she sat and stared at me.

"Now, stay there till nap time or I'll come back and put you in the shower!" I threatened with the first nonsense that popped into my head. It worked. Agnes sat still, though whimpering to herself, while I rushed to the day hall where Jennifer struggled with Diane, who kicked and punched like a demon, if indeed demons could move like that.

"Watch her legs!" warned Jennifer, but it was too late. Rosie got kicked in the head, and I caught one on the knee. Rosie hit back with a hard left, and I managed to immobilize one of Diane's legs by wrapping my own around hers. We dragged her to the restraint chair.

"Where the hell is everybody?" grunted Jennifer. We sat Diane down, and she pulled Jennifer's hair. I squeezed her wrist so she'd let go, and she grabbed my hair, until Rosie whacked Diane's knee, and she let go. I strapped the wide belt around Diane's waist and fastened the velcro on the back of the chair. Jennifer strapped three of her limbs with blinding speed while Diane howled and grabbed my left arm with her free hand and bit me. With sheer determination, I strapped her arm to the chair, feeling the ice-hot pain in my forearm as though it were not attached to my body. Two aides from D side burst through the door and took in the situation. They immediately saw Jula nodding off and went to take her to bed.

"I'll call the restraint order in," said Jennifer. "You gotta get betadine on that because I think she broke the skin." My arm felt like it was frozen. I watched the oval pattern from Diane's teeth turning purple, with little drops of blood around each puncture. I looked back through the Plexiglas window into the day hall, where Diane moved methodically against the chair restraints.

When I drove home, my arm began to ache. I kept thinking about the attack in the woods. In the weeks that followed, Tina and I had been talking to each other a lot, just like old times, but not about the attack. It was Millie who had made me aware of how

I seemed to be embarrassed about fighting back, about hitting the guy who attacked us.

"What makes you say that?" I'd asked her.

"I don't know, it's like you're apologizing for defending yourself."

"Maybe you're right. It made me feel sick inside, like I'd swallowed something bitter. It's just that I don't want to hit people, and at work—" I didn't know where I was going with this.

"Do you feel like hitting people at work?"

I'd told her, no, never, sometimes, maybe at the Cottages when Gloria was getting the best of me.

We'd gone shopping for books that day, and then to my apartment for the rest of the weekend. We were sitting on the floor, Millie between my legs, leaning back against me while I rubbed her neck. The day was swathed in thick fog, and we were sleepy. I sat still for a long while, trying to digest the things that Millie helped me to see.

"I guess I'm tired of how violent it always feels in there," I told her. "Someone's always getting hurt."

She turned to look at me, to kiss me gently. "I guess this job is a real conflict for you." She started to get up.

"I guess. Where you going?" I held her hand. She took it back to push the curls away from her face. She got up.

"I suppose that's why you've been kind of distant lately . . ."

"Have I, Mill? I'm sorry, I didn't mean to be—"

"That's okay," she said, looking out the windows into the fog. "Maybe it's good for both of us to have a little space."

After that weekend, none of our brief meetings seemed real. As I drove, I lay my right forearm on the wheel, where Diane had bitten it, so I could rest. In all the times we talked to each other on the phone, promised to cook dinner for each other, or to swing by on a Saturday, I kept looking for something left of us, something of the old me, of the old Millie. The last words I remember feeling had been said in the woods, but the memory of the attack had obliterated them.

"She's trying to say good-bye to me," I'd told Tina, and this was either the exact truth or a complete lie. Tina thought I was being dramatic.

The problem was that I was feeling something about Millie, about the two of us, but I had no idea what it was. This thing, large and heavy, occupying the entire cavity between my sternum and my stomach, had no name. But I figured the safest thing was to assume we were through. It was dramatic. I tried to think of a better word for the time where two women realize they cannot be lovers anymore. It was a place, more than a feeling.

The windshield wipers hit dry glass. The rain had stopped, and I was on my way home at three-forty-five in the afternoon; not very tired anymore, wearing a bandage on my forearm from Diane's bite. I had the whole afternoon before me. And the evening. My arm throbbed and so did my head, suddenly. The last thing I wanted to do was to see Millie, yet I ached to see her. To know it was over and to watch her struggle with something that didn't fit in her life. Something. Me.

When I got home, I turned around and around and paced the perimeter of my small apartment like an animal in a cage. Any animal, but not necessarily a tiger. An orangutan, maybe. Any type of large primate who is smart enough to suffer from being caged up but is too clumsy to attempt to get away. I was being theatrical.

I sat on the floor by the mirror-top table and thought about paying my bills, doing the things that normal people did during the day. It was barely four. I was home from work even earlier than most people, and I couldn't think of anything to do. Deliberately, I picked up the phone from its cradle of last week's clothes and dialed Tina's number.

"Yeah, I knew it was you," Tina answered at the first ring.

"What? Tina?"

"Yeah, Erica. I knew you were gonna call me. Don't ask me how."

"Well, don't answer the phone like that, you sound like—like Doña Doris."

"Who's Doña Doris?"

"You know, the espiritista my sister goes to see."

"Oh, I need to see one, too! Come over."

"What's up?" It was exactly what I wanted to do, go see Tina, but just talking to her felt better, and I began to wonder if I wasn't just making too much out of nothing.

"Oh, just come over, please! I broke up with this girl I was seeing, and I'm all upset now, so it's either you come over and make me feel better, or I go for a greasy burger at the Campus Restaurant."

"How about me *and* a greasy burger? I'll meet you at the round table in fifteen minutes."

"Deal."

I headed out of Willimantic toward Storrs and the campus at top speed. I felt full of purpose, happy to be doing something, or perhaps just happy to have something to do. I drove west on 32 and north on 195, doing almost sixty. I passed cars and delighted in the powerful rumble of my car's engine next to theirs, all eight cylinders firing in perfect pitch. As I neared the edge of University grounds, I slowed to a lawful forty-five and then thirty-five, just catching sight of a campus cruiser. The light was fading, but longer days were in the air; it was the cloud cover thickening, preparing for more rain, that gave the day a gray light, as if we were still in the core of winter. I pulled into the gas station parking lot and slid into one of Rachel's reserved spaces, under a tough willow leaning over a rock wall. Rachel, the proprietor, was leaning on the window of a green pickup, talking to one of her loyal redneck customers, and she nodded at my wave as I jumped out. Feeling strengthened by the thought that the only lesbian who owned the only gas station on campus let me park in one of her spaces, I sauntered down the sidewalk to meet Tina at our table.

"Girl, you look too good for someone with a broken heart!" I had to tell her that, because Tina did look great in her leather jacket and leather baseball cap turned backward, her smooth, brown skin aglow with the smile on her round cheeks.

"Who said my heart was broken? I got a date Saturday. You're the one who's all broke up."

"Oh, well, that was an easy therapy session! You owe me fifty bucks." I extended my open hand to her. She slapped it.

I slid over on the round booth and smacked Tina's arm, blocking with my left as she prepared to smack me back. Fleetwood Mac crooned from the jukebox. "So, what happened to the girl who threw you over?"

"Stuck-up sophomore from Trinity College, and nobody threw me over. I dumped her, just for the record. Don't have time for babies when I start graduate school . . ."

"Mh-hm." I let my reply hang in the air while I waved at Jimmy for a cup of coffee, because I knew Tina was embarrassed.

"What *mh-hm?* What do you mean?"

"I mean, so that was the bourgeois black girl with a social conscience you've been talking about off and on . . ."

"Yeah."

"Her social conscience is stamped on the back of her Sage Allen credit card."

"Mm." Tina became more laconic as the truth got closer.

"She dumped you."

"Oh, girl! Jimmy, bring us a couple of cheeseburgers and some of those greasy french fries!" Tina called to Jimmy at the counter, who signalled that he had our order memorized.

"So, who do you have a date with, Saturday night?"

"The new baby dyke working at Rachel's."

"I thought you said no more trainees!"

"Ha! It's not a real date. We're just going to Chuck's to hear some white-girl folksinger and hang out. Wanna come?" Tina made room for my coffee and the fixings Jimmy was placing on our table, a cable spool set on its side—worn smooth with the passage of time and college students. Jimmy, one of the few Chinese people in the area, worked at the restaurant with his father from the time he was a little boy. He grinned at us, letting us know he had overheard our conversation. "Thanks, Jimmy," acknowledged Tina, always perfectly comfortable talking about girlfriends and dates. It was me who was more self-conscious.

"I'll go—I'm off Sunday. I need to stay up late and drink some margaritas."

"Great! I'll see who else wants to."

"But, I don't want to go out and mope about Millie, you know? Things are not working out . . ."

"I won't let you mope, you idiot. You're my buddy, my sister. Besides, *things are not just not working—it's over* between you and Millie." Tina placed her arm around me. The jukebox went silent, and Jimmy's father turned on the rest of the lights in the restaurant.

"I feel like the bottom just fell out from this boat I was on . . ." I said, my mind wandering. I smelled our burgers and realized I hadn't eaten since breakfast.

"You have a strange way of expressing yourself, but I know what you mean. Here come the burgers, now eat! Hey—what's this bandage on your arm?"

"Nuthin'. I have a feeling Millie is seeing Scooter again," I told Tina between bites.

"Don't spoil my appetite," she grumbled with her mouth full.

"I can't imagine she wouldn't tell me, you know. I thought we could discuss anything, but it's like she can't help herself! I hate Scooter!" I sprinkled salt on my burger until Tina reached out and stopped my hand. I had been waiting two years to say how I felt about my rival.

"Erica, I hate to tell you this, but I think you and Millie have to have one more tumble before it's really over. That's what I hate, the relationships that drag on indefinitely. I just like to have it over and do my crying in peace!"

"When did you cry over a woman? I've never seen you cry period!"

"You may yet, cuz I've never fallen for anybody the way you fell for Millie, but I'm telling you, you two are going to have one last time together, and it's going to be awful. If I were you, I'd call her now and break up for real, then you can cry and be ready to have fun on Saturday night." Tina delivered her advice to me grinning, waving her right hand in front of me to make it as clear as she could. She didn't need to, I knew that what she was saying made some kind of awful sense, but I wouldn't acknowledge it.

"No," I told her, "it won't be that way with me and Millie. The last time we spent the weekend together, we got somewhere. She cried Friday night because she said I wasn't *with her* anymore, not emotionally. I was afraid to, that she'd turn cold if I told her how much I wanted to be with her. She ravaged me Saturday morning, wouldn't let me out of bed . . ." Tina was laughing at me. Jimmy was trying not to hear as he refilled our coffees.

"Then, what happened?"

"Oh, the rest of the day was fine. I thought we would get married, have a Jewish wedding, and go for a honeymoon in Puerto Rico. Scooter called that night, and Millie was a mess. It was just a short call about the self-defense class at the Women's Center, but I freaked out. I was mad because Scooter was calling Millie at my place, then I realized she was calling me about the stupid class, and I just handed the phone to Millie because I was so jealous!" Tina was hysterical.

"Go ahead, laugh. It's funny. I blew it because I gave Millie the excuse she needed to be mad at me. My jealousy."

"Did she go home?"

"No . . ."

"You seduced her?"

"Damn, Tina!"

"Yeah, I knew it!"

The worst thing about it wasn't that Tina had been right about the *one last tumble*, because she was always right about everything she said regarding other women's relationships. And I wasn't the only one who hated Tina's incisive comments. What was bad was that I could see myself walking right into the very things I didn't want to do and kept doing them.

When I got to work late, at 7:35 on Wednesday morning, I knew that Millie would call me that day. When I worked nights, she would call me about midnight, because she knew I had a little free time at the beginning of my shift. She liked to stay up late. But since I had started on first shift, I knew it wouldn't occur to her to figure out when I might have a chance to talk because she'd never be up that early. And then, she'd be off, running to her first class, late as usual. Yet at 8:45 that morning, while Kelly and I were coaxing Agnes into the steel tub for a bath and half the ward was in an uproar in their usual after-breakfast riot, I knew that the call was for me when I heard the ringing in the office. Through the hollow echoes of the shouts and squeals bouncing off the pink tiles in the cavernous bathroom, the sound of the water sloshing and Agnes's constant whimpering, I heard Jennifer calling me. I delayed answering while I soaped up Agnes's back with a wash-cloth, keeping up an energetic chatter to distract Agnes from doing her usual scratching.

"The phone, Erica, it's for you!" said Kelly. I looked at her eyes to see if she knew what effect this had on me, that it was my girlfriend calling, not just any friend. I looked at her, trying to see behind her tinted lenses whether she knew that it was women I loved. That it was on account of a woman I showed up to work with circles under my eyes. Kelly's grin could have meant she knew, or that she thought I was awfully funny the way I stood there with the soap in my hand as though I didn't know how to get my body to move.

"Erica!" yelled Jennifer from the office, and I was moving, the soap and the washcloth in my hands, dripping soapy water on the floor, and my sneakers skidding into the office to take the phone call.

"Yeah, Millie," I panted. I wrapped the soap in the washcloth and set it on the metal desk with the peeling green paint. I wiped my hands with a tissue while holding the receiver between my neck and my shoulder. Cradling Millie's voice.

"How did you know?"

"Don't ask, I'm psychic."

"Are you in a hurry? I'm sorry, I don't know your schedule now."

"Well, we're doing baths, there is a line of fifteen women waiting. Yeah, I'm busy. What's up?" I wanted to be nice to Millie, after all she did call. But I had no words. Through the Plexiglas I could see Kelly struggling with Agnes's shampoo. Jennifer was mopping the day hall.

"Do you want to get together tonight?" Millie said after my silence.

"Uhm . . ."

"You don't have to, it's just that I thought, I mean after last weekend, how we left it, I mean, I miss you, and I didn't want you to think—"

"It's not that," I lied. "It's so crazy here." Then, looking through the Plexiglas, "Someone is having a seizure, and I can't think. Can I call you today, later?"

"Well . . ."

"Never mind—"

"Okay! When you come home, call me! Bye, I miss you!"

I was running for the bathroom to catch Agnes, who was wobbling and about to fall over. She was naked, her skin blotchy red from her bath, refusing clothes and swiping with her sharp nails. I grabbed one of her favorite dresses and slipped it over her head. The dress calmed her down. She kept her arms inside the sleeves and went to sit in a chair on her own. Rosie crawled by and slapped at my leg. I caught her unaware and slipped her up onto the bathtub where Kelly caught her with strong arms and a ready chuckle.

"I didn't know Agnes had seizures, too" I told Kelly, as we soaped Rosie's brown skin, lathering up her hair with strawberry shampoo before she changed her mind and leaped out of the tub.

"Not often. So, I guess that wasn't your boyfriend, exactly—"

"Beg your pardon?" Kelly had stunned me. Rosie was resisting her bath, and I held her hands still with more force than I needed to.

"Sorry, I didn't mean it."

"Mh."

The rest of the morning grinded by; the work feeling heavy and almost unbearable. I couldn't imagine how we would ever finish giving baths, making beds, giving out meds, and then prepare for the lunch meal all over again. I was tired and hungry in spite of myself. For my lunch break I ran to the cafeteria and forced myself to eat a container of yoghurt and a ham sandwich. I drank a chocolate milk so fast, my throat hurt. When I got back to the ward everyone was calm; the after-lunch sleepiness having taken hold of the clients as well as the aides. We all sat in the day hall, talking, looking at the clouds drifting away and returning, stubbornly, to cover up the sun.

"Pretty soon, we'll be able to let them go outside, on the porch, and to sit on the swings," commented Jennifer, her round face looking happy at the prospect.

"It's only March," Kelly burst in, while she played one-handed pat-a-cake with Elaine, who still held onto her ball. "It's not going to be pretty soon. They'll be cooped up in here till the end of April. Spring never comes. I hate this part of the country!"

"Okay, already," soothed Jennifer. "So it will be a while, but I love it when they can go out. It's more normal."

"Do they keep their shoes on?" I asked, trying to imagine the Kiniry twins.

"Not any longer than now. They just get muddy." Kelly undid her ponytail and did it back up again. She had tried to talk to me while we made the beds, but I'd been too skittish to let her. I smiled at her now, to make up for it. She smiled back.

The conversation went on. Kelly and Jennifer tried to think of ways to keep sneakers on Eva Nathan's feet, so she wouldn't get dirt between her toes when she went outside in the spring. I joined in from time to time, but mostly I played with the clients. I spent time with Rosie, being extra nice to her because I was becoming more aware of my roughness. Not just with her; with many of the women as my patience wore thin. Yet Jennifer had only remarked that I was doing my job better, being more *authoritative* and getting things done quicker. I thought about my niece, the way she jumps to attention when my sister calls her. It isn't anything unusual; I just noticed over the holidays how Nélida only had to raise her voice slightly, give it that additional edge in Spanish that we learned from Mami, and already my niece was busy doing whatever she was supposed to do. But it wasn't the same thing. I just didn't like the idea of pushing people around.

"Frances! Get your hand out of Judy's hair or you'll be sorry!" Jennifer's voice startled me, but Frances barely acknowledged the warning and didn't begin to let go of Judy's hair snarled tightly between her fingers until Judy herself decided to flop down on the floor. I watched the scene, a slightly humorous scene that repeated most afternoons. Frances stood up with her arthritic hands not far from Judy's head and assessed the distance between Jennifer and herself. When she saw that Jennifer wasn't getting up to enforce her promise, she reached for Judy's head again. Then she saw me sprinting toward her out of the corner of her eye and let out a pitiful wail to make the most hardened of us take pity on her. I figured she earned my attention, so I took her by the mirrors in the bathroom and combed the hair under her helmet, even though this was reinforcing her negative behavior. But Frances was happy, and Judy's hair was safe for a while.

"So, what's Frances' story, Jennifer?" I asked her, while I combed the wavy hair.

"You mean, how she got here?"

"And where her family is," added Kelly.

"Oh, well, I heard that her mother was in an institution when she was young, under the *loose morals* statute they had in the '40s. Frances is the child of white and black parents, I don't know which one was which, but somebody else said her mother had been 'slow.'"

"What is that *loose morals* thing?" Kelly asked.

"Some law from back then, and with Agnes's mother, they did the same thing. Only poor Agnes got the worst of it."

"What happened to Agnes?" I asked Jennifer.

"When Agnes was born, the family was so embarrassed, they kept her in a basement until she was thirteen. That's where the State found her."

"You mean, she's the one they called *the tiger?*"

"You heard about that?" Kelly put in. "I did, too, during in-service training."

"Poor Agnes, everybody talks about it." Jennifer shook her head.

"Damn! Can you imagine how scared she must have been?" I could see Agnes as a little girl, being found by state workers.

"Hey, it's 3:15—where is second shift?" Jennifer looked out over the day-hall window to see if she could see anyone coming.

"Do you think her family was prosecuted for doing that to her?" Kelly and Jennifer were only half-listening to me, and getting ready to go home. I followed them.

"Hey, Jaycee Travers! What are you doing on second shift?" Jennifer was walking out to the laundry room to meet her old friend. I untied my apron and went to wash my hands. Kelly followed me.

"I'm sorry," she offered.

"About Agnes?"

"No, because I pried and teased, about your friend . . ."

"That's cool, Kelly. I'd told you things about Millie and me before."

"Are you going to be okay?"

"Yeah. You know, if that statute was still in effect today, they'd sure put me away fast . . . for going out with girls, huh?" I prodded, trying to see if Kelly was really as accepting as she seemed.

"Me, too," said Kelly, very seriously looking into my eyes, surprising the hell out of me.

When Millie and I were in bed, making love, I kept thinking. It wasn't the kind of thinking that takes up a lot of concentration, it was basically the same thought or question: what does Millie want from me? And as I looked in her eyes while she reached for me, kissed me, slid across my body, and drew me toward her, I maintained a distance with my thoughts. I looked at her amber brown eyes, and I asked the question. I pressed my cheek against the underside of her breasts to push her nipples up and then catch them in my mouth, one after the other, and I told myself it didn't matter what she wanted from me, because she was happier when I simply took from her what I wanted. What she wanted was to be detached, to take no responsibility in the fact that we were touching, tasting, penetrating each other's bodies. She wanted not to know me while I made love to her, not to have a connection with me.

This is what I had learned, instantly, the minute I got home and called her. She had started to tell me she was doing something, that she couldn't come see me, and I had been weary, feeling that whatever it was, was going to take too long. In a voice that was my voice, but one I didn't recognize, I told her.

"Millie, drop what you're doing and come. Wake me when you get here."

"Erica? You okay?"

"Yeah," I hung up.

But I wasn't asleep when she came. I heard her opening the heavy old door to the building, heard the sounds of mid-afternoon Main Street coming up the stairs. As she rounded the hallway, I visualized her pale hand on the dark bannister, heading for my door. I walked over and opened it before she had the chance to knock, and as her face was adjusting to an expression, I reached for her with my right hand and brought her close enough so I could kiss her. I didn't need to move very much, Millie was meeting me in motion. I only had to reveal my intentions.

Still, Millie tried to ask me questions, to settle the moment into something she knew, but I had already ignored her questions before she asked them. That's when the thinking started. Why, I asked myself, should Millie look for an expression for her features to adopt when I open the door? Why should she be surprised at all that I opened the door before she knocked? Hadn't I memorized her step, her breathing, the rustle of her clothes, in the two years we had known each other intimately? Between the rush of warmth in my belly, which hit me with each of Millie's moans and sighs as I held her, I felt an annoyance with her. Why do you *act* as if you love me, I wanted to ask her, why don't you just love me the way I love you?

The full moon was a few days away, but enough of its brilliance now bathed the begonias on the windowsills, the mirror-top table, my desk, and all the clothes and papers I usually let fall on the floor of the sitting room. The broad archway that connected this room to the bedroom felt like the opening to a stage. On it, my bed sat with our bodies splayed in a swirl of bedclothes and two pillows sliding noiselessly to the floor.

"It's late," Millie whispered.

"Mm, are you hungry?"

"Yes! Let's go out to eat!"

"No, I'll cook you some eggs. I've got to be at work at seven tomorrow, and you've got class." I moved to the right of the bed, turned on the small yellow lamp, and peered toward the kitchen. Millie's hands enveloped my waist.

And we made love again and again, until we fell asleep. But when I thought about it, I was mostly thinking about explaining to myself what had gone wrong. Because I thought of it in those terms; I had made the mistake of talking about something that did not need talking. As for Millie, I watched her recede, even as she still glowed from happiness, she struggled to remove her joy, her sense of satisfaction and well being. To remove it from the present plane, from her body, and place it at arm's distance where she could observe it. I could hear it in her voice, later, when she called me, still wrestling with her emotions, with my presence still weighing on her, as she catalogued our experience for me. I remember closing my eyes, imagining the course of my hands on her body moving upward from her belly, to her waist, around her ribs, and hearing Millie's voice on the phone, saying, "Erica, don't . . . !" as if she had felt me.

She was trying to remove me from her soul.

"You fill me with sexual energy," she'd said.

"Is that bad?"

"No, I mean, it nourishes me." She sounded uncertain. I waited.

"But it doesn't come from me, you know?" I didn't. "I want to find this energy within myself, I need to . . . explore, feel free!"

"You are free," I told her. I was thinking, later, that she'd wanted me to say that. That she had been waiting for me to tell her that, because she sounded relieved. We hung up then, and I didn't talk to her again.

For the next two days, I was two different people, day and night. Time dragged by in the afternoons, and it was interminable in the evenings. I fought to stay away from the phone, from calling just to hear Millie's voice. I walked on the dead sidewalks of Willimantic, and I ate at the all-night diner, feeling a sense of community with the hookers, the drug dealers, and the pimps. It was like being in church.

During the day, I got to work early, before seven, moving with energy, purpose. Friday I spent a few minutes talking with Fran and Mrs. Morse. Fran had allowed the gray hair she covered with ink-black hair coloring to come through. Then, she had frosted her hair and looked completely different to me. I had to take another look, to make sure her eyes were the same. Her skin looked a different color. On the whole, she looked younger, but less real or less like herself. I hesitated so long to give her my opinion that Fran was sure I didn't like her new hair no matter how I tried to explain it. She went off to write in the logbook and smoke a cigarette.

"And look at you, Kid!" Mrs. Morse punched my arm. She said I was skinny and seemed like I was being chased by ghosts. "You're awake, though, first shift seems to agree with you. But, whatever you've gotten yourself into out there, well, that will be chasing your shadow for a while until you let it go. Isn't that right, Fran?"

"I don't care. She insulted my hair," Fran shot back with a Marlboro hanging from her lips.

"I'm sorry, Fran, I just don't understand frosted hair!" I called to her. But she was busy, so I walked Mrs. Morse to the laundry room and helped her to carry the laundry bags to the chute, just like in the old days.

It was nice seeing them again, but what they didn't understand was how strange it was for me to look at the other side of what my life had been like. To show up at first light in the wards, when the aides were going home, almost catching a glimpse of myself the way I used to be on third shift, living at night. I felt like I was materializing into something solid, out of a fog, and stepping into myself. But not quite. In the back of my mind, Millie moved as I moved, spoke when I spoke, was silent when I stopped asking questions. Chasing my shadow.

In the afternoon, I called Tina to confirm that we were meeting that night. I took a cup of coffee in the office and made the most of a few minutes of quiet.

"Spiritual Counseling," answered Tina.

"What are you up to?"

"Oh, it's you! I've been trying my psychic abilities, but they're not going very well. I thought this was my sister calling from Bridgeport, and I wanted to freak her out. When she called this morning, I could have sworn it was you. See how you confuse me?"

"Tina, I'm at work. Are you going to keep talking about this stuff, or should I call you back?" I was actually relieved that she hadn't asked anything about Millie.

"Okay, just playin'. You ready for tonight?"

"Yeah. Want me to pick you up?"

"Your car still runnin'?"

"Hell, yeah!"

"'kay. What's that noise—some of your clients having a fight?"

"No, it's Kelly, one of the aides, challenging Jennifer to do chin-ups on the shower bar. We've been doing ten a day, me and Kelly."

"You know, I think that girl is gay." Tina said, out of the blue.

"I think she tried to tell me that, but she lives with her daughter and her boyfriend!"

"And, she has a crush on you!"

"Look, Madam Tina. Your psychic battery just ran out. I'm going to go do some chin-ups to get in shape for tonight. 'Cause we're going dancing, too, right?"

"You kidding? Natalie's driving up, and she's dying to go to that new women's bar in Hartford—I hope your car is running."

"I told you, it's fine. But what's with Natalie? She knows all the bars. Is she coming out, too?"

"My mother would die, child. Natalie just knows how to have a good time. So, can you pick me up and my date?"

"Oh, yeah. The baby dyke. What's her name?"

"Julie. We'll be ready at the station at seven. Natalie will meet us at Chuck's after nine."

"See you then." I hung up just as Jennifer was pleading for help, her arms hanging at her sides. "If you do a couple every day, you'll feel great," I told her. Kelly and I demonstrated for her, lifting our bodies up using the bar at the old showers. I involved Agnes, Diane, and even Rosie in the exercise. Elaine watched us from the day-hall door, and the Kiniry twins giggled. But it soon had to end, and we resumed our duties: replacing socks, singing little songs, and entertaining the women the best we could. In the day hall, the TV had been turned on, and hearing the theme from a soap opera, Coral twirled to the music, oblivious to everyone else, her hands wrapped tightly behind her back, her eyes closed.

Predictably, I was feeling hopeless about my relationship with Millie by the evening. I considered grabbing an early dinner at Pearl's, but the thought of eating mashed potatoes and gravy sickened me. Suddenly I wanted yellow rice with beans and stewed beef, Cuban style. But I wasn't hungry, I just felt dizzy. The last thing Millie had said to me hung about my neck, leaving a lump in my throat.

Watching the clock hit six-thirty, I decided I would eat something at Chuck's while we listened to the music. It was a steak house, and perhaps I'd be happy eating steak, drinking margaritas, and listening to the "white-girl folksinger." With any luck, she wouldn't sing anything by Judy Collins, and we'd all have a nice time. Grabbing my umbrella just in case, I turned off the lights in my apartment, locked the door, and headed down to my car to pick up Tina and her date at the Storrs gas station.

8

I hadn't noticed how March had turned into April, an April that was dry and warm, surprising the flowers probably more than the people in this cold and shady part of the state. I drove my old Valiant all over the countryside, with the top down and the AM radio blaring, going to my favorite spots to see an early spring taking root. At one spot in Putnam, behind the decaying walls of an old Spanish-style mansion converted to a school, I sat looking at my favorite magnolia trees. The thick buds seemed almost to hurry out of their fuzzy envelopes and push the flowers. Turning my face to the sun, I vowed to be happy always and from then on to push all sad memories away.

Almost instantly, a thin cloud veiled the sun. Tears welled inside me in a big gulp, showing me up for the sentimental fool I'd become. But I had too much sense to let myself get carried away so easily. I could look at the cloud as only temporary, like my troubles. May would come with a definitive sunshine, not the weak, pale glow that sunned us now, and eventually, it would really be summer in New England. And, I wouldn't miss my girlfriend anymore. I walked through the grounds of More Hall, humming to myself, picking up a few daffodils to bring home along the dry patches by the crumbling walls, then climbed back in my car.

It was Monday afternoon, the last of my pass days, and I was ready to get back to work. Since Millie and I had broken up, I had more time than I knew what to do with. Tina was busy with exams, but we still managed to slip away some nights for a drink at Chuck's or even at Rosal's, though sometimes we had to fight off the lounge lizards who thought we were just two girls looking for a guy. Tina and I would have a beer and feed quarters into the jukebox, planning how I would open a women's bar in Storrs while she was away at graduate school, and wait for her to come back and buy a house in Gurleyville near the river. It would be a lesbian house, and we would share it with the women in the area who were ready to have a room of their own. Artists, singers, writers. Julie would move in, even though she and Tina were not dating anymore, and she would teach us auto mechanics. And I would go back to school, become a potter, fall in love with a Puerto Rican girl who would materialize out of thin air, and forget all about Millie forever.

Believing in these fantasies, I drove back home, heading west along route 44, singing along to some song by the Eagles, when I caught sight of a new "health food" restaurant that had recently opened. I turned in on the gravel drive, parking the car near the greenhouse that was attached to an odd-looking wooden building bearing the sign, *The Wagon Wheel*. It looked inviting; wooden planters brimming with purple flowers lined the entrance. Dried roses and herbs hung from every rafter, and clay pots glazed in purple and turquoise decorated the wooden tables. Maybe, instead of a bar, we could open a women's coffeehouse, with music and books. I sat down near a window, taking off my leather cap, but a waitress came by immediately to let me know it was a table for two or more only. I stared at her. I could have sworn it was the woman from the Erehwon in Willimantic where I used to go with Millie. She wore the same Indian print skirt, had the same long earrings, and stringy hair. I decided to move to a small, round table for one.

"Wait!" I called back to her, knowing intuitively that she'd make me wait for a menu, and then for taking my order. She turned around in shock at my insolence, but I was beyond such slights. I figured it was because I looked so *dikey*, as Tina and I had labeled our way of dressing. So I ordered immediately in a loud voice she could not ignore. "Bring me a cup of coffee with cream and sugar and a fresh blueberry muffin, with butter."

I bet that The Wagon Wheel would have these items on its menu, and I was right. As I settled on the cane chair to wait and look around, I hoped Ms. Stringy Hair's surprise would be enough to last long enough to bring my coffee before it got cold. I mused that life was getting increasingly difficult, having to fight these small battles with people who reacted constantly to the way I looked. I was either too dark for this area of Connecticut or not feminine enough. Or both. I thought about Tina, graduating at the top of her class, always alert, always being ready to fight something off. I had it easier because I could pass. Sometimes.

When my coffee arrived, still hot, followed by a large, crusty, and sugary muffin, I looked up toward the row of hanging fuchsias in baskets, and there was Scooter, sitting down with a blonde, bony woman like herself who looked just as uptight, magically attracting the waitress to their table, and quickly becoming engaged in a chummy conversation as if they'd known each other all their lives.

Maybe I was just being bitter. Drinking the thin New England coffee slowly, I watched Scooter and her friend order lunch. I saw her very well, though she couldn't see me, sitting behind a wheelbarrow loaded with large-leaved begonias in bloom. I remembered the way her face looked then, when she and Millie were coming out of Chuck's as I was going in. Expressionless. As though the world needed to take a stance but she never needed to. That is how she looked at the table, explaining something to her friend, saying something to the waitress, her face impassive. I bit into the blueberry muffin, reveling in its freshness and the taste of the warm fruit inside. The crust was sugary and had a hint of butter. I added more butter, watching it melt into the soft dough, into the purplish blueberries, and buried my mouth in it.

I knew then why Millie liked Scooter so much; I could not imagine that she loved Scooter, but perhaps she did. The coffee was so weak after the muffin, I yearned for a big mug of Bustelo at my sister's house, sweet and milky. But perhaps I could try to find some at the A&P, or Shop Rite, and make it at home, the way Nélida made it. Across the flowers in the wheelbarrow, I could hear Scooter's exasperating laugh. I leaned back in my chair and thought about driving home, buying a whole piece of pork shoulder, and making pernil for Tina and me to feast on. I thought about going to work in the morning, and flirting with Kelly, inviting her to have coffee with me.

The thing is, I knew that I was everything Scooter was not, and it didn't bother me anymore. Or, almost. Millie was gone, but I understood. Scooter was cool water for Millie, and Millie could have all the passionate explorations she wanted, but Scooter would never know that was her appeal. She'd be too busy checking herself in the mirror to notice or get in the way.

In the fading sunshine, I drove home, the top still down, the radio off. I was a little sad when I thought about how hard it was to recover after that night. Because I wasn't surprised, just blown away by seeing them together, the air knocked out of me. Millie shouting, "Hi, Erica!" and Scooter reaching over for one of her stupid handshakes. Tina and Julie standing next to me; Tina looking like judge and jury, Julie unaware of the drama.

The night I drove to the gas station, to pick up Tina and Julie, the rain had started almost as soon as I closed my door. The Valiant was running fine, but soon the top started leaking, and I knew Tina was going to complain about that. But, perhaps because she knew I was a bit shaky about Millie or because she wanted to impress her date, the only thing she did was ask Julie for some duct tape, so we could patch up the top of my car. Julie obliged, in good spirits, all starry-eyed for Tina and looking so young in her overalls, flannel shirt, and red mechanic's cap with *Storrs Texaco* embroidered on it. Julie was from the West Coast, a short white girl with very cute blue eyes and short, brown hair. She'd learned auto mechanics from her father in Eugene, and then moved to San Francisco when she came out at the age of eighteen. Now, she was getting her B.A. and learning how to work on foreign cars from Rachel, who treated her like her star pupil.

"So, who's this singer we're going to hear, Tina?" We all sat on the front seat, with Julie between Tina and me, obviously creating a very tight fit.

"I don't know. Julie told me about her."

"Rachel says she's from Hartford, and she lives with a guy, but she has *potential*," Julie told us.

"Oh, God, Erica, I bet she's gonna do Judy Collins songs!" Tina wailed, burying her sparkling smile in her hands.

"Damn, where does Rachel get her information?" I drove up to route 32 and looked for the spotlights in the rain that would lead me to the parking lot at Chuck's. As the wheels of the Valiant crunched on the gravel, the sound of the engine audible because the rain subsided to a misty fall, I felt an odd lull enveloping me. Tina had stopped laughing and teasing Julie; Julie was watching both of us quietly as we got out of the car and proceeded toward the old barn that had become a steak house. In the twilight carved from the deep country night by powerful spotlights, one could make out the outline of a formidable silo. Tina and I loved to get the round table in the silo area inside, but we seldom managed it. Upstairs, the silo area had been made into a cozy sitting alcove where groups of heterosexual couples staked their territory.

Tina and Julie walked ahead of me; I followed them, swinging the keys in one hand, keeping my left in my pocket. I looked up to see some people leaving and met Millie's gaze full in the face. She was wearing a long, black dress under her coat, and she was holding Scooter's hand.

"I'm so glad we're all free now, Erica," chanted Scooter, bursting upon me with a practiced line out of some play, her hands gesturing broadly, stiffly. I froze.

"Isn't this better, Erica?" spoke Millie at last, imitating Scooter's way of keeping her lips stiff as she spoke. "Ooh, I feel so free!" And she tossed her head back, shaking her hair.

"Oh, yes! We can be the three Graces—oh, unless you want to join us, Tina?" Scooter leaned over in a courtly bow, trying to sweep Tina into a circle she must have envisioned. But Tina draped her arm around me and sucked her teeth loudly.

"It's raining," I told no one in particular and went inside with Tina and Julie. Warmth and bright lights met us, a fire roaring out of the oversized fireplace. As if by arrangement, the table in the silo was free, and we glided across the floor to occupy it. From then on, Tina didn't stop talking for a second, leaving me no time to brood. For my part, I ordered a steak and a margarita as soon as I had the chance, and though I couldn't eat a bite, I did plenty of drinking and talking.

"Well, how do you like that bitch, Scooter, going on about three graces and all that? Who does she think she is? Julie, would you go to bed with that broomstick? I didn't think so. Hey, Natalie! You're early, girl!"

Tina's sister joined us and was told every detail of Millie's betrayal, and she and Julie joined in plotting how they would take revenge on Scooter on my behalf. Our table got so raucously loud that when the entertainment was about to begin, the folksinger's manager asked us to keep it down. Natalie stood up, all five feet ten inches of her, and leaning back so her every curve would be clearly delineated, she placed her hands on her hips and told him, "That's okay, honey, because I can tell this singer of yours is going to rock the house with her powerful voice, and you won't be able to hear us at all. Isn't that right?" she called to the woman in the tight jeans and long straight hair who looked like a younger version of Judy Collins. "You go on, sister, belt it out!"

We were rolling with laughter, slapping the table, and ordering food and drinks. Natalie kept us entertained with stories about her latest boyfriend, and the three of us provided the audience. But it had to end. When the folksinger went into her third chorus of "Some Day Soon," Tina was making plans for the drive to Hartford and the bar.

"Okay, let me drive the Valiant, Erica. You go with my sister 'cause you're in no condition to drive."

"Okay."

"And, Natalie, see if you can get her a coffee and a donut at Bess Eaton's before we get there, 'cause this child's going to upchuck tonight."

"Okay."

"Oh, shuddup, I know how to hold my liquor."

"Oh, my God, is she singing that song about the clowns? Let's get out of here!"

I don't remember much about the drive to Hartford or telling Natalie about how I was going to open up a bar for women in Puerto Rico while Tina was in graduate school, and how I would never go back to get my degree because I didn't want to end up talking with my teeth the way Millie and Scooter did. But these were things she would tell her sister on the phone, and then Tina would tease me about them for weeks afterward. What I do remember is later on, dancing to Donna Summer at the Evergreen and rushing into the bathroom when the margaritas decided to come up. For some reason, the tequila hit me in the heart and made me cry, made me feel what my mother would have called a *borrachera llorada*, when she used to make fun of my uncles getting drunk and crying afterward.

I crawled out of the toilet stall and went to sit on the sink counter, next to a marbleized mirror with a green frame and "Evergreen" written along its oval edges. Tina came in to put her arms around me and hand me toilet paper to dry my tears.

"Did Natalie give you some coffee?"

"I threw that up, too."

"Yuck."

"Yeah."

"She ain't worth it."

"I know."

"What's all this shit about *being free*. Is this Scooter's idea about lesbian merging and all that crap?"

"I guess. I wouldn't care if she'd just told me about it, but she kept acting like it was my fault, that my feelings were keeping her from being herself. Free, I guess."

"You would have cared," Tina said.

"Yeah, I would have," I admitted.

Tina handed me another wad of toilet tissue and let me blow my nose. I was starting to see it clearly, maybe clearer than I wanted to.

"Erica," Tina stroked my head. "Listen, my friend."

"What?" I was feeling another wave of tears flooding me.

"Freedom means something different to Millie. She wants to

feel free the way you know how to be free. She wants to *be like you.*"

"Yeah, but she doesn't want to be *with* me, right?"

Back at work, with the advent of the warm weather, we were taking all the C side women outside every day after lunch. We would take turns sitting by the swings with them, playing ball, or just walking on the grass. On D side, the ambulatory clients could sit on the double swing with an aide, and everyone in wheelchairs would sit on the porch, getting some sun. For me, it was as much of a novelty as it was for the clients. I watched the Kiniry twins, wearing their one-piece gray suits belted at the waist with several tie-strings, twirling in the sunshine as if they were at home. Eva Nathan walked around, singing her silly songs just like anyone would do if they hadn't been out all winter. I looked for signs of happiness in Frances's face and Coral's and Agnes's. Rosie sat on the double swing, belted in, but apparently having a good time, with Donna, Jula, and Judy. We tried to put the women together who were either unsteady on their feet or blind or likely to have seizures.

Then, I would ask myself whether anyone else saw things as I did. I remembered the way things were in the Cottages, where the normative environment was only external. We weren't going anywhere with these women. Over and over, I would reach the same conclusions to my pondering that their families and the social workers and the psychiatrists and neurologists would have reached twenty, maybe thirty years before. That we were just there to keep them clean and pass the time.

"I want to get out of here," I found myself saying to Kelly.

"Today?" She stared at me, almost smiling.

"Oh, every day. But, ride out with me today or tomorrow.

Let's go have coffee at the Wagon Wheel, that new place. It's on the way to your house."

"Okay. I'll go with you."

"Great—the muffins there are good, but we gotta bring our own coffee," I needled Kelly.

"You mean, you're quitting."

"Huh? No, not for a while," I told her, wondering what I had meant to say.

"You blow me away," she whispered, sadly.

"Kelly, if I do, I won't be going far . . ."

"Would we lose touch?"

"Well, we couldn't see each other five days in a row, with three off, and then five on again—let's go check on the swings," I finished, when I saw that Kelly was smiling again, and pulling her ponytail out, just to tie it back up. This time, I reached over and helped her clip her hair with the barrette. It felt warm in the sun.

"Erica," Jennifer called out. "Can you check the laundry room?"

"Sure!" After making sure all the clients were fine, I ran back in through the day hall to go check the loads in the dryer. As I opened the door, Coral followed me in. Her cheeks were pink from the sun, and she had rubbed her nose raw.

"You look like you need some sunscreen," I told her. Her frown barely altered, she listened to the music piping in through the speakers high up on the wall. Someone had put on a waltz, and Coral began to dance.

Or, to turn around and around, her hands firmly wrapped with a tie-string behind her back or sometimes pushed up under her underpants like handcuffs, cutting off her circulation. She was a puzzle. We couldn't figure out why she liked to have her hands bound that way. When her hands got too red and her wrists completely white, we would distract her and give her something looser to wrap her hands, often another pair of cotton underpants.

She was everybody's least favorite because of her size, the strong grip of her huge hands, the swift kick of her muscular legs. And her screams. Coral bellowed when she didn't get her way and pounded on whatever was available. I left her twirling and went to check on the dryers.

Some were finished. I spent a few minutes shifting loads around, folding some towels, and matching some socks I figured we'd probably need when everybody came in from the yard. I pulled out Coral's special dresses and hung them up on her personal rack. Jennifer said that Coral's mother would come occasionally to visit and dress and feed her daughter, and so Coral was the only one with her own clothes and shoes, which were periodically replaced by her mother.

I didn't hear the scream. Or rather, I heard it but it did not make sense, and the next three seconds were spent beginning to turn my body toward the sound of the first scream. Then I knew it wasn't a yell to get one of the women to do something or stay out of something. It was a scream. And it was followed by another, from the same voice, but carrying the sound of my name with it, and I dashed across the floor of the laundry room, and skidded across the hallway because I definitely heard Kelly yelling my name.

She met me halfway through the laundry room across the hall, on D side, completely white, her face locked in panic. Something in my throat got steady as I walked past her into the bathroom and looked down toward the dorm. Coral was walking with her arms extended, bumping into the beds, her face showered in blood streaming from her forehead under the black leather helmet. I ran toward the apparition and grabbed hold of her, talking softly to her and yelling at Kelly to get me some wet towels and ice, and for somebody, anybody, to call the ambulance.

As I led Coral to the sink I was aware of Jennifer running for the phone and Kelly coming toward me with a chair and a heap of wet towels. We sat her down long enough to untie her helmet and apply the makeshift towels to the wound, which now appeared gaping and bloody, gushing, and showing us most of what was under her forehead. Other aides came from everywhere, handing me more towels, wet and packed with ice, which I kept replacing, using all my strength to keep Coral from swiping at the wound with her arms. "We have to get her down on the floor," I said to Kelly, who motioned to everyone to move back while the two of us eased Coral down onto the tiled floor. Jennifer was back from calling the ambulance, and she took Kelly's place, helping me hold Coral's arms and legs, which seemed to have multiplied and grown stronger. A man from Bentley West suddenly appeared, and Jennifer made way for him to hold Coral's legs. I kept talking to Coral, telling her "there, honey, all right Coral, you'll be all right, just be still, come on, stay with me" and a thousand other things, which Kelly and Jennifer repeated softly, while the aides around us chanted, "oh my God, oh my God."

In all my days of in-service training, we were never prepared for something like this. There would always be a supervisor on hand, they said, someone with more experience, and an ambulance would always materialize within seconds. But here we were, all three of us charge aides and no ambulance in sight. I don't know why I thought of Mami at that point, but her face was a veiled presence appearing before me, stubbornly, as I watched how quickly the towels kept staining with Coral's blood, and I struggled to keep both sides of her forehead together. I had never seen that much blood in my life, and the thought entered my mind and left it, as my mother's face kept appearing almost like a painting etched in sand, the lines of her face deepening as grooves marked by an artist along the shore. I tried to be conscious of what was occurring around me, to calculate the time it was taking for help to arrive, but the only thought I repeated to myself was that I wouldn't let Coral die, so I kept talking to her, holding the towel with two hands as she cried and bellowed, attempting to get up by slipping her elbows under her, and that's when I noticed the blood pooling under us on the red-tiled floor. Then, she stopped. Not a sound, not a twitch. And in the gulf of that second when everyone was quiet, holding their collective breath, I talked on—*Coral, keep going, Coral, cry, cry,* and someone said, *there is no ambulance on grounds, they're sending one from the university.* Coral moved and kept crying.

As long as the previous minutes had been, the ones that followed were suddenly short. We were in the UConn ambulance, Coral and me and the ambulance guy. What was he? An orderly? An EMT? Coral was tied to the stretcher with a sheet across her chest, and belts around her feet to keep her still. The man had done this, the best he could, but Coral was still thrashing around. Her clothes were soaked in blood, and now the sheet was getting stained with the color of it. The ride was interminable. I knew we were going to the hospital, but it seemed senseless, as though we were suspended in time, spinning wheels that were leading nowhere while Coral bled to death from the gaping wound in her forehead.

The ambulance guy put a bandage on the wound, a real one instead of the wet towel I had used to keep both sides of her head together, but Coral kept moving and I had to keep talking to her so that she'd be quiet. This worked for seconds at a time. At every lunge of the ambulance, Coral became distraught again, and she continued to wail and bellow with her thick voice, the feel of the ache in her voice being not from the pain of her wound, I was sure of it, but from sorrow, a deeper pain, or fear at finding herself unable to move, in a strange place, with my voice the only familiar thing she could place. Maybe. Her eyes were shut tightly, probably from the bandage, which pressed down on her forehead and kept her from seeing, but also because she often half-closed her eyes like this, leaving only a narrow streak of light blue showing through the heavy-liddedness of her furrowed visage. I wiped at the thick bridge of her brow, recognizing Coral's face under the brownish, caked blood, and pushed away some of the sweat and blood that had started to stream into her eyes. It would be salty, it would sting, it would make her thrash around again and harder for me to hold her.

"She's bleeding again," I said to the man in the ambulance, and for an answer he leaned toward the front and told the driver to step on it.

"The fucking siren ain't working, I can't break through traffic!" the driver yelled back, and the man and I tried to keep Coral quiet, tried to tighten the bandage some. "Blow the fucking horn, all the way to the fucking hospital if you have to!" The man yelled back, and from then on, we heard honking and the squeal of breaks and tires as the ambulance made a sharp right turn onto 195 and headed south toward Willimantic.

In the ambulance, time stood still again and again, sometimes moving as the vehicle did, careening into town, honking, bringing the promise of the hospital closer, and then slowing down to a crawl. When Coral flailed and heaved herself up I had to practically lie on top of her to keep her head down, and when she was quiet, the man took her blood pressure and told me to keep talking to her. When they had showed up at the ward, the two EMTs herded me onto the ambulance along with Coral on the stretcher; I was glued to her head, her body, and her wound. When time slowed, I recalled hearing the warning sound, Kelly's scream, and hearing the seconds that passed from there to the next sound I heard and to the next moment when I saw Coral's bloody head advancing through the dorm.

"She walked into the door!" Kelly had told me as she packed the ice in the towels. "She must have wanted to come in the dorm and the door was locked, so she banged her head and broke the window—I couldn't catch her . . ."

This is what had happened, then, the thing that the EMTs repeated to the nurses who came out of the hospital to meet the stretcher with Coral on it and me attached to her. As we ran through a short hallway to an emergency room, I tried to let go of her, telling her she would be okay now, that she was hurt, but I was there with her, and people there would help her, and whatever babble I could think of. But as we landed somewhere next to oxygen tanks and trays of hypodermics and shiny metal implements, Coral went wild, kicking, wailing, and bleeding some more. "Hold on to her, somebody," ordered a surgeon as he brandished an injection of yellow liquid, but the EMTs were gone, and the only person left was a medical student who looked horrified. I held on to Coral again, tacitly becoming assistant to the surgeon, who at that moment thought to ask if she was on any medications.

"Mellaril," I told him, stammering at first, but then blurting out the whole rosary of drugs as I had memorized them. "Mellaril, 150 mg T.I.D.; Mysoline, 250 mg O.D.; Phenobarbital, 60 mg Q.I.D.; Dilantin, 100 mg Q.I.D.—and Thorazine, I forget how much."

"Get me another 10 cc's of Valium," said the surgeon to someone in the background. "This will just be a cocktail for this girl, and you," he said to me, "hold her and keep talking to her, whatever you've been doing, just do it."

And time kept ticking. I got to see the back of Coral's left eye as the surgeon injected novocaine into her tissues and the medical student irrigated the wound over and over with water. I watched the edges of the blood stains sour and brown on Coral's clothes and begin to give off a smell like rusty metal. The surgeon kept up a constant chatter over my head, moving swiftly with sterile hands while my own, caked brown, continued to hold Coral, who had only stopped moving temporarily. The first shot of Valium had only succeeded in calming her for a few critical minutes, and she urinated slowly and copiously. The warm smell of her urine rose like steam, and the people around me tried to ignore the event. The surgeon babbled about internships and residencies, the medical student talked about her father and her boyfriend and their careers at Mass General, a nurse interjected useful information about the patient at carefully calculated breaks. The surgeon began to close the wound, stitching with a curved needle that reminded me of Mami's sewing box, her knitting, and the way she finished off our sweaters for Nélida and me.

"Surgeons use these," she had told me once. How did she know about the curved needles? Coral's forehead was sewn up and a gauzy bandage was being applied and taped with efficiency by the surgeon, who had now switched to talking about the merits of Willimantic's emergency rooms.

"Piece of cake—as a doctor, you've got it made!" To this, Coral responded by bellowing and thrashing as the surgeon and the student tried to wrap her head in more gauze. "Valium!" the surgeon yelled above the noise.

I stepped back for the first time in hours and watched two nurses remove stained sheets, cut Coral's clothes in half, and peel them off her body. My legs stood stiff and wooden under me, and I reached with cramped arms for a clean washcloth to wipe around Coral's neck. Hospital blues covered all five-feet-ten of her muscular nakedness, and she finally relaxed as the Valium seemed to take effect. With her eyes peering under the bandage, Coral looked at me, reaching for my wrist, her lips curling in a thin pout. A nurse handed me another damp washcloth, and I finished wiping Coral's face and my own hands.

It wasn't until I walked outside to get back in the ambulance, and realized that it was still daylight, that I noticed the stiff, dried blood all over my clothes and shoes. I stood in the circular driveway, watching another ambulance come around and begin to dislodge stretchers with patients covered in sheets, oxygen masks, blood pressure pumps. Seven examining rooms in this hospital, I thought, a doctor's dream. But, how much Thorazine does Coral take every day? I felt my brain starting to think again, and then I saw Jennifer in the parking lot, waving at me, standing by my car. A sudden panic seized me then, because I thought I would never be completely normal again, much less be able to drive home. But as I walked toward her, and she started to tell me how she had found my bag and my keys, and how her husband had driven her car over and she had followed, and all the details she needed to tell me, I came back to myself.

Before I knew it, I was telling her that Coral was fine, that she had a huge bandage on her head and the bleeding had stopped, and that I'd been standing there, talking to her, when her mother had walked in wrapped in a cloud of purple silks and perfume and gold bracelets twinkling on her wrists as she raised and lowered her arms, caressing her daughter and condemning the hospital, the Training School, the superintendent, the aides. She was smaller than Coral, older, verbal, but she had the same short, blonde hair and small, light blue eyes. She had the same thin lips, and through them I watched many words erupting. She looked at her daughter only briefly, while Coral smiled and moaned softly at her mother. "They're trying to kill you, my baby, but they can't, they won't, you're much too strong for them!" These words were etched in my brain, but I didn't understand what the woman was talking about. I was looking at Coral, smiling, cooing, her eyes almost closed, and I remembered thinking that it was the first sign of tenderness I had ever seen emerging from her. *The bleeding has stopped,* I said to myself, and I left Coral alone with her mother.

"So, you know where Mrs. Dombrowski was going?"

"Huh?" Jennifer's words seemed to be delayed for a second or two. I watched her mouth move. "What did you say?"

"To a gala benefit with the goddamn superintendent—see the white Caddie over there? That's hers, and that's her driver in the black monkey suit." Jennifer was pointing to the late-model Cadillac with the motor running next to my Valiant. Her round face and short, red hair reminded me that I had come out of an actual life to get to the hospital. I leaned over and kissed her cheek. I was laughing.

"What's so funny?" She was laughing, too, not knowing why.

"You see what a Cadillac gets you? Nothing. You know where Coral's going now that she's all bandaged up?"

"To a private room?"

"No way. Back to the School—to the Clinic for a few days and then, back to the ward. The doctor says she's fine. Even if your mother has a Cadillac, if you're retarded, you're retarded."

"She'll be back in our hair in a week . . ."

"Yup—"

"You all right, Kid?"

"Me? I need therapy! You?"

"A drink! See you tomorrow—" Jennifer hugged me in her motherly way and went around to her car. In my head, a conversation with myself hammered in a back beat: *I gotta get out, I gotta get out.* I started up the Valiant and roared my way home.

9

I slid back down on the seat of the Valiant and saw the fence of the churchyard approaching fast, my eyes suddenly taking in the panoramic view out of the windshield and seeing with extreme clarity in the waning moonlight. My hands reached for the steering wheel, and I coasted us, myself and the car, to the curb. I hit the brake, shifted into park, and turned the key to shut off the engine, but the engine was already off. I'd been hit from behind as I drove up Main Street, and now I saw the other car standing diagonally across the road, a block past the traffic lights at the corner. Then my brain shifted off automatic, and I began to move.

The door felt creaky as I opened it, and it occurred to me that it was probably because the chassis had been wrinkled like an accordion on impact. The top had neatly bent and sprouted up above the car like wings, thankfully not on my head or through it. The other car had its lights on, and water, smoke, and oil spurting from the hood. Inside, a woman sat in the front seat with a little dog on her lap; her chin was cut and bleeding. My thought, at that time, was that I couldn't let her sit there and bleed. I thought of Coral, and I didn't want to see any more blood. I reached over and opened her car door, which opened a lot easier than mine.

"Oh, my God, I rammed right into you!" she said to me before I could say anything. I looked at her legs. They seemed to be pinned under the dashboard. She petted the little brown dog.

"Your legs, can you feel them?"

"Oh, yeah, I think I got a cut on my knee, but it doesn't hurt so bad. Is the puppy okay?"

"Do you have a handkerchief in that bag? Here, hold it against your chin—don't move! The car's okay, I'll get an ambulance."

"I'm sorry!"

"That's okay, I'll be right back," I told her as I went looking for a phone. Strangely, there was no other traffic blocking the street; one or two cars had come by, slowed down, and swerved around us, their drivers assuming we weren't dying. Along the fence another woman came to meet me, reaching her hands out as she talked.

"I saw it—I heard it from my window. I called the ambulance, they're coming! Is she okay, are you okay? You shouldn't be running around, you must be in shock!"

"Mary, are the people all right?" A shaky old voice came from a priest running toward us, with shiny black shoes, which I noticed because I looked down and felt a little dizzy. I also saw the stone divider by the hedges along the fence, and I decided to sit down and let Mary do the talking. She escorted the old priest to the other car, where he ministered to the injured woman.

"Yes, yes, the puppy's okay," I heard him say.

For the second time in two days, I was in the back of an ambulance, heading toward the hospital. This time there was an excess of them, working in perfect order, with sirens blaring, and plenty of personnel attending to what needed doing. I was the patient, this time around, or one of them. There were two ambulances, one for each of us, and the EMTs and the police treated us as estranged relatives in a dispute, keeping us apart, the other driver and me, as if we shouldn't get too close, already establishing the tone of the battle that the two insurance companies would wage.

There must not have been any other accidents that night; I received so much attention. The cop who took down my statement praised my sharp memory and presence of mind, the nurse who helped me slip off my boots and get on the gurney in the emergency room told me the other driver's husband was a state security guard who worked third shift at the Training School.

"What shift do you work?" She asked, solicitous. It seemed everyone around us already knew the players in this little midnight drama. I looked around and tried to figure out where I'd been the day before with Coral, trying to bring my mind to some kind of order, but the hallway hadn't looked familiar. Soon, there was a man in the room, a doctor with cool hands who peered into my eyes with a light, felt my ribs, all around my neck, and my knees, and asked me questions about the Electoral College.

"Doctor, those are kind of hard questions—don't you just have to ask her what date she thinks it is and who the president is?" the nurse put in on my behalf. Suddenly, I felt very tired, realizing that perhaps I hadn't quite come off automatic pilot when I thought I did, because I was just coming to terms with the idea that I'd been in an accident.

"It's the reason why Kennedy beat Nixon," I told the doctor belatedly, who was busy making my knees jump up with a rubber hammer. "I have a pretty bad headache," I added.

"And a slight case of whiplash—you're lucky, young lady!" I winced at the sound of those hated words and looked at the nurse, who only smiled indulgently. "Give her the Demerol and let her rest," ordered the doctor. Before I could object, I had a cervical collar around me and a shot of the stuff in my arm. The headache stopped, and I could no longer move my neck.

Time in the hospital moves swiftly, usually, as it did at the Training School, and if it slows down, it's so full of routines that it moves along anyway, much faster than it does at home. This was my theory, but it seemed like it took days for Tina to find me. It was much less than that. By lunchtime the next day, she was there next to me, telling me she'd only call my sister if I wanted her to.

I sort of slept that night, the Demerol keeping me in a stupor that deadened my body but left my mind free to suffer all the anxiety of the last two days, or perhaps weeks—since Millie and I had broken up. I tried to sort out events: I had gone out to The Depot for dinner with Tina after work; how did I get into an accident? I was driving home, thinking about something, listening to the radio, and as I made the turn onto Main Street, I saw the lights change. I stopped at the red light, and suddenly I was flung up as though I had jumped straight up in the seat, and my head was almost touching the Valiant's convertible top as it unbuckled. I don't remember the impact, I just remember the car being suddenly over a block away from the intersection, heading for the fence by the church, and my body coming down to the seat again. I played the scene over and over again, each time coasting the car to the curb, putting it in park, turning off the key. . . .

I could hear everything around me, another injured person being brought in, and out in the hallway, where the clank of gurneys and IVs on wheels blended with the hospital voice paging over the intercom, I could imagine the routine duties of its personnel. I lay there with a neck brace, knowing my boots were safely in a corner and my keys in the pocket of my jacket. Coral had been in one of these rooms; in my half-sleep, I tried to imagine which one, and I remembered telling Tina everything before and after dinner, telling her I had to stop thinking about it.

"Then, stop," she'd said, pouring half of her beer in a glass for me.

"I can't stop, I was in the shower for two hours yesterday, I didn't want to get out. I must have a depressive disorder."

"What did you do then, when you got out of the shower with your disorder?" she'd asked, in that way she has that sounds like she's humoring me, but she's really being serious.

"I filled the tub, halfway."

"For a bath?"

"No, for . . . for the clothes. I soaked them."

"Good, you needed to wash all the blood off." Tina's face was encouraging. "Then, what did you do?"

"The blood, it became alive again in the water, it swirled in the tub, and I could smell it. I thought that Coral could have died—"

"But she didn't die, Erica, you saved her."

"I know, I know! I was glad I kept my head all through it, but yesterday, I didn't even know who I was when I got home."

"Well, it was traumatic, you know. You could have called me right away, I would have come then and stayed with you!"

"I couldn't, that's when—"

"What happened then?"

"I cried! I just sat there in the bathroom, and I cried!"

We sat in silence for a while. I had a few sips of the beer and then finished eating. I was hungry. Tina smiled at me, and I smiled back. The Depot was an old train station off Route 32, and through the window we could see the old train tracks winding off into the woods. The sun had already plunged, and the light was golden. Tina and I laughed and gossiped about who else in the place was gay; we knew two of the waiters were for sure.

It was early when we left, and there was still so much we

wanted to talk about. We drove around for a while in the Valiant with the top down until it started to rain, singing along to Beatles songs on the radio and laughing about our love lives.

"I can't believe she dumped you already," I teased Tina.

"She didn't dump me! I told her not to call me for a while!" Tina protested.

"Yeah, and she took you seriously, hah!"

"Oh, shut up!"

I was wound up when I drove home. We'd gone to Chuck's to listen to some more of the folk music and to have Irish coffees, only I'd had just coffee and whipped cream in mine, feeling still chastened by my overindulgence the night we went to the bar. I'd driven Tina back to the dorm, still talking, trying to tell her something I wasn't sure I was ready to talk about.

"So, what's up, García?" she finally asked me, point blank, which wasn't usual with us. And instead of hedging, I tried telling her what I didn't yet know.

"I don't know, I keep seeing something, having this feeling I need to do something. I don't know."

"Is it about your family?" Tina's eyes fixed right on mine.

"Damn, girl, how you do that!"

"I'm not doing anything. You just look like you're about to learn something, that's all. It's about your mom, isn't it."

"Damn, Tina!"

"Okay, I'll let you go. You call me tomorrow, and think about taking some time off. We'll go to P-Town—"

I'd left Tina at the dorm and driven slowly home. She'd been amazed that I'd gone right back to work that day after Coral's accident and thought I should take a long break. I thought she was right and started making plans to do something with Tina before she went away to graduate school. What would I do then? Why did I even have to stay in this lousy town? Everything had changed with Millie changing. Or with me. I wanted to get home and sleep. Wake up, start over. I wanted to stop living unconsciously. I wanted to live.

I saw the light turning yellow, and as I got to the corner, I brought my foot down slowly on the brake.

The car was wrecked, so there was no hope of getting away, driving to the Cape as we had planned to over the summer, but Tina and I longed to go to Provincetown for Labor Day weekend. With the windows open in my apartment, the sun shining, and the sounds of the traffic outside, we could still feel the illusion that it was summer and we had time, we just had to plan it right. But every now and then, a cool breeze would drift in with that sharp edge of autumn, and we could taste it on the tongue like a flavor that didn't belong. This really was the last hurrah of summer.

"We could take the bus to Hyannis and then hitch from there," Tina called to me from the kitchen, where she had managed to cook two chops with onions, zucchini, and mushrooms in my electric wok. The smell was invigorating.

"How're you gonna heat up the rice? It's stupid not having a stove in here!"

"Hey, you just keep your neck straight and let me worry about the food! And stop whining!"

"Well, if we take a bus, then we won't have money for a room. And I'm not whining!" I protested with a definite sing-song in my voice.

"Hah!"

Tina was right, of course. The cervical collar was scratchy and made my neck hot, but without it I couldn't look down, read, or tie my sneakers. Besides, I got headaches that were not related to anything, and I'd gotten intensely anxious about going away somewhere for the coming weekend.

I figured I had a right to whine, still feeling out of sorts from the accident, but I insisted that it had to do more with it being the end of the summer and the fact that Tina was a Virgo and highly sensitive about where she spent her birthday. Though mine was at the end of October, and hers on August 31, we figured I must have Virgo rising or falling someplace, so this year, we were determined to be out of the university dust bowl and celebrating by the ocean, both of us free of girlfriends and ready to cruise the scene at the Pied Piper in P-Town.

"Here, look at this food!" Tina brought the wok and placed it right on the little table in front of me. She lifted the cover, and I saw she had heated up the rice next to the chops, where it steamed deliciously. "I can't believe your sister can make rice like this—why do you only see her when you're sick or something, you fool! Let's eat."

"Damn, this is good!"

"Mm!"

"You figure Scooter and those stupid girls are gonna be in P-Town next weekend?"

"What do we care? Pass me the beer."

"I care, because I don't want to watch you mope around Commercial Street over Millie when we're supposed to be cruising! And watch you don't drink so much beer with them Valiums you're taking."

"I won't be moping. I just do that here so that cute physical therapist will be nice to me at the hospital. And the Valium is only 2.5 milligrams. Eat some more pork chop."

"Damn, you're bossy! Give me that chop."

"Thanks for cooking, Tina"

"You're welcome. You know I love you."

"I know it, I'm gonna miss you so much."

"So, move to New Haven!"

"What about my job?"

"You're on disability—now's the time to make your move!"

"Oh, God, my neck hurts."

"Don't chew so hard."

"Hm!"

I was usually okay as long as I was talking to somebody, Tina, and my sister on the phone, mostly. And since I'd been home, going to physical therapy sessions at the hospital three times a week, but not doing much else, I had time to look around Main Street and sometimes talk to the women who owned shops directly below my apartment, whom I'd met over the winter. One woman had a tack shop which was always empty, though she seemed to do quite a fair amount of business. The other two had a gift shop with all kinds of unusual things: kites, antique jewelry, used clothing. And quite often, I would stop by and join them for a smoke in the back room and some heady conversation.

But since the accident, I'd felt so moody, I couldn't remember going through so many emotions so quickly. When I was alone, I didn't feel calm the way I used to, when I would head for the woods and walk for miles. I was sad or anxious, or both. I cried or felt scared and wanted to stay home and sleep. It had been three weeks, and I'd become a face with a name to the physical therapist in charge of stretching my neck and rubbing my shoulders with an ultrasound machine. I wasn't sure this was doing any good; I felt tighter around the shoulders, and my back was stiffer when I left, but I enjoyed seeing the tough-talking therapist there, the only woman wearing white pants instead of a tight skirt. She had large hands that felt warm on my neck when she touched me, which wasn't often because she mostly used the ultrasound thing. Her face was somewhat weathered, and she seemed older than me. Across her broad mouth, on the left, there was a small scar, which fascinated me; her tan face was pockmarked, she had a large nose, and piercing eyes. I wasn't sure what color they were, I was too shy to look at her directly, but they could have been brown since her short hair was brown. It was the sense that she might possibly feel about women the way I did that produced the shyness, I thought. If she'd been straight, I would have looked at her, talked to her, and played the courtier like I did with Fran and the other women at work, without bashfulness.

And it was difficult to get her attention. Perhaps she sensed the same thing about me, and she played her cards close to her chest. She used the initials PB, so I couldn't verify whether or not she was French Canadian, which is what I assumed. As she strapped my head into the rack, I looked at her mouth out of the corner of my eye.

"PB," I managed, finally. The contraption whirred.

"What, is it too tight?"

"No, I just wanted to say—"

"Okay, just relax there," she cut me off. Hard as nails, I thought.

"Hey, PB, this used to be a medieval torture, you know!"

"What!?"

"The rack, you know, to stretch people, until they confessed!" I figured one had to talk fast with PB, she had no time for anything that wasn't business. Now I had her attention, but she was going to make me work for it.

She half-turned to me, slowly, grimacing with her sensual lips like a tough guy, "Why, you got somethin' to confess, Miss García?"

Even the charge I got from flirting with PB at the hospital, and the visits I made to the ward to remind them I was coming back as soon as my neck healed, weren't enough to dispel my moods. I had come to the conclusion that I was hopelessly sliding into some dark despair from which I would never emerge until I had enough guts to kill myself. Not that I had never considered the possibility of suicide before. I'd said it for a year when I was seventeen, but this feeling of doom was different in that it carried with it a sense of inevitability. And the oddest thing was that I could view some form of my being alive afterward. The suicide would be an actual solution from which I would emerge and continue to live, only without the same problems.

About this, I didn't dare confide in Tina. I was afraid she would decide in her sensible way that I should see a therapist or something drastic and pull me away from the almost comfortable morass I inhabited. So I kept it quiet, although I could speak rather freely in cataclysmic terms with my sister. To her, life was a disaster anyway, and she didn't notice any difference in our conversations; we still got into arguments, but at least now I was calling her more often. And I would bring up Mami, which made her get quiet, suddenly.

❈

Finally, Labor Day weekend arrived, and Tina and I had managed to pool together enough money. Staying home had its benefits, because I didn't eat in coffee shops and didn't spend any money on gas. I would walk to the hospital and try to find a ride everywhere else. The day we were leaving, Tina hitched-hiked from Storrs to Willimantic with her sleeping bag and a knapsack, and she met me by the bus that would take us to the Cape. It stopped on Main Street, a block from my apartment, almost at the exact spot where I'd been rear-ended a month earlier. Watching Tina walk down the street toward me, with a skip in her step as she swung the sleeping bag from side to side, I was seized by a slow revelation.

It stayed with me through hugging Tina, the process of buying our tickets at the tobacco shop—$32.50 each, one way—getting on board and stashing our stuff above our seats. We placed both sleeping bags at the top and kept our knapsacks on the floor, underneath our knees. *I almost died*, I thought, and kept thinking, *I could have died.*

But, I didn't die. I could hear Tina saying this to me, as well as my sister and probably everyone at the ward. Even PB at the hospital would dismiss my preoccupation with death and tell me to just relax while she lathered the jelly on my shoulders and cranked up the ultrasound. Yet I couldn't shake the awesome nature of my realization. One minute I was alive, and the next, if the impact of the collision had been greater, I could have gone through the windshield and ended up pigeon snack on the sidewalk. I talked and acted as normally as I thought I should, pulling the map out to show Tina where we'd try to find a campground when we got to Truro. But I was actually brooding.

The Connecticut roads became woodsy and meandered through the countryside; the cheapest bus took the local routes and stopped everywhere, making the eight-hour trip more like ten hours. But Tina and I weren't concerned; we were beating the crowds by leaving early Friday, and we'd have plenty of time to look around before nightfall and make connections, because we counted on meeting half the town and catching a ride back with some nice lesbians for a share of the gas. In the past, when we'd gone in my old car, we always came back with extra passengers who chipped in for the expenses. It was an unwritten rule of the Cape experience.

I didn't die, I kept thinking. *Now I'm alive, so what the hell do I do?* Soon, the road lulled us to sleep, and the last thing I remember seeing out the window were the signs for the Saybrook Bridge along I-95. I wondered if we could sleep until we hit the Cape. I closed my eyes, determined to try.

I didn't have to worry about sleeping because the small amounts of Valium I was taking to relax the muscles in my neck and back had done the work. Tina had let me sleep until we passed the town of Orleans, where the bus turned onto Route 6, and we considered this point "being there already."

"Hey," she nudged me.

"'S there a bathroom on this bus?" I slurred. Waking up, I was painfully aware that my neck had been leaning against the seat for hours. Thankfully, the collar had helped to keep it straight. Tina laughed.

"What?"

"What you said—it reminded me of that Firesign Theater album, 'We're All Bozos on This Bus.'"

"Oh, yeah, the latest one. Did you hear one of the guys OD'd on acid?"

"They say that about everybody—probably did. Oh, a bathroom! There's a smelly hole back there they call a bathroom—be my guest!" Tina scooted over so I could climb over her legs and venture to the back of the bus. We were practically the only passengers left aboard, so I called out to her, "I can smell it from here!"

By the time we were getting close to Truro, our destination, we'd struck up a conversation with the bus driver, a sort of thin, handsome white guy with blue eyes who didn't seem the type to drive a bus. He'd heard our comment about Firesign Theater comedy albums and decided we were cool.

"Listen, don't bother with the campgrounds this weekend. Go see this friend of mine. He has a place right in town."

"Oh, yeah, can we afford it?" said Tina doubtfully.

"Don't worry about it, he inherited this place from his family, and he's really nice. Just tell him I sent you, and that I'll stop by to see him Saturday night. We're buddies, you know?"

"Oh, you're buddies, okay," we chuckled, always amazed at how gay men managed to keep their romantic lives so friendly. "So, how do we get there?"

"Well, the last stop is right at the intersection of 6 and Commercial, I gotta turn around there. You just walk into town all the way up Commercial Street till it ends almost, you know that place where it makes a sharp left?"

"Wow, all the way up there?" It had been a while since we'd been to Provincetown, but one always ended up walking the length and breadth of the place. We knew exactly what he meant.

"Right. Then you keep going all the way to the end of that street, and it's the last place on the right. Up on the hill."

Jeremy, the unlikely bus driver, hadn't been wrong. The place he sent us to was the last house on the road, and we were met by a short gravel driveway and an unassuming, hand-lettered sign dangling from a white lamppost that announced, *Land's End Inn*. A copper BMW slowed to turn into the driveway and shut off its lights and its purring motor. Tina wiped the sweat from her upper lip and laid her knapsack on the ground. I checked out the smoked-glass windows rolling down to reveal two blonde men wearing green sunglasses. The sun had just gone down, and I whispered to Tina that we wouldn't get a place to sleep even by the ashes in the kitchen with the dogs.

"Come on, let's go up while these boys get their matching luggage out of the boot," encouraged Tina. "Maybe we can get hired as chamber dykes!"

We ran up the winding garden stairs, around ornamental shrubbery, rosebushes, and a birdbath near the front steps of the house. Catching our breath, we hoisted our gear down and took in the stained-glass windows and the flower boxes stuffed with purple and yellow pansies. Just then, the door opened wide.

"Welcome!" Red-haired and blue-eyed, our host was so friendly, he scared us at first. "Jeremy called me from the gas station and said two of his friends needed a place—come on in!"

Rarely had P-Town been more wonderful and less exhausting. Jeremy's friend had given us a little room by the laundry, with a fine view of the bay, for twenty dollars for the whole weekend. It was decorated in hot pink, had a huge Tiffany lamp, and stained glass along the windows and the mirrors. We doubted the money even covered the use of the water and the towels, but we were too thrilled to object. The Inn was within easy walking distance of the Pied Piper, the only bar just for women, and during the day it was a simple hike to the town beaches. There was no need to make the pilgrimage to Herring Cove, the gay beach, where the lesbians usually managed to stake out an area at the very end, so we could take off our tops. True, we couldn't let the sun brown our backs in one even tone, but we also didn't have to walk through hundreds of naked men playing volleyball. This had always been very upsetting to Tina.

❧

That evening, after having settled comfortably in our little room, we were making quick work of our dinner by the pier at Mojo's.

"At this rate, we could even buy a bus ticket back if we want!" Tina was calculating our finances.

"Oh, we'll find a ride, have faith!" I was savoring the mozzarella-covered mushrooms in my submarine sandwich. The menu wasn't varied at Mojo's, but one could easily live on cheese and mushrooms and midnight slices of Spiritus pizza, across from the Pied Piper.

"But we have to eat here every night and no soft ice-cream cones and no pizza at Spiritus—it's overpriced!" Tina had come up with a strict budget.

"What? I love that pizza at two in the morning, after last call!"

"Wouldn't you rather save the money in case you get to buy a girl a beer?"

"Oh, I see your point," I conceded.

"And we could get coffee and Portuguese sweet bread at the bakery in the morning!"

"Can we stretch it to include saltwater taffy and fudge? It's traditional when we come here—"

"All right, either taffy or fudge, pick one."

"Fudge! Are you kidding?"

There are certain aspects of spending a weekend in Provincetown that never change; at least for Tina and me and most of the women we knew, who weren't that many. First, there was the heady rush of seeing so many gay people all in one place, the narrow streets crowded with us, walking up and down, holding hands, laughing, smiling at all hours of the day or night. Then, there was the thrill of that first evening at the lesbian bar, three-deep along the counter, the tables, and every corner taken up with groups of friends talking or couples kissing. But this doesn't always last; as it happened that first night, Tina and I were so relieved to be in each other's company that we walked directly out onto the deck to enjoy the sound of the surf, after getting ourselves a beer.

There was the unavoidable realization that we didn't know any of these women, and that they knew it, too, as they looked at us appraisingly or not at all, when we first walked toward the bar. There was the group who'd been there the whole summer, looking down on the newcomers, the weekenders, like ourselves. And there was also the realization that women hardly ever showed up alone; you either walk in with a group of well-dressed, affluent-looking dykes, or hand in hand with a new lover. Because nobody you don't know is really going to talk to you, unless you intend to go to bed with them, and neither Tina nor I were prepared for a one-night stand, though we teased each other about it.

On the deck, we found a corner where we could lean and sip our beers, enjoying the breeze and the dark sky, the moon barely suggested by some shimmering clouds above the horizon. All the brooding of the past few weeks had become a habit, and now I felt as though I were noticing everything with aching clarity. Hopelessly, I tried not to sound like a downer while I extemporized to Tina.

"This isn't such a friendly town, you know."

"You mean those stuck-up chicks out there? Forget it, when the music gets going, we'll dance, and we'll meet the friendly types."

"Doesn't it bother you? You realize this is the only place for women in the whole town?"

"There's Womencrafts—" suggested Tina.

"That's a store—I mean a social place, like the guys have . . . in every corner."

"But you get the 10 percent lesbian discount when you buy something, and the guys don't!"

"That's true. Do you know that one time, when me and Millie went in there, a woman was asked the question at the cash register, you know: *Do you qualify for our lesbian discount?* And she says, Oh, no, I'm not a lesbian!"

"Get outta here! For five minutes she can't be a lesbian? Was she afraid the discount was contagious?"

"I know! I hollered, and Millie poked me in the ribs."

"Look," said Tina. A woman with long hair was dancing alone in the middle of the dance floor. She seemed to be enjoying herself, as she swayed and twisted seductively. Everyone watched her with practiced boredom.

"I know what her deal is," I proposed, cynically.

"What?" Tina egged me on.

"Her boyfriend is waiting for her at the Atlantic House while she's over here exploring her sexuality."

"Oh, you're no good!" Tina chided me, but then, more thoughtfully, she agreed. "You know, I think the A House is like, the bisexual bar. That's where all the boys without dates hang around at two in the morning, after last call."

"How do you know that!?"

"The power of observation, Watson. Stick with me, and you'll learn a lot!"

As it turned out, Mark, the happy hosteller, invited us to share the continental breakfast in the morning with the rest of his guests. My cynical take on this development was that he must have been beside himself with joy at the prospect of Jeremy's visit, and that we'd probably be kicked out on Sunday morning. But Tina seemed to feel that he was a genuinely nice guy, which I had to concede.

"I'm just always prepared to be ignored or stepped on by rich guys in P-Town. They're always so much taller!" I whined.

"Well, unprepare yourself. I feel propitious cosmic winds blowing our way!"

"Oh, Tina—"

"What is it, my child?"

"You're serious about feeling like something good is coming, I mean, it's not just your fortune-teller routine?"

"Would I lie to you?"

"No, I believe you, but I think I might cry."

Tina never ceased to amaze me. She made faces at me and made me laugh, we finished our coffee and croissants with extra strawberry jam and marmalade and butter overflowing onto the plate. We sat in the lavish, if gaudy, breakfast room of Land's End Inn, surrounded by gilt mirrors, Tiffany lamps, brocade, and stained-glass windows that looked out onto the beautiful view of the ocean. Mark was most gracious and made sure all of his guests were on a first-name basis with one another. Tina and I chatted amiably with architects from Long Island; bankers from Colorado who were windburned from skiing; a sweet-faced gigolo from Tennessee who had everyone roaring with his tales of woe, being, as he said, a child of a child of the Depression. He was there with an older man, a rancher from Texas who went out of his way to be polite to us, the only "young ladies" in the place.

With our bellies full, we headed for the center of town to window-shop with the rest of the weekend throngs, and Tina announced to me that, thanks to having free breakfast, we were comfortably over budget.

"Let's go to Womencrafts," she urged. "There's something we have to have for our birthdays."

We walked along the sidewalks, taking in the manicured gardens still sporting late summer roses, daydreaming about retiring here one day when we were old. Cutting through parking lots, we walked and jogged the rest of the way along the beach, as the sun hit the peak of its midday heat. Picking up little stones and shells at low tide, I reconsidered the retirement idea, and so did Tina.

"Besides, we'd get arthritis—you know this place is hell in winter?"

"Yeah, it's Puerto Rico or nothing!" I cheered.

"Or the Old Dyke Home!" cheered Tina.

"Oh, God," I sighed, feeling my heart caught in my throat.

"What is it?"

"Nothing," I lied, almost sobbing.

"Come on," urged Tina, dragging me toward the boardwalk where the shops were. "Put your sneakers on, we're here!"

I followed her without argument; I didn't want her to see me cry, though my tears had started to flow behind my sunglasses. As we entered the gallery of shops and headed for Womencrafts, I sniffled and distracted myself, looking at the displays of exotic seashells, silver jewelry, leather caps, tied-dyed shorts, and of course, all the women holding hands.

Tina definitely had a plan, as she walked us purposefully up to the jewelry counter of the store. She let me browse around while she picked up a couple of handmade whatnots, asking prices.

"Look," she said finally, pointing to a display of silver dangling things. "We have enough money to get one of these for each of us."

Several dozen charms, pendants, and earrings made of silver were displayed on top of the counter. There were half-moons, Isis wings, labryses, goddesses, ankhs, and a variety of less-symbolic designs. Under the glass counter, one could appreciate similar pieces, but made in gold; some with garnets or amethysts. I touched a heart-shaped pendant. Tina guided my hand toward a pair of woman symbols dangling together with a little price tag.

"Do you like these?" Tina's eyes were expectant.

"Yeah, I've always loved these," I assured her. It was true; I'd admired the dangling silver earrings on the lobes of many a trendy lesbian, but I'd never thought of anything so extravagant as owning a pair.

"We can get a pair—friendship earrings," said Tina. "While I'm at school in New Haven, I want you to know we'll always stick by each other, no matter what."

I nodded enthusiastically, sucking in my mixture of anguish and elation, which had brought me copious sniffles, and watched behind my sunglasses as Tina paid for the earrings, and got our 10 percent lesbian discount. Once outside, I grabbed Tina, and we started running back to the beach.

"Wait!" she yelled. "Don't you want to put it on?"

"Yes, I do!" I yelled, crying. "I'm just having a nervous break-down!"

Breakdown or not, I grabbed a bunch of napkins from the ice-cream stand and held them against my nose until we got to a safe place on the beach, by some rocks. I ran into the water up to my ankles, sneakers and all, and sat on the rocks to blow my nose.

"I love you, Tina," I bawled between napkins. "You're my sister!"

"I know, I know, calm down, you'll be all right," Tina soothed.

"Let's put them on right now—they're real silver? They won't rust if we go in the water? Here, let me do it!"

"God, Erica, you're such a kid! Here, oh, it looks great!"

The tide was coming up, swirling around the rocks, but it didn't matter. We put our legs up, and Tina held my hand as I talked on, between sobs.

"It all started when Coral split her head open or maybe when Millie broke up with me, I'm not sure. It's just that Coral could have died, right there, in a split second, and I couldn't really help. And then I almost died, or I could have, but I didn't, and then I wanted to die—I thought I was going to, I was so sad I thought the only way out was to kill myself, but now I know I'm going to live, and I don't know what to do. I mean, your life could be over in a second, so how do you know what is important? I mean, I know, your family, and your friends, but your friends could leave you . . ."

"Not this friend."

"I know, that's why I'm so happy, but I haven't been good to my family! Oh, God, Tina, I have to tell you about my mother."

"Finally. It's about time you trusted me."

"I do trust you, I just didn't want you to think badly of me . . ."

"Erica, I never would. You told me she was sick in a home somewhere, but you always told people she wasn't around anymore, making them think she'd passed on."

"No . . ."

"Is that why you and Nélida always fight?"

"Yeah, she doesn't want me to see her."

"Does Nélida see her?"

"Yeah."

"Where is she, Erica, where is your mother?"

It took me forever to answer. The gulls flew by and chanted their short yells, somehow calming the storm I felt raging in my heart. I thought at that moment that I wanted to hear the bellow of the horn from the lighthouse, and as if by arrangement, it happened. My senses felt sharp, full, as if I was being touched by everything at that moment. I could feel the sun, the water, the breeze, I could hear Tina's question, hold her hand, watch the gulls in their swirling flight, and I felt like the answers to everything were in the sky, in the scent of the breeze. I told her. Mami was in a nursing home, but I didn't know where. Nélida wouldn't say because I wouldn't accept that she couldn't come home. It had happened over three years ago when Mami had a stroke, and I tried never to think about it. My niece didn't even talk about her grandmother. From Puerto Rico, sometimes we received holiday cards from relatives who wrote as if Mami had indeed died.

"Would she recognize you if she saw you?"

"I don't know, she doesn't talk much. Nélida says, what she remembers most of the time is that she's in New Britain, in 1945, when she and Papi were young, working at the factory."

"Is that because of the stroke?"

"It left her right side paralyzed, but you see, she always . . . I can't, Tina, I can't."

"It's okay, take it easy."

"But I want to tell you . . . the doctors told Nélida there was no hope, that we couldn't take care of her at home. I wanted to, though, I know I could have done it!"

"Erica, you were a young kid—seventeen, eighteen—what could you do?"

"Something, anything!"

"Yeah, I know, it's okay, don't cry." Tina hugged me to her, smoothing away the last of my tears. "Now I understand why Nélida insisted you go to school."

"And why she was so upset when I quit, went to work. I've been such an idiot!"

"Hey, don't knock yourself!"

"But you know, the worst of it is that this whole time I didn't know what I was doing. Why I quit school, why I worked so hard. It was like I wanted to set up a life somewhere!"

"To bring your mother home, maybe?" Tina asked, almost whispering.

"To bring my mother home."

There are some things that always stay the same in P-Town, like the Saturday night of Labor Day weekend being the biggest night for reveling, cruising, and dancing till it hurts. Our plans were no different. After our usual dinner at Mojo's, and a chunk of rich chocolate fudge, we were ready to join the crowds. The music was blasting in waves out at the Boatslip, where one could see hundreds of men in bathing suits dancing to Donna Summer. At the Atlantic House, the rock-n-roll crowd was breaking through the door, and at the Café Blasé, the cappuccinos and white wine coolers were being served by a bevy of handsome gay waiters, all wearing the colorful T-shirts and de rigueur tight black pants. At the silversmiths and leather shops, the locals patiently catered to gay and straight tourist alike, and except for the women at the candy shop, I was convinced that all snobby heterosexual women had to have long hair and long Indian print skirts that year, to differentiate themselves from us—the fearsome short-haired dykes.

The Pied Piper was packed that night, and the music was as loud as possible. Tina and I squeezed through the crowd and found a space to dance near the deck, which, if not the center of all the attention, was at least close to the fresh air and away from all the cigarette smoke. Knowing this was going to be a hot night, Tina and I had saved our best clothes—jean-shorts and black tank tops. And on our left ear, we each wore one bright silver earring.

10

After I figured out I wasn't dying, I threw away all the Valium and concentrated on getting ready to ask my sister where our mother was. The fog that had followed me everywhere since the accident was lifting, and though the pills probably had little to do with my mood, it didn't matter, I wanted to be free of everything. Besides, it wasn't going to be easy, because when I looked back, it seemed that the fog extended to the time I left New Britain to come to school, or before, when Mami got sick.

It was on the way back from Provincetown that I began to look forward to things, to make plans that I couldn't wait to set in motion. Tina was amused with the change in me and encouraged my almost nonstop chatter. I was overflowing with ideas. We had met three very nice women from New York on our last night at the Pied Piper, who had asked us to ride back with them in their old Volvo. Tina was happy to meet them, all three undergraduate students at Yale, two white and one black. The black woman had been born in Panamá but had been raised in the Bronx with her aunt, and she piled in the backseat between her girlfriend and me, so we could speak Spanish together. I was a little shy at first, because my Spanish was rusty from disuse, but I found hers was just as peppered with Spanglish as mine.

I hadn't put on the cervical collar since Friday night, and although my neck was sore from not wearing it, Tina could not persuade me that it looked interesting at the bar. I seemed to feel better whenever I was relaxed, even dancing. Perhaps the strain on my neck was healing, or perhaps it was the relief of having confided in Tina, but I was beginning to feel like my old self, though I wasn't really sure what that was. Our new friends dropped us off right at Tina's dorm, before continuing to New York City. I stayed with Tina that night, helping her to pack the last of her things as she got ready to start school.

It was good that the change in my outlook had begun just as Tina was leaving. Neither one of us wanted to think about it, so I kept busy packing and cleaning the dorm room when she could hardly keep her eyes open. My energy was enough for both of us, and it probably kept us from crying. That's how I walked Tina to the bus the next morning; she, barely awake, and me, full of promises about how I'd come for her at Christmas.

"But you don't even have a car anymore, Erica."

"Ye of little faith. I'm gonna have one by then, you'll see," I insisted.

"One that doesn't leak and has heat?"

"You don't want much, do you? Yeah, it'll have heat and an FM radio!"

"Wow," Tina hugged me.

"Study, you hear me?"

"I hear you. I'll call you!" She climbed up on the bus. I ran beside it and followed her to her seat by a window.

"Don't call too much, you've gotta save your money!" I yelled at the bus.

"You're always saving money!" she called back.

"I love you, Tina!"

"I love you, Erica!"

The bus lumbered away. I walked a couple of miles in the brilliant sun before I got a ride home.

The next two mornings, I got up early to walk in the crisp September air, making notes in a notebook, a way to help remind me of things. I would walk to the old bridge by the thread factory and sit on the edge, dangling my legs over the trickling water beneath. From there, I could see the big Victorian houses on one side and the tenement buildings on the other, down by the embankment where the old building of American Thread Company stood, now practically all closed. Only a small section of it was still in operation, and I could see the rows of women sitting inside through the wide windows. Polish and Puerto Rican women, whom I endowed with my mother's face, my mother's walk, my mother's pañuelo over her gray hair.

It was May 1974, a hot day in New Britain, when I heard my sister yelling at Mami to cut it out. They always had fights, screaming fights that I avoided entirely, knowing there was no point in my trying to reason them out or end them. I stayed in my room, thinking that at least I'd be going away to school soon, leaving the maddening regularity of these fights.

I was a mess of confusion in those days, not that my state of mind improved much in the following years, but I remember being angry with my mother and my sister a lot. I blamed my sister for being so boy-crazy that she had to get married because she was pregnant and for making things worse for my mother's illness with her constant arguing. And I blamed my mother for the schizophrenic episodes that had made our lives a roller coaster ever since I could remember. A scary ride of unpredictable shifts, this definitely described the García family. As I got older, I knew it wasn't Mami's fault, and as she got older, the episodes lessened in intensity and duration but were still just as upsetting.

My niece was only two then, and she had just come to live with us that winter. Her father had left my sister the same way my father had left us when I was two, and we hadn't seen him since. I suspected the same would be true of my sister's husband, but she insisted that his absence was only temporary. At any rate, my room was also my niece's, while my sister shared my mother's room. I watched the baby sleeping in her crib, hoping that the yelling from the kitchen wouldn't wake her up. Along the windowsills, I had made room for her little girl's toys next to my seashell collection, and I had given up my desk for her clothes. On my dresser, I kept all my books and papers that had come from UConn, the only school I'd applied to, and the one that had fortunately accepted me. I sat on my bed, looking over the brochures with photographs of the dorms, Mirror Lake, the science labs. My sister screamed.

I ran out of my room and skidded into the kitchen because the scream wasn't normal to my ears. And there she was, on the floor, holding Mami and loosening her collar and urging her to breathe. My mother's face was ashen, her dark face suddenly blending with the blue-gray paisley of her bata. I reached for the yellow wall phone and dialed for the ambulance. I remember that my throat was stuck dry and that I could barely speak, that I could hear my niece waking up and wailing in the other room, and that I was so scared that there seemed to be a wall of sound surrounding us, booming in my ears, while everything, time and movement, slowed down to a crawl. I didn't know what else to do, so I untied my mother's shoes and took them off.

My sister was almost a nurse; she had worked at the hospital as a nurse's aide ever since she was in high school. Now, she had placed Mami on her back, and she was giving her mouth-to-mouth resuscitation with precise movements.

"It's a stroke," she stopped to tell me.

"Should I go get the baby?" I asked her, suddenly hearing my niece's wails again.

"Wait till the ambulance comes and open the door for them."

Her presence of mind had saved our mother's life, and her insistence that she had suffered a stroke, and not another psychotic episode, made the EMTs take her to the correct pavilion of the huge New Britain hospital. I remember this time vaguely, the edges of it getting more blurred as I try to avoid feeling again the desperation, the frustration, and the shame that surrounded us as we tried to get the nurses and doctors to listen to us. I stayed by the admissions desk, holding my niece on my hip while she sucked her thumb and looked at all the adults with her big eyes. It was my job to convince the nurse on duty that my mother's pension would cover her treatment, and that she wasn't on welfare, in which case she would have to wait to see the doctor on duty.

Getting up from my perch on the bridge, I walked further toward Windham, where there was nothing but houses, then back over the river into Willimantic, where I would decide whether to cook something at home or eat at a coffee shop. The special treat of eating somewhere else—at Pearl's or at the little railroad diner across the street from my apartment—was that I could have an item like toast. Lately it had been grating on me not to have a toaster or even a stove on which to cook real food. But it was a needling that was waking up certain parts of me I hadn't had time to consider in the two years I had been living alone; these things hadn't been important before. I had my red electric wok, and I could cook practically anything in it, except rice. Or toast, for that matter. And I could get coffee across the street. Other than this detail, the apartment was perfect.

My solitude had been perfect. For the first year, I hadn't had music, not even a radio or a television. I accompanied my thoughts with Mami's old guitar, singing, "En mi viejo San Juan," or some tune I could play by ear from Patti Smith or Santana. I didn't think this was unusual, until Millie had become impatient one day and fretted that my apartment was like a sanatorium. She had been lying in bed with me all morning, seemingly at peace, when suddenly I noticed her look of desperation. She was tired, she complained, of having nothing to listen to but our thoughts. That weekend I went to the junk and antique shop and bought a used stereo.

Millie's words had stung, touched something that I now realized made me think of my mother.

"A sanatorium?" I'd asked her. "Doesn't it feel like a monastery—I like to think of it that way. It's got these high ceilings, white walls, tall windows, quiet . . . except for the street."

"You would think of it that way. I'm not Christian, so I don't have that point of reference. Jews don't lock themselves away to commune with God. We go out in the world and do it!"

"Oh, I see." I remember her thoughtful face, the curls around her forehead, and then the frown she got when something worried her.

"Except for old people. We put ours in nursing homes . . ."

"Millie, don't get so serious. I'll get a stereo, all right?"

"Is that where your Mom is?"

"Baby, I told you I can't stand to talk about it—"

"Sorry. I was thinking of my Aunt Barbara."

It seemed odd to remember Millie and the conversations we used to have, to remember the things we had discovered together, without having the intimacy that had bonded us anymore. I didn't want to dwell on those days. I wasn't angry with her exactly, but I was beginning to enjoy feeling separate from her. I was beginning to feel a certain joy in making plans for myself again, the way I had when I was preparing to go to school. Memories of Millie were becoming a burden I no longer wanted to carry.

Probably because of this, I delayed going to see my sister for a few days. I knew she would ask about Millie, since she had become sort of an ambassador in the strained relationship between us. I wanted to tell my sister the decisions that I had come to, the plans I'd made on my own, and that I wanted to see our mother. I went instead to the insurance adjustor to negotiate a fair price for the wreck of my car and then to the office of continuing education at UConn. And, putting my collar back on because I wasn't actually supposed to be without it, according to the advice of my physical therapist, I stopped in at the Administration Building of the Training School to get my disability paycheck.

"Hey, García!" Kelly rushed to greet me, hugging me carefully as I came out of the brick rectangle. "Your neck still hurt?"

"Nah, it's much better," I sort of lied. Kelly looked tanned, her eyes seemed softer to me.

"Can you do chin-ups yet?"

"Haven't tried. What are you up to? You look good!"

Kelly looked down, blushing a little and shrugging. I asked her about the ward and her daughter, as we walked together through the parking lot. She told me she missed me three times, and I didn't tell her I wasn't coming back. She knew. I said good-bye and asked her to call me, so we could go have coffee at the Wagon Wheel after work, then I hugged her quickly, before her skittish body could move away.

But the surprise was on me. Kelly moved her face and kissed the edge of my mouth, leaving a tickle in the pit of my stomach. I watched her walk away, tucking her shiny brown hair in the usual ponytail, just like in the old days back at the ward.

That night, I called Nélida.

"To what Saint do I owe your call, you ingrate? It's been months!"

"To Saint Whiplash and don't exaggerate because I called you before Labor Day."

"Yes, to tell me you were going on a bus to who knows where, camping in the woods, alone, where you could get raped, and the long ride was probably no good for your neck. Are you still doing the physical therapy?"

"Listen to me, Nélida, I didn't get raped. Tina and I slept in nice, soft beds, and my neck is better. And I've seen the light, okay? I'm going back to school, and I want to come see you and talk to you about it."

"Ave María, you really did get shaken up! You're coming voluntarily, and it's not even a holiday? It's a miracle! Is Millie coming with you?"

"No, we broke up." I decided to be blunt.

"Ay, bendito! Don't tell Marisol, she doesn't understand these things. When are you coming?" And then, without waiting for a reply, "Come Saturday, early, for lunch, and stay for the weekend," she ordered me.

"Okay."

"Okay," said my sister, unused to my compliance.

Not knowing how I would approach the subject of our mother, and fearing some of the old confrontations—the fights that would last three days, eating meals in silence and having to withhold my real feelings for the sake of uneasy peace—had me anxious and restless. I almost regretted having dumped the last prescription of Valium down the toilet, but I reminded myself how distant it had made me feel, if calmer. Without having work at the Training School to drain my energy, I hitched a ride to the river and walked until my calves ached. Then I walked to campus and spent the rest of the day in the library, until it closed.

But Saturday arrived, and I had attended to all the outstanding business on my agenda; I would know exactly what to tell my sister when she asked. Whatever she asked. The bus was rounding the corner as I ran into the tobacco shop to buy a round-trip ticket to New Britain.

"Where's Millie?" was the first thing my niece said when she opened the door.

"We broke up, Marisol, give me a hug, " I tried.

"No!" she yelled at me, hands on her hips, skinny legs protruding from a starched white dress. "Girls don't break up!" she informed me. I grabbed her and hugged her, nuzzling her tightly braided hair, while she giggled and squirmed out of my arms, running up the stairs.

"Why not?" I followed her up, slinging my knapsack over one shoulder. I could smell my sister's cooking already, and it was only 11:30. I was hungry. "Why don't girls break up?" Marisol stared up at me with serious brown eyes. She had grown tall for her age.

"Because," she gave me her hand-on-hip explanation. "Because they love each other."

"Well, Millie and I probably still do love each other, we're just not girlfriends anymore."

"Don't talk to her about those things, Erica!" My sister yelled from the kitchen. "She doesn't understand!"

"I do, too!" protested Marisol, then turning to me, she asked: "Do you love Tina, then?"

"Yes, of course I do, but Tina is my best friend. Like Raquelita is *your* best friend." I wasn't sure if I was being very clear, but I had a feeling I should speak frankly to my niece, instead of hiding things from her. Then she asked what was really on her mind.

"Are you going to get another girlfriend, or a boyfriend?"

"Another girlfriend, I'm pretty sure."

"Okay," she said, satisfied, and took my hand. "Come see my Barbie!"

It wasn't until the afternoon that my sister and I sat down to "talk about things." We were in the kitchen, she fussing with the spice rack or wiping down the formica table that had been witness to so many of these family talks since we had been children. I sat holding my favorite blue mug full of sweet cafe con leche. I felt strangely comfortable, and her questions didn't bother me. I answered them slowly, evenly.

"So, if you take nine credits, you can just register?"

"That's right. I did that yesterday."

"And you had enough money, from the . . . insurance thing?"

"Yeah, I settled on my car. They gave me nine hundred dollars, and I'll get another chunk for the damage to my body," I tossed it out, laughing at her concerned face. Nélida was getting to look just like Mami when she was young.

"Don't joke like that, God will punish you. So you're not going back to work? You know you can come here and live with us!"

"Gracias," I told her, touching her hand just lightly because I felt grateful, but a little embarrassed that my sister was being so nice to me, and I had been so afraid to talk to her. "I'll get something part-time and be okay for now, but I was going to ask you if I could do that next semester."

"You know you can, nena, esta es tu casa!"

"See, next semester I'll get financial aid, and I can work here at the hospital on weekends and finish my B.A. at Central. I'll even have money to give you for the house."

"You don't have to give me any money, Erica. I want you to save it for graduate school. And, what are you going to do at the hospital? I don't want you washing bacinicas and mopping floors!"

"Oh, it's no big deal! You forget I'm an experienced aide now. Just put in a good word for me, and I'll be the favorite of old Mrs. Horton in no time. She won't make me wash pissing pots, you watch!"

Nélida and I laughed about her old supervisor, and she reached over with her left arm around my right shoulder, and my niece promptly came to slip in between us, trying to catch some of the good feeling. I watched my sister with her daughter, her features stern yet loving, her eyes tired, her lovely, thick black hair beginning to gray at the temples. I waited until late, after dinner and a walk, an ice-cream cone at Dairy Queen, and bedtime for my niece, to ask what I'd been waiting to ask. We watched a movie on television and then the news. The "Johnny Carson" show was on. Neither one of us was watching it.

"Why do you want to go now? You'll get upset and talk crazy all over again about taking her to live with you in the country."

"Did I say that?" This was a surprise to me, I didn't remember very much.

"Don't you remember?" I shook my head. "Erica, you swore up and down you would save money and move with Mami to PR. You called me a bitch and said I didn't care about her. And then you cried for a week, and I was so afraid you would try to . . . I don't know, hurt yourself." My sister took a deep breath. I added an ice cube to her glass of Ginger Ale.

"I'm sorry," I told her. "I didn't know what I was saying."

"I know."

"You're not a bitch. You saved her life— remember?"

"Well, I am a bitch sometimes, but I love Mami. She just needs constant care!"

"Where is she?"

"In Manchester. I'll give you the address."

That night I slept in my old room, next to Marisol. Her dolls were on the windowsill, and my seashells were still there.

With the address of the nursing home in my hand, I wasn't any more ready to go visit my mother than I had been for the past three years. I began to play games on the way back from New Britain, sitting on the bus in the early evening, a regular student going back to school after visiting her family. Or maybe I was a nun going to the convent after taking her novice exam and meeting the Bishop—or whatever nuns have to do to graduate. My best idea was that none of the past few years had ever happened, and I was a basketball player going to defend UConn against Notre Dame, only I didn't know whether Notre Dame had a girls' basketball team.

But the fantasy worked, it kept me calm. I remembered when Nélida was still in high school, and she had a boyfriend who had a car. They dropped me off at the middle school sometimes, letting me ride in front with them, and I felt like we were rich, lucky, far away from our lives. Nélida and Ricky smooched at all the red lights, and I pretended they were Archie and Veronica or that Ricky was the older brother from "My Three Sons," only he had a Puerto Rican girlfriend. Ricky was Italian and Polish. This fantasy worked, too. After her job at the hospital, Nélida would come home in her nurse's aide uniform, and she would stand at the door calling, "Mom, I'm home!" laughing hysterically when Mami would look at her as if she were nuts for calling her *Mom* and speaking in English to her.

I would laugh with Nélida, but uncontrollably, in spasms, and join in the farce by going to the refrigerator to get a glass of milk and cookies, like the kids on TV, only we didn't do that at home, and we didn't eat cookies, so Mami would smack me for taking out the milk, and Nélida would smack me for laughing so much. She'd have to smack me a few times because I'd continue the game in our room where I'd pretend my name was Shirley and hers was

Debbie and her boyfriend's name was Biff. My problem was that I didn't know when to stop. Sometimes I'd call my sister *Debbie* when we were in the car with Ricky, and I was busy pretending we were rich, fiddling with the radio, and I couldn't stop laughing because Nélida wouldn't hit me in front of Ricky. He couldn't figure out what was going on, but when they broke up and Ricky moved to Forestville to marry a Polish girl named Debbie, Nélida swore it was all my fault.

On the bus, I tried to fantasize that maybe my name really was Shirley, and I had just finished school, and I could really do anything I put my mind to. Only Shirley would probably not know what to do, in a case like this, because her mother wouldn't be in a nursing home, and she wouldn't know what to do in the morning, when she woke up in her own little two-room apartment, with only the insurance money to last her through the semester and no car. I figured Shirley wouldn't know, but I would.

When I woke up, everything was different. For one thing, my begonias had bloomed over the weekend, and my neck didn't hurt at all. I knew the physical therapist had told me not to get too confident about sudden improvements because some back problems were sure to show up later on. I stashed the cervical collar in a drawer.

After I checked in on my three literature courses and saw that the professors did indeed have my name on their lists, I had the odd feeling that I was starting over. I walked on air for the rest of the day, looking at books I could take out at the library and those I would have to buy. I floated by the Humanities Building, thinking that school had gotten much more interesting in the time I had been away. Or was it me who had changed? I was taking two Women's Studies courses and one Latin American literature course, and I had the feeling that there were lesbians in every class.

But this certainly couldn't be, I had to be imagining things, and at any rate, there was no way of knowing. I just wished I could check with Tina, because she had her foolproof ways of knowing who was a lesbian, and who had "QT," *the queer quotient,* as she put it. With these thoughts, I hitched a ride back out of campus and into Willimantic, where I had a very important appointment to see Jack, the mechanic at the Mobil.

"Yo, Erica, my friend!" Jack's legs rolled out from under a blue Pinto. The garage owner, a grouchy guy named Mike, checked to see that I was someone who should be there and continued working on a white Datsun with black pinstripes inside the bay. I sniffed at the familiar smells of the garage and felt at ease. Jack was dusting himself off and adjusting his red cap. "Fantastic weather we're having, eh?"

"You mean this heat wave, Jack, you like it like this?"

"Yeah, man, my muscles feel like they've been oiled, I can move. I hate to be stiff and cold, working under these cars. I'll show you what I got."

We climbed over the wreck of an old Ford pickup, which separated the garage area from the junkyard behind it, Jack's lanky figure folding and unfolding easily through the obstacles. He helped me jump off the hood down onto the pile of tires on the other side, behaving like a regular friend helping a friend with shorter legs than his own. There was a feeling of respect and unobtrusive consideration I got from my interactions with this man; I wondered if this was how guys treated each other.

In the small, fenced-in yard, there were enough pieces of junked cars to provide parts for Mike's garage. There were piles of fenders and bumpers, side-view mirrors, headlamps, and stacks of hubcaps gleaming in the sun. To the right of the tires, parked like day-old donuts against the fence, four used cars bore the chalk marks on their windshields that indicated a low price and their best feature: *Low mileage $750,* said a red Opel Kadett; *New*

Transmission $500, said an ancient gray Volvo, broad and sturdy; just the opposite of the neon green Corvette, which was simply marked, *Runs $300*. Next to it was a beat-up, dark green Karmann-Ghia, with spots of putty antirust Bondo on both front fenders. There was nothing written on the windshield, and the canvas convertible top was rolled down.

"The Ghia?" I said to Jack.

"It's a great date car," he winked at me. Wiping his hands on his blue overalls, he took two giant steps over to the car and climbed in from the top. I opened the other door and got in, not even attempting to copy his maneuver. The dashboard was all wood, the seats were brown leather, and the steering wheel was covered in black. I grasped the round wooden gearshift and smoothed my fingers over the red-and-black inlaid numbers—1, 2, 3, 4, R, and 5.

"Five!" I exclaimed at Jack, while he reached for two wires under the dash and rolled them together, pressing the button for the top to come down over us, which purred smoothly. I reached up along with Jack to grab hold of the top as it glided obediently forward, nothing like my old Valiant. We snapped the top in place and turned to look at each other.

"It's a real Porsche engine, from some guy who wrapped his import right around a tree out in Chaplin. I brought the shift along with it 'cause it's got an overdrive gear—nice touch, huh?"

"What were you going to do with it? Hey, I can see daylight through the floorboards!" I slid the rubber pad over to look at the rusted holes underneath my feet.

"Nothing! I can't get a good body to go along with this great engine, so this was the easiest thing to do with it before Mike snatches it up—" Jack unhooked the wires. "He doesn't know I got it for nothing. Give me $400, and we drive over to Motor Vehicles right now."

"I got $200—you said you had a trash can with wheels for me

that would hold me till next year! This is a trash can with a Porsche engine—"

"Okay, okay. $300. I can't do anything with it anyway."

"Plus, I gave you my wreck—"

"Yeah, the V-8 is still good, the body's shot, you know!"

"Saved my life, though, that was a lot of metal behind me." Jack laughed, remembering the state of my late automobile, which he had towed after the accident. I knew he could get something out of the front end, though, and apparently he had.

"Okay, $250. Help me push it over to the gate, you've got to jump-start it."

"Right." We pushed the car out of the lot onto the back street, and after Jack secured the gate, we gave it a running start and hopped in, popping the clutch into second. If I had any doubts about the car actually running, the throaty sound drowned them out. We roared away to the Motor Vehicles office.

On a blue-sky Monday after classes, I was scheduled for my last physical therapy appointment. In the brisk end of September, the wind changes directions as many times as it seems necessary for that abrupt cold that tinges the leaves to descend and to drive away every single cloud so that there is only blue. Blue and the uncertainty that it was ever summer or that it will ever be winter. I would have felt sad again, even apprehensive, thinking about the snow on the roads, but I had a car. It made all the difference.

On North Eagleville Road, I had found a short hill, steep enough to jump-start the Ghia, and not too far from my classes. I walked quickly, leaving the campus behind, feeling already that I was outside of school, not a campus student, naturally, since I got further and further away toward a car and not a dorm, but it was something else. I'd lived outside. School didn't mean the same to me any longer. I watched my classmates from Women's History walk in the opposite direction, toward the library. I wanted to go with them, do my research, and talk about Rosa Luxemburg and the social democrats, but I was already outside the class and moving toward my car, and Rosa and the rest were moving back into history away from my life. I tossed my books on the passenger's seat.

I drove faster than usual down the hill from school toward the Willimantic Hospital. The sky continued blazing blue over the hills, kites on either side fluttered orange and red in changeable winds. I had canceled one appointment after returning from Provincetown and received a stern chiding from PB. I had told her I'd felt fine, but she'd insisted that if I didn't care about my health, the least I could do would be not to mess up her insurance report on me, so she could send it in, and I could get my money. I saw the wisdom of this and promised I wouldn't miss my last appointment. I was also looking forward to seeing PB again, though she never said anything more to me than was strictly necessary.

When I arrived, though, I was met by a tall stranger, very blonde, who talked very loudly. She seemed not to know who PB was or to understand that I regarded her as my personal physical therapist. Feeling completely disoriented, I prepared myself to undergo the usual treatment of stretching and shivering under the cold gel and the ultrasound massage. But the blonde therapist surprised me with an order to take off my T-shirt, put on a hospital gown, and lie face down on a cold, black leather table. And she proceeded to massage my back and my neck with warm hands and quantities of hospital lotion. No stretching and no ultrasound. I felt great but was terribly embarrassed every time the paper gown opened and my sides felt exposed. I was sure the sides of my breasts were visible, and I slipped my arms down to my sides. The therapist simply gripped both my arms in her large hands and gave them a good pull. I felt an odd stretch in my spine and a certain relief. I received a slap on my jeans.

"Okay, Miss Gracia, you're done!"

I grabbed the gown around my breasts and tried to reconcile to the fact that the therapist had just slapped my butt and mispronounced my name. I figured it was the last time I had to go there, so I let it go. I wasn't so happy anymore; PB was gone, and the day outside had deteriorated. It was late, and the sky was quite gray. I got dressed quickly and didn't even thank Miss Warm Hands for the completed form as she handed me a copy. She would take care of sending the original to the insurance company. I was filled with regret. My back felt great. My name was spelled correctly on the form. What more did I want?

"Thank you," I called from the door.

Pacing back and forth in my apartment, I decided it was my state of uncertainty that made me act so childishly. I couldn't continue this if I was actually going to go to the nursing home in Manchester to see my mother for the first time in so long. I had to have a plan. No. I didn't need one. I could just walk in and say I wanted to visit. No. I couldn't even go to my physical therapy appointment without acting foolish just because the person I expected wasn't there. But it wasn't that, was it? I didn't really know PB, and she wasn't really expecting me. I just felt outside of things. But there was something I had to do, and I felt better acting alone. Without my sister or Millie or even Tina. I wanted to tell Tina, though, but not until after I had been there, after I had seen. I had to see for myself.

I waited until dark.

The drive to Manchester only took about fifteen minutes. I knew the roads, Tina and I had passed nearby when we took a shortcut off the highway on our way back from the bar a few times. If I had only known, perhaps I could have told her, "Look, Tina, that's the nursing home where my mother is." And she would have asked, *When do you go visit her?* But I didn't know where my own mother was. That's why I had to do this alone.

The moon hung oblong and distant from a black canvas night in the suburbs. The quiet of the streets carried no songs of crickets, but instead the humming of mercury lights and fluorescent signs maintained the illusion of a habitable place. There was no one on the streets. I drove around the Crescent Hill Home for the Aged and pulled in the empty parking lot of the gas station next to it, which still advertised several grades of octane even though it was closed. I decided not to shut the engine off, and I sat there, with just the parking lights and the purring of the motor, watching. I stared at the parking lot of Crescent Hill, with its brick complex wedged on the side of a hill that could have been as much crescent-shaped as a thousand others in the area. I hoped my mother had a view from her room.

Near a dumpster by the edge of the lot next to me, there was a slight incline I thought I could use. I followed the sidewalk with my eyes to the front entrance and imagined myself walking that way on a Sunday afternoon, as a regular visitor. The place looked small, sort of like an elementary school. I half-expected to find a swing set and a jungle gym on the other side. On the grass, leaves were already spreading their territory. Almost on cue, a gust of wind swirled an eddy of them up over the sidewalks. I came back to myself.

On the way back, my head full of memories I wasn't sure were mine, I took a long time. I tried driving back east using all the streets and avoiding the highway and the major rural routes. I tried to imagine what the state had looked like thirty years before, when there had been no easy access to service roads, four-lane highways to accommodate rush-hour traffic to and from the major factories, the major employers of the state in those days. I knew nothing about how people lived or how people worked. I studied literature of the past and tried to live in the present, with nothing in between. Suddenly, driving at night by myself, the wind whistling through the soft top of the Ghia where canvas met metal, and metal met worn-out rubber seals, I thought that I knew more about cars than I did about how my mother had lived when she was young. I heard Tina's jokes to me about my theories of a new world, my sister's digs about thinking I could get anywhere with an English degree, and I even heard Millie's question from long ago, *Well, do you want to study, or do you want to work?*

Meandering, I ended up in the back end of Willimantic by the old railroad track, on a street I seldom passed, but where I knew there was a bar. A bar frequented by women.

"You mean, old dykes, don't you?" Tina had said, when she heard this from her sister.

"No, young women, like you, fool, only a lot tougher."

"And how do you know these things, Natalie? You don't even live in this town, you're not even gay, and you know more than me and Tina!" I quizzed.

"I make it my business to know, you couple of hot-house college girls who've never been outside your own dorm. You think life stops at the edge of your campus? Why don't you take a drive and go see the world for a change!"

That's all Natalie had to say to us, because the first weekend we could, Tina and I went looking for the bar, only we got lost. I didn't have a car then, and it was only through walking for miles and hitchhiking that we got back to campus. When Natalie heard we'd gone in search of the old bar, she laughed in our faces.

"Oh, you're lucky you didn't find the place, those white factory dykes might have thought you two were looking for trouble and given it to you!"

Sometimes, Natalie wasn't very helpful to us, but she did open our eyes. This night, I found the bar easily enough.

It was painted dark red outside, one window completely darkened, and the other, too high for anybody my height to look inside, had a neon sign blinking "BEER" on and off. I walked in and almost bumped into the pool table in the semidarkness. But it wasn't all that dark, once my eyes adjusted, and the place wasn't that big. There were two wooden booths on the right, a few round tables on the left, and a bar in the back that looked more like a pizza counter. There were men strewn throughout the joint, but they all ignored me. And when I saw the women, I recognized a couple of faces from the Training School, though I didn't know their names. I did the smart thing and nodded in greeting, then went to get myself a beer. A low hum confirmed I had done the right thing.

Turning around, beer in hand, and preparing to watch the action at the pool table wasn't that simple, though. My eyes met another pair of eyes I hadn't expected at all, and the owner of these cool brown eyes held my gaze. All I could think of doing was to nod again, and take a sip out of the cold brown bottle. In front of me, PB stood with her legs spread slightly, thoughtfully chalking up her cue, a long cigarette dangling from her lower lip. She put down the chalk, removed the cigarette from her lip, and set it smoking on the edge of the billiard table, bent forward with a straight back and legs apart to make her shot. She sank the eight ball.

11

The bar had no other name, it was just known as *the bar*. I hadn't gone in there looking for anyone, but I couldn't seem to make PB understand. She insisted on following me home, just to make sure I got there safely. She parked her gold Oldsmobile Cutlass next to the Ghia and pointed to it with her chin.

"Oughta get that thing painted."

"Just got it last week," I explained.

"I know, 'cause you used to come to the hospital on your sneakers," she informed me, draping her arm around my shoulders. I wasn't sure if I was glad PB seemed interested in me; she was suddenly too real and made me too certain that she had something in mind. The subtle flirting had lost its thrill.

"PB . . ."

"What is it, honey?" I almost got a kiss then.

"What's your first name?" I asked her with my hand on her

chest, my fingers spread wide, until PB noticed I wasn't ready to accept that kiss.

She looked into my eyes, placed both arms down by her sides, then asked, "Can I come up for coffee?"

"Sure you can."

We talked while I made the coffee, PB looked at my books, the guitar, my hiking boots. She complimented me on my begonias and began telling me about herself. She was twenty-six. I told her she looked older. She certainly acted older. I placed the cups on the table, and we sat on the floor next to each other. PB laughed and told me I had looked very young to her at first, until she looked at my chart and noticed my age when she filled out the final insurance form. She looked shy, all of a sudden.

"What is it?" I asked her. I liked her smile. Her eyes sparkled.

"Oh, I realized I liked you, you know? So I asked Brenda to fill in for me today. I didn't think it was right that I do your treatment after . . ."

"What?" Now, I was the one drawing closer.

"Well, you were always so friendly when you came in!"

"I shouldn't have been? I liked you, too," I admitted.

"Yeah, well, with a job like mine, you gotta be careful. Anybody could think something, you know, the other therapists, the patients, and then you're out on your ass."

"Have you seen that happen?" I was very close to her face.

"You know, you ask too many questions," she reached for my hand. "It's Patricia."

"What is?"

"My first name," she said, as she stood up. I followed her to my bed.

It was odd at first, being so conscious of how bossy PB seemed to me, but I liked her again. She excited me with her sharp movements, the low tone of her voice, accustomed to giving orders. I kissed her first, and she let me continue until we became used to each other. She had a way of grabbing my bottom lip with hers that felt like she was drawing me in, until I could close my eyes and almost feel sleepy with desire. PB's laughter was throaty, full, and I told her she sounded like my car. She laughed more and asked me if this was good or bad. Oh, very good, I told her, I like cars. She wrestled me down between my pillows and kissed me passionately, exciting my nerve endings out of their stupor, until I moaned with a thirsty pleasure, watching her mouth move between my neck and my breasts. Until PB was slowly waking me out of ecstasy with small kisses on my chin, my mouth, and my eyelids.

"You okay?" She asked, her fingers gently touching my cheek.

"Mm hm . . ."

"Excuse me," she said, and got up to wash her hands at my kitchen sink. I went to light a candle by the bed and turned on the radio. Then I joined her by the sink and washed my hands, got a glass of water to share.

"Patricia, huh?" I took deep swallows of the cold water.

"You asked—" I watched her throat move in small gulps.

"Yeah, PB suits you fine," I told her. She embraced me from behind and began to nibble my neck while her hands, deliberately, stroked my hips over my jeans and then my thighs. My knees began to buckle, but I wanted to stand, leaning back against her until she unbuttoned the rest of my shirt and slipped her fingers down to caress my belly. That's when I began to collapse, kneeling on the bed and taking PB down with me.

I tried to catch my breath at that moment, but PB grabbed my leg back with hers to hold me tightly, and I swooned again, if that is possible when one is lying down. I liked everything she did to me, how she touched me and explored my body, asking questions silently, sometimes whispering something in my ear from behind me and making my skin shiver from head to toe. I don't know how I ended up naked in her arms, but I liked the feel of her clothes as she held me and slipped her fingers between my legs. I think I drifted away for a few seconds, in waves of consciousness and abandon, and when I opened my eyes, I groaned again because I could see PB's hands turning my nipples hard in her fingers.

"Have you got school in the morning?" she asked me suddenly in a breathy voice, and I laughed, turning around and straddling her. Her face was flushed and smiling, her lips gone soft while I unbuttoned and unzipped her clothes. I had some ideas, and her body felt willing. I figured I could miss my morning class.

In the morning, I stood on the sidewalk with the paper. Cool wind and dust swirled in eddies around my feet, but the sky was a brilliant blue again. I held the paper under one arm and the milk I'd gone to get under the other, fishing the keys out of my pocket slowly. There was a sense in the air that I no longer had to hurry, so I turned the key in the lock, pushed the heavy door on its old hinges, and waited. Nothing. The bus to Providence came soundlessly to a halt in front of the cigar shop, while my ears were trained on the door upstairs.

Another gust of wind brought leaves from the walnut trees around the corner, and PB came bounding down the creaky stairs. She stopped, with her hand on the banister. I knew we both smelled the dusty wooden steps and the crisp air of fall out on Main Street. For a second, she stood there.

It was probably her line, but I stole it.

"I know. If I see you on the street, don't say anything."

She winced. Her eyes looked hazel in the morning and her face smooth. I decided it was the way her top lip twitched in a smile under her scar that had made me swoon and could do it again if I remembered how she kissed. But PB was in a hurry. She reached to pull me inside and closed the door. She kissed me affectionately, almost too slowly. I couldn't feel her lips anymore.

"It's better," she said, "it's better like this." And she was gone, closing the door quickly as if one of us would change her mind. I went upstairs to make fresh coffee and read the paper, wondering if Patricia had ever stayed in any woman's bed long enough to have breakfast.

It was still early when I got dressed in my best tan slacks and a blue sweater. My hair still felt wet from a hot shower, and I noticed the day would be warm after all. Jumping in the Ghia, I drove back to Manchester, sticking to the major roads this time, following Route 6 to the new section of Interstate 84, a brand new patch of highway where I hit 80 much too easily, and had to slow down again. I had no budget line for speeding tickets, but the car handled like a dream or like the racing engine it really was under all the Bondo that covered its puny metal body.

More than anything, I had a tremendous sense of freedom while driving. It still didn't feel quite like my car, not like the Valiant had been. But I was developing a sense of kinship with the machine. Both of us a little banged up, survivors of a crash, gliding by undetected. The Ghia handled much better than the Valiant, fit anywhere, and even rattled less. It would grow to be my car soon, maybe after I drove it to New Haven to show Tina. I just didn't want to like it too much too fast.

As I approached the nursing home, I shifted down and coasted into the parking lot for visitors. There was a spot all the way at the end, by a dumpster, that had a small incline near the exit. It was the best I could get and simply had to hope I could start here as easily as I could on my other hills. I parked and shut off the engine. Then I had to envision myself walking resolutely into the lobby several times before I actually opened the door and got out of the car. The building spread out crescentlike under its crescent hill, looking oddly like a fortress of red brick in my path in the daylight. I had to move.

The glass door opened wide, and the lobby met me with supermarket music and the smell of fresh flowers. Roses, I think. I felt like I was putting down a payment I couldn't get back. I swallowed hard when I saw the visitors' area, the information desk screaming out a welcome from a yellow smiley face. I couldn't do it.

I'd vacillated long enough between the two courses of action available to me, and I couldn't go the straight way, the civilian way. I headed right for the Chief RN's Office. Before I knocked, I slipped an *Application for Employment* form out of the wooden box outside her office. Then, I knocked.

"Hello," I chanted. I was shaking hands with a Mrs. Saunders, very tall, black, with beautiful eyes and perfect hair. "I'm Erica García, and I'm looking for a job!" I thought she could see through me down to my socks. But she asked me to sit down, gave me a brand new Bic pen with a blue cap and a wooden clipboard with a yellow smiley face stuck on the right-hand corner.

Nélida would be frantic by this time, waiting for me to tell her what was happening with my visit to Mami, but I didn't have time to explain. Besides, though she might have done something similar herself, she would never have admitted it to me. But I had to call her, and I did. When I knew she'd be in the shower, and my niece would be alone in the kitchen having breakfast. The coward's way, but the most effective, so I told Marisol everything Nélida needed to know: I had a lot of studying to catch up on, that's why I hadn't gone to see our mother yet. But I would call again as soon as I did. I told myself I was proceeding in the only way I knew.

Or almost. I actually did have a great deal to read, so I piled my books in the car, thinking I would get some of it done over the weekend. It didn't help that Mrs. Saunders had hired me immediately, to begin that Friday night because they were very short-handed over the weekends. I was almost regretting having told her I wanted to work on third shift, suddenly being faced with the prospect of fighting sleep again, after having gotten used to working during the day. But it was one of my most attractive features as a possible nurse's aide, besides my experience, and a great cover. Student walks in needing a job for two, three nights a week. She's got to go to school, so night shift is the perfect solution. And for me, the only way I might be able to see my mother for real, the way she was really being treated at the home. No phony nurses dressing her up for Sunday visits. If it was bad, I wanted to know it, but I wanted to do it my way, from a distance . . .

Mrs. Saunders looked at my application, and for a moment, I thought I was lost. Would she recognize my face or my name? Would she have seen Nélida coming to visit? And it was unusual for a black nurse to be chief administrator, especially a woman so young. Perhaps she was from another town, perhaps she only just started to work there and wouldn't be familiar with the residents or their families. That was it. She looked quickly over what I had written and asked why I had left the Training School. When she said it, it was kind of a shock, so I told her.

"You know, I hadn't even gotten used to the idea that I wouldn't be working there anymore—I loved my job, but it would be too strenuous now. I was in a car accident over the summer, and I can't do any more heavy lifting for a while."

"You worked there for over a year, you must have gotten very attached to the women in the ward—"

"Yes. I went back to visit, but my coworkers didn't even want to see me as long as I was wearing a cervical collar! Not during the day, anyway, perhaps at night. But then, it's very difficult to get hired part-time at the Training School, and I really want to finish school this time."

"I'm glad to see that. More young women should finish their education before they think about getting married and starting families. Is there a young man waiting for you to finish school?"

Mrs. Saunders was looking so kindly at me, I didn't want to disappoint her. But I had no idea how she'd gotten on that track.

"Ah, no," I told her. "Between work and school, you know . . ."

"Good!" She said with surprising cheer in her voice. "Then you'll be a reliable weekender. Can you start tomorrow night?" She'd gotten up and was extending her hand to me across her desk. I took it, half-standing, and nodded vigorously, thinking of course I would work there for years, just to prove to her that she could count on me. How could I be so devious?

I walked in that night at midnight and went right up to the nurse's station on the second floor. It had been a breeze finding a nurse's uniform at Goodwill for $3.50, never-worn white nylon pants and jacket. I already had a pair of white sneakers. I was met by a broad pair of welcoming arms and a lot of faded blonde hair on the head of Miss Lubarski, who seemed to be out of breath and too busy to lift the hair from her eyes. I thought I liked her right away.

"You're brand new, from the Training School, aren't you? God bless you! Isn't Mrs. Saunders a dream? She just came here from Darien and she's going to turn this place around. Come, come, it's just you and me, but we got no crazies like you had at the School. Piece of cake!"

Miss Lubarski seemed like a basket case, but she was thoroughly organized. In fifteen minutes, she covered the East wing, male geriatric, and the West wing, female nonambulatory. I was taking temperature, pulse, and respiration readings in the men's wing by 12:20 and folding laundry by 1:30. The layout was familiar, somehow, and it wasn't hard to figure out the rhythm of the work. I wouldn't have to clean or wash until the morning when I would bathe the women and bring them breakfast by 7:00. And I wasn't required to swab floors unless there was an accident, which suited me fine. Having been away from the smell of betadine and human waste for a while had made me realize how I despised it, but I didn't pay much attention to details. I had a mission. I discovered Mami was on the third floor, moved from the nonambulatory wing for some reason. I'd have to sneak up there during my break, if I could make Miss Lubarski think I was studying. I'd brought my books.

"So what are you studying, honey?"

"Oh, literature, you know."

"Oh sure."

"Are you always this short-staffed?"

"Just since the cutbacks, but the patients aren't difficult, poor dears."

"Anybody ever die during the day?"

"No, just at night. That's when they go. Nighttime."

"Is everybody as nice as you?"

"Oh, you're a sweet girl, bless you, sure. We love them dears, but they can be trying, you know. There's rubber lady in 206, she goes off walking right out of her wheelchair, that's why we have to keep her tied up, but she slips out of everything. And Mr. Collins in 235, he cries for his reading glasses every hour on the hour and they're right on his nose. But no crazies like you got over there at the School, no siree."

"No, I guess not. Should I put in another load of laundry now?" The laundry room was right by the stairs. I waited by the dryers until I heard Miss Lubarski wheel her medicine tray into one of the rooms, and then I ran upstairs two steps at a time. Gasping, I looked through the metal mesh in the glass door. I had the nurse's station in my sight. No one. The light was dim, mixing with the red glow of the exit lights on the blue-tiled floor. I heard soft laughter. Women. One man. Room 307 was to the right of the desk. The door was open, and the room looked dark. Mami must be sleeping. I turned around and ran back downstairs.

When I got to the second floor landing, heart pounding and ears ringing, I moved like a cop on a stakeout. Look first, walk.

Look first, walk. Until I rounded the corner of the laundry room and dove into a pile of unfolded towels I had left. I began to fold them feverishly. It was 3:30. Time for a complete bed check of the floor, Miss Lubarski had said. I went to the desk and picked up the clipboard with the list.

One by one, I made sure each old woman and old man was sleeping peacefully or lying awake but comfortably in their beds, like at the Training School. I met Miss Lubarski halfway down the corridor, and she entrusted the rest of the bed check to me, since I was doing such a good job. I tried to imagine someone not doing a good job. Most people slept but woke easily when I entered the room or when I leaned close to check their breathing. White-haired grandfathers and grandmothers opened a blue eye or a brown one to check me out. There were two black grandfathers, one Chinese grandmother, and one black. She was the only one with her own teeth. Everyone else was a white New Englander, it seemed, and I saw no one who looked like Mami. The urge to see her was growing huge in my heart. I got to the end of the list, and everyone was breathing. It was the second time I had passed through everyone's room on this first night, and I already remembered half their names. I tucked the clipboard under my arm and headed back to the desk.

"Break time," chanted my new colleague. I followed her into the small locker room, where she took her brown paper bag from the refrigerator and handed me mine. From her locker she took out a stack of magazines, and I grabbed the three books out of my knapsack. As soon as we were settled behind the desk again, I sank my head between the pages of my books and gobbled my sandwich. Miss Lubarski didn't mind, her magazines took all her attention.

As for me, I had made a serious miscalculation. There was no way I could slip away during a break, that's when everyone would be gathered around the desk. Had I made a mistake in asking to work at night? Would it have been easier to do it during the day? But maybe I wouldn't have been hired so easily. I turned in my chair and caught sight of a swift pair of feet slipping by. A trail of bedsheets and restraining straps lay on the shiny floor. The door to the hallway lavatory slammed shut.

"I think we've got an escapee," I told Miss Lubarski, throwing my books and my sandwich on the desk. "I just saw rubber lady slip away."

"Damn, and it's barely 4:00! Well, let's go!"

I wouldn't have believed how fast Mrs. Tompkins could move, but she was out of the lavatory by the time I slid to a stop in front of the door and off in the opposite direction. "Whee!" she squealed.

"Where is she going?"

"To the kitchen," said Miss Lubarski, panting, her hair bobbing.

I walked in and saw Mrs. Tompkins, thin as a rail, opening another door and almost slipping away as I caught her. She was about to go down the dimly lit backstairs. Her hospital gown was all wet and wrinkled, and underneath, her thin form was shivering with cold. "Hello!" she said to me. I began to walk with her back to her room, but Miss Lubarski gave her a shove and scolded her, making the old woman scamper in front of us. I know my jaw dropped, but I didn't let Lubarski see my reaction in the dim light.

I gave Mrs. Tompkins a sponge bath in her bathroom while Lubarski changed her bed and fluffed her pillows quietly, so as not to disturb her roommate. But her roommate snored, and the thin old woman was amazingly gregarious.

"I remember you! You used to come and see your dear old mother, didn't you, dear?" she said to me. "I'm so hungry, you know, they don't feed us here. A milk shake, that's what I'd like. You get my purse and go down to Friendly's for me, get the chocolate malted in the big cup. Ask Eddy, he'll make it for you. Here, I'll give you a nickel, and ask your mother what she'd like . . ."

"Here we go, Mrs. Tompkins." Lubarski, now calm and solicitous, and I helped the old woman onto the clean, perfectly smooth bed, tucking and retucking until we had almost packaged her in white sheets and blankets. She placed fluffy pillows all around, the smell of clean linen blending with the sour smell of the wet laundry in the hamper.

"I'll get you a carton of milk, okay, Mrs. Tompkins?" I asked the old woman, as we slipped sheets and fabric restraints over her legs and arms, fastening her to the bed. I could see her slim arms already working themselves free of the restraints. She reminded me of Madeleine and Rosie and the Kiniry twins.

"She can't have milk now, she brushed her teeth already before bed," objected Lubarski, checking the chart for the last TPR readings.

"Her teeth are in a glass, over there—" I pointed to the green metal nightstand. Mrs. Tompkins nodded emphatically and patted my hand. She'd already pulled her right hand free.

"Oh, all right, get her cookies, too, and dunk them in for her and maybe she'll get some sleep, right, you rubber lady, you rascal?"

"Oh, yes, dear. You're so smart, just like your mother. Nobody thought she could talk, but she could talk, that's why they took her upstairs. Chocolate malted, that's what I like." Mrs Tompkins was looking right at me. I had the uneasy feeling that she knew me and really was talking about my mother.

Saturday I spent sleeping, reading for my history class, and making sketches of the layout of the nursing home. It wasn't something I really needed to do any longer, I had seen what I wanted to, but the idea of making a concise plan, a map for my actions, felt soothing to me and kept me from noticing the uncomfortable feeling that was settling underneath the place where I thought my heart should be. Memories of my childhood with Mami and Nélida were surfacing in my half-sleep, things I didn't expect to remember so clearly after so many years, showing me different sides of us.

The nursing home was easy to navigate, not very large. A three-story, crescent-shaped brick building, it had staircases and elevators in its middle, and narrower stairs at the end of the east and west wing corridors. The nurse's station was in the middle of each floor, with a small TV room and patients' rooms numbered consistently, left and right. Down on the main floor were a large dining room and two visitors' lounges.

The dining room was utilized apparently only when there was a special event and the families of the residents came to visit, but daily it functioned as the occupational and creative therapy room. Mami would be taken there, along with everyone else able to participate, for a dose of drawing or cross-stitch embroidery after breakfast. I knew I couldn't stay that late, unless I mentioned that it had something to do with a school project. Perhaps I'd be able to mingle among the therapists, in case I failed in my night-time mission.

I preferred this, the first visit alone, without gawkers or anyone judging how things worked out. Getting ready for work, I imagined Mami during art therapy, smearing pastels or watercolors, or fooling with a plastic needle on a prepainted net with a cat or a bunch of pansies. I thought she would hate it, she who was the fastest pieceworker at the factory in New Britain, who had never had time for these frivolities. I remembered the day Nélida brought home a bunch of patterns from her home ec teacher and told Mami she was going to decorate the apartment. Mami did her best to encourage Nélida to express herself and bought her the yarns and the threads she wanted. Mami put up a brave front when my sister crocheted rows of peach lace on the edges of our lime green cafe curtains in the kitchen and proceeded to create colorful doilies for the back of the sofa, the armchair, under and over the lamps, the coffee table, the bed pillows and the pot holders. When Nélida was measuring the top of the toilet tank for a powder blue cover full of pink rosettes, our mother put her foot down.

"Qué muchacha," she muttered under her breath, loudly enough so I could hear, I suppose, but not Nélida. "She'll have us looking like every other Puerto Rican family on the block!"

I remember being shocked, taking this as a message. I never thought Mami noticed or cared how things looked, but I paid attention after that. She liked them simple, uncluttered, and I decided I did, too. I scraped off my neon flower decals from our bedroom door and my school ring binder, threw out my hot pink fishnet stockings, the bright yellow plastic go-go boots I'd inherited from Nélida, and the flouncy lavender umbrella Aunt Cuqui had given me for Christmas. No more big hoop earrings from the bargain counter at G. Fox, and I had my hair cut short as soon as I could so I could donate all the elastics with the neon ballies for ponytails to the girls in my gym class. I wasn't sure what I was reacting to then, the excess of frill which was beginning to tire me in any case or the dormant self-consciousness about being Puerto Rican. I'd always had a vague sense of shame about how we were seen outside the neighborhood, and I knew that the shame itself was wrong. I knew I wasn't strong or stubborn enough to be proud, and this I wanted to hide. But scrambling around these memories I hadn't touched in so long, I did remember knowing that Mami was a practical woman, that she wasn't ashamed, and perhaps because of her illness or because of the life she'd led, hard and unforgiving, she was a person like nobody else, and I loved her. And I was feeling the excitement of seeing her again seep into me slowly.

It began to rain in the afternoon, and at night when I went to start the car, I took an old towel with me out of habit, to dry the points and the spark plugs. I didn't need it. The car started a little roughly as I pushed it down the hill on Walnut Street, but it kept running fine. I used the towel to dry the seat and myself after I jumped in. Inside, the top was not leaking at all, as the Valiant's would have, but the defroster didn't work, so I had to keep the windows rolled down a bit to keep the windshield clear. I arrived at work with the left side of my head all wet.

The night was dense with fog. I walked into the nursing home feeling practiced and ready for another night, even though my body was tense and twitchy from the lack of that sleep that people can only seem to get at night. I knew it was written all over my face when Miss Lubarski, her curls newly peroxided and permed, met me cheerfully.

"Hey, Kid, got the second-night blues, don't you? Come, come, the coffee's ready!"

The second night of work did begin to feel blue around 2:30 in the morning. Almost as soon as I'd arrived, Mrs. Tompkins had escaped her room and performed her ritual run, trailing her wet clothes down the hallway as she sped in only her underwear to the small refrigerator in the nurses' locker room.

"Mmm! Tuna fish!" she had exclaimed to me, and I'd taken her back to bed with promises of a whaler special at Friendly's later on and a chocolate malted. I was busy in the men's section for a while and didn't see her when she broke free a second time and ransacked Lubarski's brown bag for the tuna sandwich she must have smelled the first time. In two seconds, the old woman had plunged her thin fingers into the sandwich and poked out a lump to stuff in her mouth. The rest she dropped on the floor when

Miss Lubarski grabbed her and practically flew the frail body like a kite back to her room.

"Wait, let me help!" I called behind her.

"You stay with Pop Jones, I'm giving this old lady a bath!" The door to Mrs. Tompkins room shut with a slam. I bent down to pick up the mess on the floor, thinking, *this is what happens to old ladies in nursing homes, somebody treats them bad.* There wasn't a peep out of Pop Jones's room, so I turned on my heel and rushed up the middle stairs to the third floor. When I got up there, not panting, not breaking a sweat, I stood again by the screened-glass door and peered at the nurse's desk. Empty. Three long steps put me right against it and my right arm swiped a clipboard. A young nurse's aide looking greener than me was walking along the hallway; looking straight into her face, I asked her if someone had already checked Mrs. García for bedsores. I knew she wouldn't fight me for the job, so I slid into room 307 while the aide busied herself with a meal cart.

The room was still, two women slept peacefully. It took a second to adjust my eyes to the yellow glow of a night-light, to distinguish the black face of the grandmother whose gray curls were spread on the pillow of the bed on the left. On the right, there was a fat woman, also with gray hair, but cropped short, all atop her round, very pale face. It was not Mami. I noticed my own intake of breath, and the fact that I could smell rose water, a little mustiness, and stale tobacco. I heard my steps moving toward the bed, though I tried to be quiet, then I took up the tag on the bed pole and read, *García, Guillermina L.* I looked at the sleeping face again, this time every part of me conscious, but it was not my mother. On the nightstand, were greeting cards, pastel blue and green, and on the bed was a light green crocheted quilt covering the woman's feet. I don't know why, standing in the twilight, I wanted to know who this was, somebody's mother, but it was definitely not my mother. The ache under my heart was returning, and it was time to go, though the thought did occur to me that I could put an end to everything, right then, and just ask. But I didn't. Still clutching the other clipboard, I rushed out and ran down to the second floor.

Reaching the doorway, I slid back in surreptitiously, and was caught immediately by Lubarski, her curls all in a shambles. "Where did you go?" she asked, facing me, giving me just a fraction of a second before she would form a judgment about my escape, but I just started talking.

"God, you should have seen it! That was no mouse, I'm pretty sure it was a rat, brown, and it squeaked as it came in the locker room, I was cleaning up the sandwich, wow, the rat must have smelled it all the way from the basement, and I chased it up the stairs, trying to hit it with the clipboard. Don't they have an exterminator here?" Lubarski's face had changed from disbelief to fear to complete trust in what I was saying. She turned to the desk, waving her hands. I took a breath.

"Oh, that's disgusting, we can't have this, you could have been bitten! Come, come, help me fill out a report."

She filled out a report while I scrutinized the third-floor list to find my mother's name. There it was, room 307, still, so I figured either the staff had killed her off and placed some other woman in her bed, or Nélida had been wrong about the address. I was working at some nursing home for the hell of it, while my mother was miles from there in another nursing home. But Nélida couldn't be wrong, it had to be a mistake. I read the list again, looking for another Spanish surname, and there was only one, Martínez, Dora M., in room 324. That would be the room directly across the hall. Could the staff have switched my mother with someone else?

Lubarski was muttering about the rubber lady destroying her sandwich and being hungry and having nothing to eat for break. It didn't take me long to get her interested in my cheese omelet sandwiches and entertained with my stories of the ward back at the Training School, where food fights and tripping on mashed sweet potatoes were daily events.

"I should go up and warn them about the rat," I said calmly, getting up and walking to the stairs with resignation.

"Oh, now, there is no need until 5:30 when security comes in. I'll just call Mary Ann up there," offered Lubarski, brushing off crumbs and reaching for the phone.

"Okay, but they'll be scared and not know where to look. I'll go, I'm not afraid—I'll just take a peak in each room . . ." I called to her as I walked up.

On the third floor, break was over, and I found Mary Ann, a nurse who could have been Miss Lubarski's twin for all of her blonde curls and flustered looks as she reviewed medications. She picked up the call from Lubarski just then, and all I had to do was wave and smile and run over to room 324. The door was almost closed, and there was no night-light in there. As I pushed the door open, the hallway light broke the shadow of the room, first the left side, with an empty bed, then the right side, the standard white bedspread covering a small, thin woman. She was turned away from me, toward the windows, but I knew it was Mami. I smelled her cologne, something that I would never forget, lavender water, and I could smell the talcum powder from the nursing home overpowering the other scent, so that I thought I only imagined it. I walked closer to her, and looked at her profile. On the tag around the bedpost I read, *Martínez, Dora M.* The noise from the hallway called me out, and I left the room to find Mary Ann and three young aides preparing to look for the rat, brooms in hand.

"Do you think we can get it with a broom?" asked the aide I'd seen earlier, her face flushed.

"How big is it? I hate mice!"

"It's a rat, Bernice!"

"Can you help until breakfast?" asked Mary Ann. I tried to look doubtful for her sake, but naturally I agreed.

The rat search was made to order. It kept the two floors busy and woke several of the residents, who thoroughly enjoyed the excitement. Mary Ann dispatched two of the aides downstairs, and Lubarski traded me because she said I had more experience with ambulatory patients.

By 5:30, everyone was awake, and I slipped back into room 324 to find Mami. She didn't recognize me, but she seemed perfectly willing to let me help her out of bed and into the wheel-chair, and then to the bathroom, where I sponged her and changed her gown because it was all wet. If I was angry or upset I squelched it, because I was being just another aide. I didn't know how much time I had there. I washed my mother's face, her hands, and brushed her teeth, her own still intact in her mouth. Her right side was completely paralyzed, but with her left, she helped with these tasks. She was so small, it was simple to rotate her weight against my knees, to help her in and out of the chair. She seemed to know the rules and placed her left arm around my neck when it was necessary. I imagined the countless times a nurse's aide must have instructed her in this procedure. I wheeled her back to the side of her bed. I pulled the wet sheets off and dumped them in a corner of the room.

Day was breaking above the bluish hills that were visible from the room's eastern window. There was a thin aura of soft pink light crowning the hills, a glow that turned pale gold when I pulled the blinds all the way up. I thought I saw my mother smile a little, her left eye crinkling just a bit. Draping a robe around her thin shoulders, I asked her if she wanted me to help her comb her hair. She pointed with her hand to the nightstand. In the drawer, I found a blue-handled plastic brush, probably one Nélida had brought for her.

I began to brush her hair, still thick, down to her shoulders, and a little tangled at the nape of the neck. In a voice I knew would be soothing and reassuring, I told her I would take out the tangles and began to comb through the hair with the edge of the brush, a little at a time, the way she had fixed my hair when I was a little girl, with unruly braids that got all matted when I was sick in bed. Mami was quiet, she breathed slowly, and looked at the sunrise out the window, her dark face lined and tired as I remembered her, but not tense, not angry. When I could pull the brush freely through her hair, I asked her if she wanted me to braid it. She didn't respond.

"Mami," I said in my own voice. "Do you want me to braid your hair?"

"Mm," she uttered in a low voice, almost nodding her head. I braided her hair from the top and tied it with the rubber band I found on the nightstand. Mami moved her left hand, quickly, then slowly. Up, down. She patted the side of the chair. "Mm," she said again. I understood.

I moved a little metal chair from the foot of the bed next to the wheelchair and sat next to my mother. Her hand came down on mine, and she left it there. We both looked at the edge of the sun, just emerging above the hills. The moment felt long, and very still. I felt the silence, then the certainty that someone was at the door. I turned to see Mrs. Saunders standing there, with Lubarski and Mary Ann behind her, squeezing their blonde mops of curls into the doorway.

"Good morning, Mrs. García, good morning, Erica," chanted Mrs. Saunders, but I couldn't tell from her inflection what she really felt.

"Good morning," I answered, breathing a little. Mami continued to look out the window.

Mrs. Saunders walked into the room, and the two nurses stumbled at the doorway. Their boss, dressed impeccably in her white uniform, hair coifed, and her manner as crisp as toast at six-thirty in the morning, barely flinched at them, and they were off to make themselves busy. I stood up when Mrs. Saunders sat on the edge of the bare mattress near my mother and me, but she sat me down again with a nod. She was smiling.

"Perhaps you'd like to stay for breakfast with your mother."

"Uhm, yes, I mean, if she wants me to," I stammered. I stroked my mother's hand.

"She wants you to, Erica. Don't you, Mrs. García?" Of course, Mami didn't say anything, but she did seem to be aware of everything around her. As for me, I started to feel the uncomfortable welling of tears in my throat and my face getting hot. Mrs. Saunders placed her hand lightly on my shoulder. "Erica," she whispered.

"Uhm, yeah?"

"After you go home and get some sleep, you can come back and visit with your mother through the front door—from six to eight on Sundays. Will that do?"

But I don't think she expected me to answer, because she was already beginning to leave the room. I squeezed my eyes shut for a second, heard her speak softly to the nurses and the rustle of the very starched white pleats of her uniform as Mrs. Saunders walked briskly away. I opened my eyes and kept them focused on my mother's face.

12

Waking up has always been hard for me, ever since I was a kid. Even in the summer, during school vacation, during those sultry New Britain days when the window in our room was open all the way, and the lace curtains billowed in early with the bright sun and inner-city breeze, I wanted to stay in bed. Nélida would be up at seven, filling the room with the scent of coconut shampoo from her shower. I liked to stretch slowly out of my sleep, lingering in the haze of a dream I could never quite remember once I opened my eyes. Stretching my arms to touch the headboard and my toes as far as I could, I made the broad jump from dreamland to the world of feeling my body again, of opening my eyes like the curtains to the theater on Main Street, lifting gracefully to see my sister sitting on her bed, in a full white slip, drying her black hair with a lime green towel.

It was then that I'd remember, sometimes, that my dreams were about water, green water I'd never seen except in dreams, and that the billowing curtain seemed to help me feel I was at sea, on a boat or a raft, adrift. I know I wanted to tell my sister about it, but she was off to her summer job, and Mami had already left for work. Waking up has remained a hard transition from more than just dreams.

Coming home that Sunday morning, keeping my eyes on the road and my mind on the face of my mother sitting in the wheelchair, looking out the nursing home window, I wondered if I was waking up again, for real. Hadn't I known exactly what I was doing, hadn't I been awake? I knew how Nélida would react, just as she had been there when we were younger, my sister would be there to let me know the day had started, a little rough, a little bumpy, and I'd better catch up. She was just as stubborn and steady as she ever was.

When I got home and found the phone ringing, I knew it was Nélida. I wanted to pick it up and say something smart, but I was too tired.

"Listen," she said after my hello. "I know you have to sleep now, but are you going back to see Mami tonight?"

"Yeah, of course—"

"Okay, I'll see you there at six. You bring the flowers this time."

"Nélida, wait!"

"Oh, and I'm bringing Marisol with me." She hung up. I lay face down on the bed.

And didn't wake up until the sun started to set.

In five minutes, I was back in the car, driving toward the nursing home eating an apple, a piece of stale Italian bread, and some slightly stiff licorice twists I'd bought ages ago. Looking in the rearview mirror, I tried to smooth out the splash of powder I'd dusted on my chest after washing with my shirt on. At least it was clean and not too wrinkled. I decided not to think about the smooth lines of Mrs. Saunders's uniform or the ridiculous thought that she would have to fire me. After an interminable red light, I pulled into the parking lot next to Nélida's car. My niece was crying in the passenger's seat, and my sister rolled the window down. She looked surprised to see me in the Ghia.

"I'm going to park on the hill," I told her. "Meet you out front."

I backed out, waving at Marisol who was smiling and sniffling, and parked on the little hill I'd been using. The ignition would have to get fixed, soon.

"Erica, Erica!" Marisol ran toward me with her arms wide open. I hugged and twirled her around, making her little legs fly and her feet kick with delight, clicking her patent leather shoes together. I stared at her bright brown eyes and the missing front tooth in her smile.

"Why were you crying in the car?"

"'Cause Mami said I couldn't change the radio!"

"She wants to hear the Partridge family," Nélida explained to me, wrapping an arm around me and giving me a quick kiss. With her other hand, she grabbed hold of the back of Marisol's coat and held her firmly as we crossed the parking lot. We walked in silence, and when we reached the tiled walk in front of the nursing home, my niece straining against her mother to go running inside, Nélida let her go but not before smoothing the flyaway hair around her ears. Her little blue coat lifted in the air.

Nélida adjusted her own blue coat and looked at me. "Your hair is still wet," she informed me.

"And I forgot to buy the flowers! I'm sorry—"

"That's okay, you'll bring her some next time."

I looked at my sister; she reached over and brushed something off my pea coat. I flicked something off her sleeve, and then I hugged her.

The thing is, I'm not forgetting years of my life anymore, but some parts of certain events do seem like hazy dreams. But I can remember conversations, word for word, an exact memory of what everyone said. Like my niece, yelling at the door of the nursing home.

"Come on, you guys, I want to see Abuelita!"

And me, asking Nélida in the elevator, "How did you know I was here?"

"'Cause you're a nut, Erica."

"No, really, did Saunders call you?"

"Yeah. When Lubarski heard about the rat story, she called security but the guard was sleeping. Mrs. Saunders was told as soon as she came in. When she saw you in the room with Mami, she understood, and she called me."

"Were you mad?"

"What do you think? I've known her ever since she was fresh out of nursing school—I was embarrassed! Come on, Marisol, we're going to see Abuelita."

In my mother's room, which had now been permanently changed to room 324, my niece behaved as if we were all home. She kissed her grandmother on the cheek, chattered to her about school and her missing tooth, and helped herself to the candy in my mother's drawer. My sister got fresh water in the pitcher and got Mami to drink some. I felt like a fifth wheel and occupied myself with checking her chart, her TPR readings, her medication schedule. I don't remember much of that visit, except that my niece sang her a song, and Nélida and I joined in at the chorus. Her new neighbor, a very old Polish lady, had no visitors that day, and she seemed to enjoy all the activity.

As we were leaving, Mami said softly, "Adiós, niñas."

I stood speechless, at the door. My sister's eyes clouded over while she cleared her throat and responded with a calm, full voice, as if nothing was going to stop her from behaving normally, "Adiós, Mami, see you next week."

"Adiós, Abuelita!" my niece sang.

It must have been during the week of finals, when I was moving my things to New Britain, and I took Nélida and Marisol to a new steak house for dinner, that we talked about bringing Mami home. Nélida was glad not to have to cook, and my niece was thrilled with all the variety of food. She picked at everything and ate nothing, finally demolishing a piece of black forest cake and eating only the cherries.

"Listen, Nélida. You think they got the point about the toileting after midnight? I mean, some people need to go at night and withholding liquids after dinner isn't gonna do it. That's plain cruel!"

"I know, Erica, you're right." My sister agreed. "That's the first thing I yelled at Saunders about. I couldn't stand the thought of Mami having to lie in bed while she was wet all night. Saunders took care of that right away."

"And, did you know that the second-shift aides lost Mami in the wrong room?"

"Yeah, I made a big stink about it the first time it happened—" She sipped her coffee. "Thanks to your crazy stunt, though, they tightened up their bed checks, got more aides, and won't lose anybody else again."

"They could have killed her if they had given her somebody else's medication, like the heart medication for Mrs. Martínez!"

"I know, but fortunately Mami only takes her pills from the nurses she knows, that's why they moved her from the second floor."

"What do you mean—what else had been happening?"

"She used to be in the same room with Mrs. Tompkins, the rubber lady—"

"You're kidding, you know about her?"

"Sure. Mami liked her. She used to give her the candy I brought, because the poor lady was always hungry. One day, the evening nurse got transferred upstairs, and Mami wouldn't take anything from the new aides. She told them, *Don't give me that shit!*"

"Oh, my god!"

"That's when they figured out she could talk, when she wants to. And almost walk. The physical therapist thinks she might be getting better."

"Enough to come home?"

"I don't know, Erica. It takes time, but who knows?"

And, I remember another time, soon after Christmas, when I'd already moved in.

"You might want to get married again . . ." I told my sister, without knowing why. I was brushing my niece's hair, while she squirmed and fidgeted, tying up her new tennis shoes. Nélida was heating the milk for coffee on the stove, and on the radio the polls were predicting a sure win for Carter in a second presidential term. She harrumphed my suggestion.

"And you might get a girlfriend and move out!"

"And who would take care of Mami, when she comes home?" I countered, a little surprised at my sister's direct reference about a girlfriend.

"And, who's gonna take care of me?" demanded my niece, undoing my careful styling with a quick turn. "Erica, can you cut my hair real short like yours?" she whined in a plaintive voice, before either her mother or I could respond to her first question.

"Ask your mother," I told her.

"Go ahead, she drives me crazy," said Nélida.

"Yipee!" yelled my niece, running off.

"So," continued my sister.

"So?" I asked, cleaning the brush over the trash can.

"You're not seeing anybody?" Two steaming cups of coffee and milk were on the table.

"Nope," I said. "You?"

"Nope, and if I do, I'm not about to marry some fool so he can take my money."

"Okay." We sat down for breakfast.

The snow was two feet deep on the ground when I drove the Ghia down to New Haven to see Tina. I parked right in front of her house on Whalley Avenue, in the spot that somebody had just dug out and left waiting for me to occupy. Tina and I sat on the wooden porch watching the slow traffic, drinking mugs of hot chocolate.

"It'll be nice here in the spring," she was saying to me, her right hand brushing the back of my recent haircut. "There will be flowers on this porch and wicker chairs for us."

"Tina, I can't move here with you—I just started at Central!"

"If you could transfer to Central, you coulda transferred to Yale, and then we'd be together," Tina pronounced, crossing her arms.

"You know I couldn't; I gotta live with my sister or I can't afford it. Besides—"

"Mm?" Tina looked tired. Tired but beautiful. Her hair was short, cropped close to her head, and her face had thinned out since I'd last seen her. Her profile was regal, dignified. She looked like the silhouette of the African queen in my Art History book. But I didn't want to tell her that, or she'd think I was stupid.

"Well, besides, I have to be there for when Mami comes home."

"Erica."

"What?" I said, defensively.

"Well, you know that won't be for a couple of years. In the meantime, you could live here with me and we could be together again. I've missed you," Tina returned her hand to the spiky hairs along the back of my neck.

"Quit it," I told her, batting her hand away without much spirit. "I've missed you, too. You don't know how much."

"I could introduce you to some nice women, and—"

"What? You're all in graduate school. Why would your friends wanna hang out with me?"

"Because you are my best friend and because you're cute! Come on, Erica!"

"I'll think about it."

"And you could join our group; we have a Third World Women's alliance and we're organizing a conference."

"Wow—"

"And get this, we might have the funding to bring a black women's singing group!"

"All women? What's their name?"

"Sweet Honey in the Rock."

"Wow."

"You've got to come, it's on March 8, International Women's Day."

"Cool. I'll be here." We sat with our arms around each other, Tina's head on my shoulder, until the afternoon sun faded and we got cold. "Let's go for a ride to the ocean," I proposed.

"And lose this parking spot?"

"I can always dig out another one. Don't you know I can do anything?"

"You can do anything!" Tina clapped me on the back as we

hopped down to the street. It was the first time I would give her a ride in my new car, which now had heat, new ignition, and floor boards so that the ground was no longer visible under my feet.

"Wow," said Tina, as we sped away toward the beach in winter. "Overdrive!"

In the spring, the roof at Tina's house sprang a leak that their landlord couldn't fix. Or so he said, but Tina thought he was actually trying to make them move out, but the landlord himself had moved to Florida.

I drove to New Haven on a wet weekend, with a bunch of tools, and got to work on the roof. All those odd jobs I'd had before the Training School had been good for something. Tina was perched with me by the brick chimney, holding an umbrella over both our heads while I slathered tar on roofing planks and covered the holes. Tina had a new lover, and from time to time she stared dreamily into the horizon, letting the umbrella fall to the side.

"Hey, you gotta keep this stuff dry for awhile yet!" I chided her.

"Sorry, I was thinking—"

"Yeah, I know, Imani, the only woman in the world for you!"

"You know, I like your hair like that, real short. It makes you look . . . like one of the Sharks in *West Side Story!*"

"Don't change the subject. Hand me that cutter, please?"

"Here. But I'm serious! You oughta spike it up in the front, put some of that dippity-do gunk the white girls use on their hair."

"Spike it *up?* Tina, you crazy? You know how long my sister subjected my poor head to lemon juice and gomina to make my hair lie down? Hold the umbrella."

"You would look so cute. You know, Imani has somebody

she'd like for you to meet—" I gave the patch a good whack with the rock I used as a hammer to seal it in place. I stared at my friend in disbelief. She was grinning.

"Tina, you would set up your best friend on a blind date?"

"She's gorgeous!" Tina protested.

"That's not it, you know I'm shy about meeting women."

"Well, PB might have something different to say about that!" The rain had stopped. Tina closed the umbrella spraying both of us with water.

"Watch it, you'll knock us off the roof!" I cautioned her.

"Don't change the subject—"

"PB was different. It just happened!" I grinned at Tina.

"Well, this could happen, too. Or, are you still hung up on Millie?" Tina looked at me carefully. Drops of rain dotted the face of the friend who had seen me through my worst times. And the best.

"Nah, I've seen Millie, and things are cool." I brushed the rain from Tina's face with my sleeve. She raised her small eyebrows just a touch. "Now, let's get off this roof if we're gonna have enough time to spike up my hair for this hot date, eh?" We practically rolled off the roof until we got to the ledge of the attic window. Tina never knew when to quit laughing at me.

The first time I'd run into Millie was around Thanksgiving. It was a snowy day, and cars were sliding all over 195, unprepared for the weather, just like every winter in the beginning. I pulled into Storrs Texaco for a fill-up, waved at Rachel, and started to pump the gas myself. As I was pondering whose blue Saab was parked all crooked over by the bank, I turned around and almost knocked Millie off the gas station island. I bit my lip a little, but more from habit than excitement.

"Erica!" Millie's face was flushed, her eyes shining as though she were about to cry, and she threw her arms around me.

"Hey, what are you up to?" I hugged her.

"You know, school. I've been wondering why I haven't seen you—" Her eyes were tearing up a little, and she wiped them with a blue woolen mitten.

"I'm only taking three courses," I put the nozzle back in the pump and gave Julie a ten dollar bill.

"Big tank in this little thing!" she smacked the side of the Ghia. "Hey, Millie!"

"Hey," answered Millie. I wiped my windshield. I tried to feel something that would explain to me what I should be feeling. But there were just big flakes of fluffy snow in the cold air, sticking to my lips.

"What's with the Saab?" I asked Millie.

"It won't start, and when it does it stalls. I was coming over to ask Rachel for help—"

"It's probably your points again; I can set them for you."

"Can you?" Millie placed her hand on my arm. She looked down, then up. She was crying.

"And then, you could get us both a hot chocolate at the Campus Restaurant," I continued, feeling stupid, because that's probably not what she wanted to hear. But it was. She burst into a smile and sniffled, shaking the snow from her black hair and hugging me. I kissed her cold cheeks.

Regapping the points in her car hadn't taken long. I parked mine under the old willow, and we left Millie's right next to it after starting it up and making sure it ran smoothly. We walked over the wet snow, sliding a little and laughing about something. It was a little scary to me how easily we fell into the rhythm of our talk. At the restaurant, Jimmy brought over two hot chocolates and asked about Tina. We chatted for a few minutes; Millie asked for a powdered donut.

Everything wasn't the same, although it seemed to be. Millie and I held parts of each other's lives, and yet we could never come back to that time again. We asked ourselves how that could be, sitting there at our same old booth, around an old table that was a cable spool once, where countless people had etched their names, and where the ancient grime of the Campus Restaurant had smoothed it over with its powerful magic. We watched the new students streaming in, establishing their favorite perches, and ignoring the history we were leaving behind like so much graffiti on a wall. But before we got too existential, Millie laughed and snapped us out of our indulgence.

"We think we're so important to this place, but—" she began.

"That sounds like a line from *Casablanca*." I put in. I'd taken my pea coat off, and I was wearing the blue-and-green shirt she had given me for my birthday over a year before. Millie looked at it, then at my face.

"I know, but Erica," she put her hand over mine, tentatively.

"Millie, just talk to me," I fought the impulse to bring her hand up to my face and hoped that I could give her what she was about to ask. I knew it was something, I did know her well.

As it turned out, it was friendship. It was what I wanted, too. I figured we could try.

Time has a way of appearing to be something it is not. Of returning in cycles, perhaps, of appearing to move while it's standing still, and it's only us who run around in circles. Getting nowhere, sometimes, and thinking that time is catching up with us as we come around a bend. The thing is, as I finished school and worked on weekends at the New Britain Hospital, I would some- times feel that I had done everything already once before and I was stuck doing something completely pointless with my life. And sometimes I would feel so sad I would just cry, standing in our old apartment feeling like the time for changing anything was gone, long gone. Mami would never come home, I would forever be scrubbing a floor or watching a patient getting pushed around by overworked nurses, ignored by doctors. But then, Nélida would come and give me a cup of coffee. Or, Tina would call.

I was listening a lot more to Nélida, and I'm glad that I did. She told me I was too sensitive, that things would work out and that, believe it or not, this is what life was about as we got older. Doing the same things for different reasons and trusting in ourselves. Who else did we have to trust?

And Tina, she would tell me the same thing but in other words. I knew what I was doing, she would say. I had to know, we were all part of the sisterhood, and she needed me to be strong, not to despair. There was a lot more work ahead, she told me, and I had to become resilient, not to get broken by the little things, the day-to-day things. Because, Tina said, I was the kind who would be willing to fight one battle at a time, to see the injustice other people were too busy to see. And I would fight, she said, for all the people who couldn't fight, or even speak, for themselves.

Sometimes, I admit, I didn't know what she or my sister were talking about. But as we got to the end of school, when I was calmer, whenever Tina and I got together I felt stronger. And this strength lasted, stayed with me, even when I was alone. Sometimes, usually at night, driving with the top down, I'd stop the car on a quiet stretch of highway and look at the sky. The world did make some kind of sense, and there was a part of it, a small part, that was mine.

Other Titles Available From Spinsters Ink

Spinsters Ink was founded in 1978 to produce vital books for diverse women's communities. In 1986 we merged with Aunt Lute Books to become Spinsters/Aunt Lute. In 1990, the Aunt Lute Foundation became an independent nonprofit publishing program. In 1992, Spinsters moved to Minnesota.

Spinsters Ink publishes novels and nonfiction works that deal with significant issues in women's lives from a feminist perspective: books that not only name these crucial issues, but—more importantly—encourage change and growth. We are committed to publishing works by women writing from the periphery: fat women, Jewish women, lesbians, old women, poor women, rural women, women examining classism, women of color, women with disabilities, women who are writing books that help make the best in our lives more possible.

Spinsters titles are available at your local booksellers or by mail order through Spinsters Ink. A free catalog is available upon request. Please include $2.00 for the first title ordered and 50¢ for every title thereafter. Visa and Mastercard accepted.

Spinsters Ink
32 E. First St., #330
Duluth, MN 55802-2002
USA

218-727-3222 (phone)   **(fax) 218-727-3119**
(e-mail) spinsters@aol.com
(website) http://www.lesbian.org/spinsters-ink

Photo by June Chan

Mariana Romo-Carmona, a native of Santiago, Chile, has lived in the United States for thirty years. She teaches in the MFA program at Goddard College, Vermont. Ms. Romo-Carmona is co-editor of *Cuentos: Stories by Latinas;* editor of *Conditions* magazine from 1988–92; and co-editor of the 1992 volume of the *Queer City: Portable Lower East Side* annual anthology series. Her work has also appeared in several anthologies, including *Compañeras: Latina Lesbians,* and *Beyond Gender and Geography: American Women Writers. Living at Night* is Ms. Romo-Carmona's first novel.